THE SCORPIO LETTERS

VICTOR CANNING

'His inventiveness never flags for a moment.'
—*The Daily Telegraph*

'One of the finest six thriller-writers in the world.'
—*Reader's Digest*

'A top thriller-writer who writes the pure thriller, that is the story told for the sake of excitement and not to convey a particular view of the world or insight into human nature . . . the overall weight is achieved by sheer good writing and sheer hard thought.'—*The Times*

THE SCORPIO LETTERS

'Canning spins an ingenious plot, and manoeuvres his cosmopolitan cast across half Europe with never a dull moment.'—*The Irish Times*

VICTOR Canning, one-time feature writer for the *Daily Mail*, has worked as a scriptwriter in Hollywood and written very successful serials for the BBC. Highly praised on both sides of the Atlantic, *Queen's Pawn* is his latest title to join the Pan list. It is his thirty-second novel, each characteri̶ high-class planning and meticulous atte

D1331544

THE SCORPIO LETTERS

VICTOR CANNING

UNABRIDGED

PAN BOOKS LTD : LONDON

First published 1964 by William Heinemann Ltd.
This edition published 1966 by Pan Books Ltd.,
33 Tothill Street, London, S.W.1

ISBN O 330 10523 X

2nd Printing 1967
3rd Printing 1971

PRINTED AND BOUND IN ENGLAND BY
HAZELL WATSON AND VINEY LTD
AYLESBURY, BUCKS

PROLOGUE

ANTONIO BARDI came out of his bedroom, and went into a small study whose windows gave a view of the Mediterranean and a distant high sprawl of a headland topped by the white walls of coastguard buildings and a lighthouse. In the room was a desk with a pale-golden leather top, a chair behind it padded with the same leather, and a wall safe behind the desk. To one side of the door was a very good copy of the Bosschaert painting of irises, tulips and roses from the Mauritshuis.

He pressed a buzzer on his desk, then turned and opened the wall safe, pulling out a worn, bulging briefcase. The door opened and Lodel came in. He was a tall, dark-haired man of about forty with a greyish, deep-frozen face. He crossed to the desk and set down a silver tray holding a decanter, soda siphon and a glass. Without a word he poured whisky into the glass and gave it the merest flick from the siphon.

Bardi pulled three or four files from his case and, without looking up, said, 'When Maria's finished, you can both clear off for the evening. Take Gian with you.' He spoke English with no more than an ancient echo of an accent and he brought the words up from deep down in his throat with a resonance that seemed to make each one throb a little as it hit the air.

Lodel nodded and just for a moment his eyes looked with curiosity at the files on the desk before they went to the large face beyond them.

'Send her in now,' said Bardi and, before the other was clear of the room, picked up the top file which had a number in red crayon pencilled on the front and opened it. It contained Press-cuttings, and about a dozen pages of white foolscap paper. Alone on the first page, like a title, was the name – *Ronald P. Dean*. He began to turn the

5

pages over slowly. Near the end of the file there was a page divided into columns and marked with dates and amounts in sterling against them. He studied the figures carefully, his ice-blue eyes full of glacial coldness in the big, blank face.

There was a light knock at the door and a woman in a green silk dress came in, carrying a notebook and pencil. She was about thirty, attractive, with long dark hair drawn back behind her ears.

Bardi, now smiling, said, 'There are some letters, Maria. Quite short. I want them done before you go out.'

The woman nodded. Outside the setting sun began to lay a scarlet and gold carpet across the sea and, away to the east, dusk took a few mauve and grey steps along it.

'The first,' said Bardi, 'is to Professor Ronald P. Dean, DSc, FRS, Lower Lodge, Godstow, Oxon.'

He began to dictate and, as he did so, he stood up and walked around the desk, sipping at his whisky.

The letter read:

My dear Dean,

I am a little late writing to you this year but, let me assure you, this is not because I have forgotten you. It simply is that I have been very busy in the last few months.

However, from time to time, I have had news of you. I have read, too, your survey of recently collected plants from Madagascar in the last issue of the *Journal of the Royal Horticultural Society*. Most interesting.

You will be a little disappointed to learn that I propose to increase my annual charge this year by twenty-five per cent. I do not have to tell you why. Will you please make the usual transfer for the new amount to Scorpio Holdings by the end of this month.

My kindest regards,
Yours sincerely,

The first letter done, he reached across the desk behind Maria and picked up the second file. He opened it and stood at her back, going through the pages without hurry.

'The second,' he said, 'is to Sir Alexander Synat, Lawton

House, Curzon Street, London, W.1.' He paused and said, 'He was long before your time, Maria. He was in a rare hurry to make his first million.'

He did not wait for any comment from her and she made no effort to give one. He went on dictating his letters, taking up the files as he needed them. Once, without stopping his dictating, he stood behind her and let his hand drop to the nape of her neck and held it there, the brown fingers curling gently around one side of her throat in an absent-minded caress. For a moment the shadow of a smile touched Maria's lips, then was gone, the response in her as distant and undisturbing as the past which they had once shared.

When he had finished he said, 'Leave them in your room with the envelopes. I'll see to them later. Have a good evening. And don't let Gian drink too much. Something's getting into him.'

Maria, halfway to the door, paused and her words came with a surprising tenderness.

'He's young. Life's a big bursting rocket and the sparks are in his hair. Surely you can remember?'

He sipped his whisky thoughtfully, his eyes on her, and then said, 'It's like that?'

She nodded. 'It's like that. I can't stop him. There's no need. He'll grow out of it.'

'While he's growing, teach him to be careful or one of his rockets might burst in his face. There's a point where even Lodel can get jealous.'

She shrugged her shoulders and went.

An hour later, as he sat in the main room reading the *Daily Telegraph* airmail edition, he heard the staff car go past the front of the villa. One of the men was singing and he knew that it was not Lodel. He got up and went into Maria's room. The letters she had typed were laid neatly on her desk. Bardi took a pair of lightweight cotton gloves from the top of her typewriter, slipped them on, and then sat down, read each letter through carefully, and signed it. The signatures were all the same – Scorpio.

The sitting-room looked out across a tiny garden, iron-railed along a low brick wall, part of the rails broken away. Beyond the cars parked on both sides of the road was an asphalted public tennis court where, in the early June sunlight, two young men sat on a bench changing their shoes.

Mrs Luigi Fettoni picked up her handbag from the sofa and said, 'Well I'm off. Sure you can manage for a few days?'

'Yes.' The man sitting on the sofa, reading the *Daily Mail* with the help of a large magnifying glass, stirred his stockinged feet which were propped up on a chair.

'Yes, what?'

Without looking up, Luigi Fettoni said, 'Yes, love. Thank you.' He did not say it as though he meant it or even resented it.

Mrs Fettoni looked down at him as though she felt she ought to make something out of it and then decided that she had not got the time. She walked over to a wall mirror and adjusted her hat with little pecks of her fingers in much the same way as a wood pigeon tidies up a nest which will never be anything but a mess.

'So long, then.' She left the mirror and put her hand on the door knob.

'*Ciao* . . .' He paused, looked up, and with the hint of a smile, added, '. . . *cara*.'

She lingered at the door as though even now she might change her mind and not go.

Luigi, aware of her hesitation, eyed her with unexpected firmness. 'You go on – I could still handle a six-course banquet for six hundred. What is there here? Just me and the cat. Why do you fuss?'

'All right, then. I'm off. So long . . .' She went out on the breath of the last word. Luigi heard the front door go and, a little later, the squeak of the front gate.

He was an old man, nearly bald, with an ascetic face that had two deep clefts either side of his chin which gave him trouble when he shaved. There was a little patch of fluffy cotton wool, flushed with pink, at the top of the right-hand cleft now. He wore a cheap brown sports jacket, too big for his thin body, a faded blue shirt without a collar and crumpled black trousers. One of his patterned socks had been put on inside out and a black silk scarf was knotted around his neck.

After half an hour he finished the paper, put it aside on the sofa with his magnifying glass and stared at his feet. He shook his head and smiled, leaned forward and changed the odd sock the right way round. Then he reached under the table and pulled out his boots. They were black, laced part of the way up and finished off with metal hooks around which the laces went before being tied. You could have bought them in any shop in 1918, but now they were museum pieces. It took him a little time to find his hat, a well-worn brown velour, which was on the window-seat hidden by the overlap of one of the lace curtains. From the top of the sideboard he picked up a large envelope which had come in the post that morning. He slit the flap open and shook out four smaller envelopes. They were all that the covering envelope contained. From a little pot below the mirror he pulled out a book of stamps, eased out four threepenny stamps and stuck them carefully on the envelopes. The last letter – all of them had their inscriptions typed – was addressed to Prof. Ronald P. Dean, DSc, FRS, Lower Lodge, Godstow, Oxon, and it was franked, *Private and Confidential*.

He put the four letters in his pocket and picked up the large covering envelope. He struck a match, watched it begin to burn and then walked across the room and dropped it into the empty fireplace.

Luigi Fettoni went out into Fentiman Road, paused for a moment to watch two young men playing tennis in Vauxhall Park and, taking his time, moved off into South Lambeth Road a few yards away. As he turned the corner he took a cigarette from behind his ear and lit it. Smoking, he walked slowly up towards the Albert Embankment, debating with himself whether he would cross the river

9

by the Vauxhall or Lambeth Bridge. In the end he decided he would walk to Lambeth Bridge and get a bus from there. It didn't matter where he posted the letters so long as it was well outside the radius of his own house. Those were his instructions and Luigi had been obeying instructions meticulously for many years.

He walked along enjoying the morning sunshine, hardly hearing the rumble of riverside traffic, keeping his eyes on the pavement about a yard ahead of him.

Nearly a mile away from his home he came to the roundabout at the foot of Lambeth Bridge. He waited at a pedestrian crossing to make the move over to the river side of the Embankment, looked left and then right, and was about to step off into a clear crossing when, his head up from sighting the traffic, he caught the sudden flight of pigeons' wings over the river. Sharply, pleasurably, they reminded him of a pigeon loft in the backyard of a Brighton house many years before, and he watched them, smiling, memory clear and vivid. Then he stepped on to the crossing, his eyes beginning to drop from the flighting birds. He saw, too late, the red loom of a London bus, and the arched vault of a mudguard.

He died an hour later from multiple fractures of the skull in St Thomas's Hospital, a little farther down river, without regaining consciousness. He had no papers on him which could identify him. Nobody knew him. To be knocked down and killed a mile from your home in London is like dying in a foreign land. It can take days before the news reaches home. All he had on him was a half-empty packet of Player's cigarettes, a box of Bryant and May's safety matches, two pounds in notes, three shillings and sevenpence-halfpenny in coin, a dirty handkerchief without a laundry mark, a cheap penknife, a small dirty visiting card in a Perspex holder on which was printed the word BIANERI and, under it, an inked-in 6, and four unposted letters. There was no Bianeri listed in the London Telephone Directory, the police found later. They were left with the four letters. Of the two which bore

London addresses one carried the name of a man who rated a visit by a District Deputy Commander on his best behaviour.

So died Luigi Fettoni while his wife was away visiting a sister in Reading; died because his eyes had caught the chequered flight of London pigeons and memory had tricked his sense of time.

1

GEORGE CONSTANTINE came down the garden path carrying an old hickory-shafted mashie in one hand and a linen bag of golf balls in the other. He had found the club and balls in the boot room. The sun was beginning to dip behind the poplars that fringed the edge of the orchard and, distantly, he could hear the hum of summer traffic on the Oxford by-pass. He was thirty, a big man, built like a full-back, sandy-haired with a sun-burnt, square, almost pugnacious face.

As he reached the garden gate a police car drew up in the road outside. It was polished to hurt the eye, and the driver had his peaked cap pushed a little too far back for regulation wear, though this was understandable in the heat of the June afternoon.

A police officer got out on the far side and came to the gate.

He said, 'Excuse me, sir, are you Professor Dean?'

George shook his head. 'I'd want another twenty-odd years. Also a first-class brain. He's in the house.'

The officer went by him towards the house, not looking very amused.

George said to the driver, 'What's the old boy done? Pinched the college silver?'

'I wouldn't know, sir,' said the driver, stiffly.

'Keep things from you, do they?'

The driver gave him the cold look which goes with a uniform and a police car, and George, smiling, went across the road to the orchard. A girl went down the road on a bicycle, dark-haired, her summer skirts flaring out. George watched her. Girls in summer dresses on bicycles. Well, there was that much to be said for being back in England. He glanced at the car and saw that the driver was watching the girl, too.

13

George shook his head at him and went into the orchard. He found an open line between a row of apple trees and began to bang away at the balls. He was not very pleased with his performance and after a time he lit a cigarette and lay on his back under a tree, smoking. A perfect day. As a boy he could remember making himself sick on green apples from the orchard. He thought of the big, fat trout lying under the bridge down by the river. Perfect. Everything was perfect. It always was for the first couple of weeks after he got back.

He didn't see the Professor until dinner-time that evening. Mrs Dean was away and they had it alone, and all through dinner he got the impression that something had happened. It wasn't anything much. Just a small brightening of the old boy's manner. The Professor was sixty, almost bald, one of those thin, gentle-mannered men who look as though they had never really stood upright in their lives. If it had not been for his wife, he could easily have got elbowed away in the rush of life and lost in some corner. George was fond of them both. After his father had died they had looked after him, treated him like a son. It was a pity, he thought, that he saw so little of them.

When the maid had gone, the Professor went to the sideboard and brought the port decanter. At the first taste George raised his eyebrows. It was the Warre 1927, and there were only half a dozen bottles left.

He said, 'What are we celebrating?'

The Professor took off his glasses and polished them on the edge of the tablecloth. He put them back on and then, with a little grunt to himself, said, 'I hope I'm right. I've been thinking about it all the afternoon. Not that I could tell Lucy, anyway.'

George, who was familiar with this manner, the Professor talking to himself more than to anyone else before he could make a point, said, 'You're making it crystal clear to me, sir.'

The Professor smiled. 'How like you, George! Straight to the point. Still, there's virtue in that.' He reached for

14

the decanter. 'You see George – I've just been reprieved. After serving a very long sentence.'

'Sounds interesting. What were you in for?'

The Professor filled his glass, one long thin hand like fragile china against the decanter neck.

'In for? Oh, yes.' He gave a little laugh. 'I was in for innocence, romantic innocence and impulsiveness. Mostly, I suppose, for being young.'

George said nothing, playing with his glass.

The Professor sighed and then pulled an envelope from his pocket. He pushed it across to George.

'Read that. Of all the people I know, I think you're the only one I could tell. Also, you might be able to help clear up the last little anxiety in my mind.'

George pulled the letter from the envelope and read it.

'What's this all about? Why do you have to make an annual payment to someone called Scorpio?'

'I don't any longer. That's the point. But I have done – for more years than I like to think about. You see, George, for many years I've been blackmailed.'

'Blackmailed! You!' George heard his own voice go high with surprise.

The Professor said, 'Keep your voice down, George. The maid may still be here.'

'But I can't believe it. What on earth would anyone blackmail you for? Is that why the police were here this afternoon?'

'Yes. You see, they brought me that letter. It had been found on the body of a man who was knocked down by a bus in London. I think they said two days ago. He died without regaining consciousness in St Thomas's Hospital. They wanted to identify him and thought if I opened the letter it would help them. Well, I recognized the envelope and the typing at once and I knew what would be inside.'

'So what did you tell them?'

'Not the truth, I'm afraid. I said it was an anonymous letter, no signature, no address, about an article I'd written in a magazine.'

'But didn't the police want to see the letter?'

'Yes, but I said it was my letter and wouldn't help. So they couldn't insist.'

'Did they tell you anything about this man?' George stood up and walked to the window.

'They said he was a man in his sixties. There were three other letters on him, but the policeman did not say to whom they were addressed. But he did say that the only personal thing on him was a kind of visiting card with the name Bianeri printed on it and the number six written in ink.'

'Does that mean anything to you?'

'No. But that isn't the point, George. Don't keep shooting questions at me, because I'm trying to tell you the real significance of this. This man was blackmailing me. And now I'm free. You can have no idea how I feel.'

'And you can have no idea how much I'd like to have known about this before and got my hands on that bastard. A bus was too good for him.'

'George . . . sit down. And listen, like a good chap. I want to tell you, and then I want you to do something for me.'

George sat down slowly. 'All right, sir. Go ahead. I'll try and keep the pressure down.'

'When I was a very young man just down from the Varsity,' said the Professor, 'I had an illness and went to stay at Brighton with a maiden aunt. I met a waitress at a restaurant called Morelli's. Her name was Jane Barnes. It was my first love affair and I didn't conduct it very wisely. She conceived and, of course, I offered to marry her. But Jane was a very level-headed girl. She knew such a marriage would be a failure. A sum of money was paid to her by my father and she married a motor mechanic from her own village who was prepared to accept the child as his. Jane, her husband, and myself were the only ones who ever knew the real father – except my aunt and my father, of course. Some years later I married Lucy. You know Lucy, what a sweet person she is. I never told her. Maybe

I should, but I didn't. In 1939, two years after our marriage, I received my first letter from this Scorpio. I had to pay him two hundred pounds or he would tell Lucy and also see that the story was spread around Oxford.'

'So you paid him.'

'Yes, perhaps it was weak of me. But Lucy had just lost her baby – you know about that, of course. And we could never have another. I couldn't bear to upset her . . . and so it went on, year after year. For the last five years I've been paying four hundred.'

'Four hundred! But how on earth have you managed?'

'Somehow. That was the dreadful part. It meant not being able to give Lucy some things I would have wanted to. And I've worked at my books, articles . . . Somehow I've always managed. This Scorpio was shrewd. He never pressed me to any desperate limit. This letter was to increase my payment, because I've just had a small legacy from my aunt.'

'The bastard was very well informed, wasn't he? Anyway, it's over now.'

'Except for one small thing, George. And this is where I'd like your help. You see, this man has certain of the letters I wrote to Jane Barnes. To be absolutely easy in my own mind, I'd like them back. Sooner or later he's bound to be identified and his address known, and I wondered . . . well, I know it's asking a lot.'

'It isn't asking anything. You want the letters back and you shall have them. I'll see to that.'

'I know you will, George. But, please, try and do it diplomatically.'

'I'll try. But tell me, this Scorpio – have you never had any idea who he was?'

'No.'

'What about Jane Barnes? How did this chap get hold of the letters?'

'That's always been a mystery. She thought she had destroyed them all – but obviously some had been stolen.'

'What about her husband?'

'He was killed in the war. She remarried and they now live in Canada.'

'How did you pay this Scorpio?'

'I made a transfer to an account in a City bank – Scorpio Holdings.'

'And you never tried to trace him through that?'

'I did write to the bank once and ask for information, but they sent me a polite letter saying that they could disclose nothing of the account.'

'But couldn't you have got the police on to it? They would have made the bank cough up.'

'The last thing anyone who's being blackmailed usually wants, George, is to have to tell the story to the police and then go into Court as Mr X. How would I have kept it from Lucy? All I'm worried about now are the letters. Scorpio is dead.'

George got up and went to the window, pushing it open. A late thrush was pumping out a song from one of the poplars. Thinking of the Professor as he was now, he found it hard to imagine him as a young man getting involved with some Brighton waitress. He'd probably given her Shelley and Keats and found that they weren't much of a guide when it came to being close to a girl in the dark on the beach, the pier lights winking in the distance. But if all that was remote, hard to imagine, the rest wasn't. Year after year the old boy had been sucked dry by this damned Scorpio . . . damn it, even when he was living here, being brought up by the two of them. And Lucy going without things the old boy would have liked to have given her. . . .

Behind him, the Professor said, 'Let's finish the port, George. It won't keep. I can tell by the way you've got your shoulders up how you feel. Just forget it, and let us have our celebration.'

George was up early the next morning and drove back to town in his Mini-Cooper. He had a top-floor flat in Montpelier Street, near Harrods, which he kept on even

18

while he was abroad. Sometimes he had thought of letting it while he was away, but he knew that that would have meant tidying it up and the effort always seemed too much for him. It had one large room overlooking the square, a small bedroom, a smaller kitchen, and a bathroom in which he could just turn round so long as he kept his head down.

He dumped his case in the bedroom and then called a surgeon in Harley Street whom he knew. The surgeon said it was a pleasure to hear his voice, he didn't know he was back in the country, they must have a game of golf sometime, and what could he do for him? George said that he would like an introduction to someone at St Thomas's Hospital so that he could go round that morning and make some inquiries about a man who had died there a few days ago.

Fifteen minutes later the surgeon rang back. A friend of his was Acting Medical Secretary to the St Thomas's Medical School and would be glad to see him if he called round.

It was five minutes to eleven as he came over Lambeth Bridge and then got side-tracked in the one-way system beyond the roundabout. You turned your back on London for four months and the whole damned place changed. He finally found his way back to the Lambeth Palace Road. There was a row of cars parked outside the hospital. As he cruised past them a car pulled out ahead of him. He went past the empty space and stopped to reverse back. As he did so a blue-painted MGA gave a warning honk behind him and slid, bonnet first, into the space he had thought to make his own. It was a very neat piece of poaching.

George, indignant, backed level with the MGA, and got out of the Mini. He stepped over to the MGA. A girl was in the driving-seat, her face hidden from him as she bent down changing her shoes.

George said angrily, 'I suppose you think that was very clever.'

The girl looked up at him. She had blonde hair, blue eyes, a nose that wasn't much, and a long, lively mouth that at this moment was showing the owner's pleasure.

'Well, yes, I did – actually.'

'I see. I suppose you're one of these damned feminists who believe in extra rights for women.'

'Could be. Do you always swear at strangers like that?'

'Only when I'm angry. I had a stake on that place before you.'

The girl eased herself up from the seat, sat on the back and swung her legs over the side to the pavement, a process which reveals a lot of leg and one which George, despite his anger, watched with the eye of a connoisseur.

'There's no survival,' the girl smiled, 'if you stick to the rules these days.' She stood up and straightened her skirt.

'Well, I must say—' began George.

'Don't tell me,' said the girl. 'I've probably heard it before. What's the matter with you men? Just because women are better drivers and can get into a place front-wards when you have to back in with an even smaller car, you get all steamed up. Anyway, if it helps, I'm sorry.'

George, who had heard people sound sorrier, said sarcastically, 'Well, that makes me feel better.'

The girl, beginning to move away, said, 'There's a car pulling out just ahead. If you hurry you might make it this time.'

She turned and walked back along the pavement towards the main hospital entrance. George watched her with the interest any man would have shown. He liked the way the fair hair swung against her neck, the easy sway of her body in its light-blue linen suit, and the trim movement of the long legs, the stiletto heels tapping a Morse code against the pavement. She was about twenty-three, knew that her good looks helped her to get away with things like this, and was well aware that he was still watching her. Handled differently, this could have finished up with a dinner date which was not something to pass by lightly when one kept coming back to London and finding all the girls one knew engaged or married. He turned to find that he had lost the other parking space.

Fifteen minutes later, he was sitting in the office of the Acting Medical Secretary. He explained to the Secretary what he wanted to know. The man was very helpful. He made a long telephone call and then pushed over to George a page of notes which he had made as he had listened.

George said, 'Could I see the body?'

The man shook his head. 'Not without some proper authority, I'm afraid. He's been taken to the morgue. There's still the Coroner's inquest. I should imagine if you have some real interest you could easily get it. From the police or his widow.'

'His widow? So he's already been identified?'

'Late last night by his wife. Her name and address are on the sheet you've got.'

'I don't think I'll bother then. And thank you very much.'

George went back to his car. On the way he noticed that the blue MGA had gone. He sat in his Mini and studied the sheet in his hand. There were six names and five addresses on it.

Professor Ronald P. Dean,
Lower Lodge, Godstow, Oxon.

Sir Alexander Synat,
Lawton House, Curzon Street,
London, W.1.

The Rt Hon. John Hope Berney,
1074b Queen's Gate, London, S.W.7.

Miss Nadia Temple, Catwell Manor,
Horsmonden, Kent.

Deceased: Luigi Fettoni
Widow: Mrs L. Fettoni, Rix Villa,
Fentiman Road, London, S.W.8.

Two of the names on the list meant something to him. They would have meant something to most other people in the country. Berney and Temple. Synat, too, rang a very distant bell somewhere, but for the moment he could not put anything to it. One thing was clear, though; if they had also received letters from Scorpio, then the man had had a distinguished clientele.

He fished his *'Geographia' Greater London Atlas* from the dash pocket and looked up Fentiman Road. It was not very far away, up the river beyond Vauxhall Bridge.

He drove up the Embankment and, beyond the bridge, took the South Lambeth Road. He turned into Fentiman Road, went a couple of hundred yards down it and then parked. He had no very clear idea what he was going to do. The best thing, he thought, was to play it as it came.

A West Indian in a bus conductor's hat and trousers was washing down a Ford Anglia on the other side of the road and a coloured woman in an apron and a purple headscarf was leaning over the front gate, smoking and watching him. Both of them looked relaxed and happy, safely lodged in the Land of Promise. A fat child, naked except for a pair of yellow plastic drawers, was digging with a table fork in the garden, about to give a rose bush a root trim.

George went over, lit a cigarette, and said to the man, 'Do you know where Rix Villa is?'

The man straightened. Water ran down his bare forearms.

'This is a long road, mister. Mostly numbers.' He turned towards the woman. 'Rix Villa, honey. You know?'

The woman said, 'Who live there?'

'Fettoni,' said George. 'A Mrs Luigi Fettoni.'

The woman nodded. ''Bout twelve up, this side. The rails is broke. You can't miss it.'

George went back up the road. He didn't miss it. Grimy-stemmed laurels, cut low, backed the broken rail and wall. He went up to the front door and tugged at the bell. The iron grip came out and hung, prolapsed, on its wire. Somewhere in the house a bell gave a couple of protesting clanks. He fed the wire back into its slot. Down the side entrance that led to the back door were a couple of dustbins, one with a piece of old three-ply over it for a lid.

The door opened and Mrs Fettoni stood in an angle of sunlight. She wore an overall and a headscarf from which grey hair escaped as though the stuffing were coming out of her head. Small, dark eyes looked without curiosity at George.

'Well?'

'Mrs Fettoni?'

'Yes.' She bent and picked up a folded copy of the *Daily Mail* which lay on the floor at her feet where it had been pushed through the letter-box. She glanced at the headline and tucked the paper under her arm.

'Is your husband in?'

'No, he's not. And what's more he won't ever be in.'

There was no change of expression on her face.

'I'm sorry . . . I don't understand.'

'He was knocked down by a bus a few days ago and killed.'

'Killed?' The surprise he put into his voice gratified her. A little gleam livened her eyes. She was right in the centre of the stage.

'Came as a shock. Though to be expected really. Always wandering around with his head in the clouds. I felt really bad last night. But I'm over it now. I'm off to my sister's again this afternoon. Couldn't stay here, you know, all on me own. Last night was enough. Perhaps you're insurance?'

'No, I'm not. I wanted to talk to him about a letter he sent to a friend of mine who lives in Oxfordshire. Would you know about it?'

'No. And he wouldn't neither. Not even if he was here.'

'Why not?'

'Because he never wrote letters. All he was was accommodation. Did it as a little business. Not that he made much. And I never liked it anyway.'

Momentarily, he remembered the Professor drinking port, celebrating. Somewhere at the back of his mind a cloud began to form with the name Scorpio on it. No, no, it couldn't be, he told himself. Life couldn't be that bloody.

'You mean this house was used as an accommodation address?'

'That's it. People used to call and pick up letters. Never brought their fancy cars down here, though. Walked. But you could tell they were fancy-car types. Carryings-on. Women some of them.'

'He posted letters on, too, did he?'

'Not often. You a detective?'

'No. Why do you ask that?'

'We had one here some years back. Little bald-headed man, I remember. Very took with the cat he was. And very took with that cat I'll be, too, if I don't find him. Got to get him packed up in a hamper to take to my sister's. Can't leave him here now on his own till right after the inquest and funeral. Poor Luigi.'

It was the first expression of sorrow she had made and she did not put much into it.

'Had you been married to him long, Mrs Fettoni?'

'Five years.' Her eyes held him, suddenly intelligent, but without anger. 'I know what you're thinking, too. I don't seem very upset. Well, I'm not. We liked one another. It was just an arrangement – two oldish people who wanted a bit of company. He could be very irritating. And I never liked this accommodation thing. That all you wanted to know? I got to be packed and there's still that cat to find.'

For a moment he debated whether he should press her further. He decided not to risk it. The best thing he could do was to wait and hope that she did find the cat and got away safely to her sister's house.

'No. No, thank you, Mrs Fettoni. In the circumstances you've been very kind. Anyway, this business of my friend's letter isn't too important.'

'That's all right then. I must say for a moment I thought you was coming to collect a letter. There's a few there. But you don't look the kind.'

He went back to his car and squeezed himself into it.

Definitely not the fancy-car type, he told himself. He drove on down the road and was suddenly aware of the loneliness of London. Two streets away and you were in a foreign world and nobody knew a damn thing about you or your business. And then he thought again about the Professor. He was beginning to feel more and more certain that the Professor had celebrated too soon. Luigi Fettoni was dead, but Fettoni, who ran an accommodation address, didn't strike him as likely to have been Scorpio – unless the Professor was his only victim. He was now very interested in the other three letters which had been on the dead man. He hoped he was wrong about all this – my God, he hoped he was wrong. He didn't fancy telling the Professor that it wasn't all over.

He drove back across the river, found himself a meter slot outside the Athenaeum, and walked around the corner to the Travellers' Club. He settled himself down in a corner with a copy of *Who's Who*.

The entry for John Berney read:

BERNEY, Rt Hon. John Hope, PC 1960;
    CBE 1960 (OBE 1958); MP (C)
    Llangwll Division of Cardiganshire since
    1949; Minister of Industrial Development
    since Jan. 1961; *b.* 28 June 1919; *s.* of
    late G. V. H. Berney, MA. *Educ.*: Uppingham,
    Exeter College, Oxford. Barrister Gray's
    Inn and Northern Circuit, 1947. Service
    throughout War, 2nd Lt. (TA) June 1941;
    Capt. Feb. 1943; Maj. April 1944. General
    Staff Officer on HQ Second Army to
    surrender of Germany. *Address*: The Manse,
    Llangwll, Cardigan; 1074b Queen's Gate,
    S.W.7. *Clubs*: Carlton, Turf.

It was quite a picture. Berney was still in his forties and well on his way to the top . . . faster than most people made it. Here was another Welsh wizard, a thrusting, brilliant young barrister not giving an inch of space or wasting a second of time. It didn't take any crystal ball to tell where his sights were set.

The entry for Sir Alexander Synat read:

SYNAT, Sir James Alexander, KBE, cr. 1950;
Public Works Contractor; Partner Lince,
Synat Ltd; *b.* 7 Sept. 1910; *s.* of James
Synat and Katherine Agnes Hall. *Educ.*: The
Academy, Ayr. *Recreation*: Golf, yachting.
Address: Corbels, Falmouth, Cornwall. *Clubs*:
Riggs, Royal Automobile, Royal Thames
Yacht.

George remembered now why the name had seemed familiar. One saw the familiar purple-and-white boards at the foot of so many hoardings from behind which London was sending up new skyscraper growths. Lince-Synat. Scorpio, perhaps, had had – or still could have – a stake in the changing skyline of London.

He looked for Nadia Temple and couldn't find it in the book. There was no doubt that she should have been there as a celebrity, but maybe she had objections. In a way, he supposed, there came a grading in public life when it was more distinguished not to be in *Who's Who*.

He wandered into the smoking-room, ordered himself a Travellers' Joy – equal quantities of gin, cherry brandy, and fresh lemon juice – and read the *Evening Standard*. He was flushed once from behind the paper by a literary agent who paused long enough to give him, 'Hello, didn't know you were back in England,' and then was gone, reluctantly, on the heels of his guest, a well-known actor who was announcing too loudly that if he didn't have a large whisky right away he would die and he didn't care who knew it.

It was three o'clock when he got back to his flat. He flopped out on the settee and took out the Professor's envelope and letter which he had brought with him. He sat staring at it, his face screwed up into a frown. He hated what was in his mind and tried to fight it down. Scorpio had to be L. Fettoni. Had to be.

The telephone rang and it was a man from the BBC Television studios with a lot of unnecessary questions about his last piece of film. Would it be all right if . . . ? Did he think . . . ? He bore with him with remarkable patience, for him.

Afterwards, he lit a cigarette and walked to the window to see how the tulips were doing in the square. An Aston Martin went flashing up the road, breaking the speed limit handsomely, showing a CD-marked tail to the world. The Professor thought that his blackmailer was dead. So he could be. But it was a gamble, and with just the facts he had before him he knew what odds any bookie would give. Although it was much too early he poured himself a large whisky and soda to get the dirty taste out of his mouth. Fentiman Road, he told himself, would have to come up with quite a lot if the dirty taste was to go for ever. The least he would want to find would be a typewriter that could match the typing on Scorpio's letter.

At ten o'clock he took a taxi to the south end of Vauxhall Bridge and walked the rest of the way. He went past Rix Villa. The front-room curtains were drawn. No light showed from the room, or from the dirty scallop of glass over the hall door. The West Indian's car now had an old sheet over it. He turned back to Rix Villa. Outside the gate he lit a cigarette. A hot, sour, summer smell came up from the poisoned earth in which the laurels languished. He went through the gate and down the side entrance to the house. Somebody had knocked the three-ply lid off the dustbin and he held his breath. At the back there was a concrete yard with an old mangle standing up against one wall. The back door was in a small extension from the main house wall. Light showed from a window beyond the dividing wall of the yard and a radio screamed in record-breaking agony.

He tried the handle of the door and it opened. He went

in and shut it. He flicked a pencil torch on and saw that he was not in the house but in a small wood and junk storing extension. Half a dozen cockroaches wandered around the fringe of a wood pile looking as though they wished they had somewhere to go. The back door proper was half glass-panelled and had a Yale lock. If Mrs Fettoni had tripped the catch on the inside he would have to break the glass, but Mrs Fettoni hadn't struck him as a meticulous type, except about the cat. He took a thick strip of Perspex from his pocket and slipped it between the door and the lock. A little pressure and the door opened. A smell of wet flannel and boiled-over milk wrapped itself around him. He flicked the torch again and saw that he was in the kitchen. It would have taken a 'special mention' anywhere for untidiness. Another door took him into the hall which ran through to the front door. There were two doors to his right and a flight of stairs on his left. The first door opened into a small dining-room. It looked tidier than the kitchen because there was less in it. The second door was to a sitting-room. He looked in briefly and decided to leave it until he had checked upstairs. He didn't want Mrs Fettoni coming down in a wrap and curlers, working up to her first scream. There were two bedrooms and a bathroom upstairs, the untidy hand of Mrs Fettoni written all over them. In the small, spare bedroom there was no bed, but a bicycle leaned against the wall and the floor was covered with piles of old magazines and newspapers. He went back to the sitting-room and switched on the light. There was a table, a sofa, a sideboard, three chairs, a television set and a fireplace with a mantel over it that held a bowl of plastic flowers flanked by an assortment of stuff that would have taken an hour to sort out.

He stood in the middle of the room and looked round, trying to make up his mind. There had been no sign of a typewriter anywhere. By now, though, this gave him no surprise. He stubbed out his cigarette in a table ashtray that looked as though it hadn't been emptied for a week and decided to try the sideboard drawers. The first one was unlocked and held a few packs of worn playing-cards, a shoehorn with the arms of Margate Corporation as a handle, some old copies of a weekly called the *Caterer and Hotel Keeper*, and a half-knitted child's vest with needles stuck through a ball of wool. The other drawer was locked. It took him a few minutes to find the key which was in a tobacco tin on the mantelshelf.

Inside the drawer were three partitions made of cardboard. The partitions were divided laterally with more cardboard strips marked in groups of three letters throughout the alphabet except for the last group which contained five letters, VWXYZ. It was a neat little job and, obviously, not the work of Mrs Fettoni. There was a letter, stamp-franked, under ABC addressed to a Mrs Valerie Apps at the Fentiman Road address. There were four other letters under various sections. They all had English postmarks.

George examined the letters and then began to put them back, wondering if their owners would ever get them. He put back the last one – Valerie Apps – and shut the drawer. As he did so, something caught his eye in the dead fireplace. He bent down and picked it up. It was part of a large white envelope, nearly a third of it burnt away. The stamp and postmark were untouched. The stamp was French and the postmark said St Tropez. What was left of the typewritten inscription read

    Mr L. Fett
    Rix Villa,
    Fentiman Roa
    London, S.W.8.
    Anglete

George compared the type with that of the Professor's letter. The envelope had been addressed with the same typewriter. As he acknowledged this, he acknowledged, too, that the Professor for sure had been celebrating too soon. For a moment he stood there quietly punching a fist into the palm of his hand.

He began to fish in his pocket for his cigarettes, wondering whether there would be any point in going over the house more thoroughly when his eyes were caught by the slightest movement at the bottom of the thick curtain which ran across the entrance to the bay window. Just showing beyond one of the folds was the tip of a black shoe.

He hesitated for a moment and then began to step towards the curtain. As he did so it was suddenly whipped aside. A girl moved sideways swiftly and stood facing him across the small table. Her left hand clutched a handbag up under her arm and the right, low over the table, pointed the muzzle of a gun at him.

Sharply, she said, 'Don't move. Stay where you are.'

He looked from the muzzle of the gun up to her face, and then let his eyes drop slowly back to the gun. He was no fool. An armed woman, backed up into a corner, was an unreliable quantity. The handbag was comfortingly feminine – but not the gun. It looked a small, but efficient number.

Very calmly, he said, 'For God's sake be careful with that gun.' As he spoke he saw the gun tremble a little in her hand. She was nervous, but it could be the wrong kind of nervousness.

'Then do as I say,' she said. 'You've taken something from the fireplace. Put it on the table.'

Very slowly he reached into his pocket for the thing she wanted. He'd recognized her almost at once, but he was not putting any faith in their brief acquaintance. The first hadn't been any too friendly. There was no mistake about her, the same blonde hair, the small stubborn nose and the large blue eyes, and the same blue suit showing through a loosely-hanging summer coat. Slowly he put the charred envelope on the table in front of her.

He said, 'You make a habit of taking things from me, don't you? Who are you and what are you doing here?'

She said curtly, 'I'll ask the questions, not you.'

She said it like a line from a play, putting all she could into it, but not quite bringing it off. Still, he told himself, even an amateur with a gun could be effective enough.

Slowly she put her handbag on the table and then reached out for the envelope he had surrendered. He watched her pick it up and slide it awkwardly into the left-hand pocket of her coat. It was that movement which betrayed her. Her left shoulder hunched up momentarily with the effort and her right hand wandered a couple of inches so that the muzzle no longer covered him. He swept his right hand out across the table, taking her handbag and slamming it against her right wrist. The pistol was knocked from her, flew across the room and hit one of the partly-drawn curtains.

He jumped for it and got there ahead of her. She tried to grab at his hand but he stood up and pushed her away so that she staggered backwards and, her legs catching the edge of the settee, sat down.

'Stay where you are!' he snapped.

She looked up at him, made as though she were going to say something and then her mouth-line tightened stubbornly.

George went back around the table, jerked the magazine from the pistol and saw that there were no shots in it. It was a nice neat weapon, though, a ·22 Walther 'Manhurin' pistol. He put the magazine back and slipped the pistol into his pocket.

'All right,' he said, 'let's get this sorted out. Did you know this thing wasn't loaded?'

'Yes.'

'Well, that's a point in your favour. The only damned one so far. Women and loaded guns don't go.'

'I only wanted it to —'

'I know. Just to give anyone a kind of fright. Well, you did.' He pulled out his cigarettes and matches, lit himself a cigarette and tossed matches and cigarette packet to the settee at her side. She ignored them.

'Have you got any right in this house?' he asked.

'No.'

'Neither have I. How long have you been here?'

She reached out then and helped herself to one of his

cigarettes and lit it, and studied him carefully through the smoke.

'A few minutes before you. I heard you come through the back door, and I hid.'

'How did you get in?'

'Through the front door.'

'With a key?'

'Yes.'

'Clever girl.'

Calmly, she said, 'She keeps it on a little ledge up by the fanlight. I watched her go.'

'She's a careless old biddy. What's your name?'

She hesitated, and then said, 'Meade. Nicola Meade.'

'Mine's Constantine. George. What did you think it was? Scorpio, perhaps?'

It touched her. He saw the slight upwards movement of her chin and the moment of surprise in her eyes. She made no reply, though. He hoisted himself sideways on the table and looked at her in silence.

After a moment, he said, 'Well, somebody's got to go on from there. I suppose it's me. I've a feeling that we may be interested in the same thing.' He paused, and then said quietly, 'Blackmail?'

In the V of her buttoned blue jacket a little triangle of white silk showed, topped by a tiny edge of lace that stirred against her brown throat as she breathed quickly.

George smiled and said, 'You don't have to answer, of course. But there it is – that's why we've both paid a visit to nice old Mrs Fettoni.'

She spoke then, sharply, her voice full of contempt. 'I don't think there's anything nice about anyone connected with blackmail!'

George said, 'Neither do I. But I don't think she knows anything about it. What I do think is that you and I should go somewhere and have a drink and talk this over. Agree?'

She hesitated again, but not for so long and then she nodded. 'Yes, I think so.' She got up, moved around the table on the far side from him, and paused when she got to the door. 'My car's parked down the road. Although my name's Nicola Meade – my mother is Nadia Temple. Temple is only her stage name.'

'You don't surprise me too much.'

He motioned her out ahead of him, and then followed her to the front door. Refreshing in the stuffiness of the house, he got a breath of her scent. He liked it and wondered what it was.

2

SHE DROVE him back to his flat in her MGA. In the sitting-room she took one look around and said, 'How on earth can you live in a muddle like this?'

'What's wrong with it? I know where everything is, and when I want to work I clear a corner of the table.'

'But where did you get all this junk?' She picked up an African tribal mask and put it over her face, turning towards him.

'Oh, round and about. You look good in that.'

'Thank you.'

'All you need is a grass skirt.'

'What I really need is a drink.'

He fixed a couple of drinks and she dropped into a deep armchair, first taking a pile of books from it; then, legs crossed, she raised the glass to him. The table-lamp behind her made a little nimbus about her blonde hair. She looked very good to him and if his mind had not been full of the Professor and Scorpio he knew that he would have been hard put not to try and do something about it. Instead, without giving the Professor's name, he told her how he came to be at Fentiman Road. When he had finished, she was equally frank with him. The letter from Scorpio had been brought to their house at Horsmonden. Her mother had said that the letter was from an admirer of her acting, no name or address given. After that the two stories were almost parallel. Her mother had been excited and happy, and Nicola, for the first time, had learnt about the blackmail. But, instead of letters, there was a photograph in Scorpio's possession which Nadia Temple had wanted back. Nicola had got Fettoni's name and address from the main reception desk of the hospital. She had gone to see Mrs Fettoni, pretending that she was from the local paper, learnt that she was going to her sister's house and had waited until she had seen her go and put the key over the door. She had been in the house only a few minutes before George arrived.

George said, 'When she left the house was she carrying a typewriter?'

'No. A wicker hamper and big shopping-bag affair.'

'Did you know that there were four letters on Fettoni when he was knocked down?'

'No.'

'One to your mother, one to my friend and two others to people in London. I've a hunch that they were blackmailing letters, too. Can I ask how much your mother paid?'

'A thousand a year.'

'What!'

'It was three hundred originally but it's increased over the years.'

'A thousand from your mother, four hundred from my friend – and I wonder how much from the other two people, and perhaps other people we don't know about. It could add up to a pretty big income. Does that suggest anything to you?'

'Yes, it does. Poor Nadia . . . it's going to be too awful to have to tell her.'

'I'm with you there. But we've got to face it. All that money doesn't point to someone living in Fentiman Road. I'm damned certain that Fettoni was just a postbox. This bastard Scorpio is still alive.' He put his glass down on the table and looked at her with a sudden grim smile. 'In a way, you know, I think I'm glad about that. It gives us a chance to get at him. That's something to look forward to.'

'But what can you do?'

'Find the so-and-so. When we get our hands on him we can work out the next step. And I do want to get my hands on him!'

He moved angrily away from the table and stood staring at a framed colour photograph on the wall. It wasn't one of his. It was a view of the Zaskar Range from the Kuari Pass, a long ridge of snow-crested peaks in the background and a little splash of red and pink flowers in the foreground. Willow herbs and potentillas. He thought of the times he had brought plants and seeds back to the Professor, of the old boy's pleasure in his work, and then of the shadow that had been over him for years and years, a shadow that still remained. Oh, Mr Bloody Scorpio, he said to himself, just be alive and let me find you . . .

He turned back to Nicola.

'Are you staying in London?'

'At my mother's Kensington flat.'

'Then just leave this with me for a while. Maybe I'll ring you tomorrow. In the meantime don't tell her that Fettoni has been identified. You'd like a crack at Scorpio, wouldn't you?'

She stood up. He liked the way she did it. Uncoiling and suddenly on her feet. She nodded. 'But when we find him, I'll be content just to stand by and hold your coat.' She paused, watching him and then said, 'You must be very fond of this friend of yours.'

'I am. He and his wife brought me up after my father was killed in the war. Another drink before you go?'

'No, thank you.'

He walked down to the car, smiling to himself at the thought that it took exceptional circumstances for a girl to get out of his flat without a pass being made at her. At the car he handed her the automatic pistol.

'Where did you get the thing?'

'Nadia brought it back from France after some trip.' Already in the car she bent down and pulled off her high-

35

heeled shoes, slipping on sandals. Looking up at him, she said, 'You are the George Constantine of *Amazon Aspect* aren't you?'

'Yes.'

'I thought so. My mother loved both your books.'

'Not you?'

'No. I don't go for all that animal and jungle stuff and all those plants.'

'Not even orchids – in a cellophane box, of course?'

She smiled. 'Try me sometime.'

She started the motor and swung away, waving a hand to him. The headlights flicked up full for a moment and then dipped.

He was up early the next morning, his line of action clear in his mind. If you were going to do something there was no virtue in sniffing around it having a debating match with yourself. Sir Alexander Synat was a business-man and he would have trouble getting near him at his office. He drove along to Curzon Street and was ringing the bell at half past eight. A tall, burly butler opened the door and gave him an unwelcome stare. Probably he didn't reckon to start opening front doors before ten.

George said, 'Has Sir Alexander left yet?'

The butler said, 'Sir Alexander is breakfasting, sir. You wish to see him?'

'Ask him if he'll see Mr George Constantine – and if he starts to say, "Who the hell is Constantine?" just say I want to see him about a man called Scorpio. He'll see me.'

'Very good, sir.'

The butler led him along a hallway which had a beauti-ful flower arrangement of lilies and tulips in a mahogany brass-bound tub. He was shown into a room with a thick white carpet, and furnishings in pastel shades. There was another flower arrangement near the window. George wondered what Synat's monthly bill at Moyses Stevens was. The butler went away and through the half-open doorway a black poodle with a diamanté collar came in and attacked George's ankles in a businesslike way. George endured this for a few moments and then – poodles weren't anywhere in the top ten of his favourite dogs – got his right foot under its stomach and lobbed it on to a sofa.

At this moment Sir Alexander Synat came into the room carrying a coffee cup.

'Milligan,' he shouted. 'Get this damned dog out of here.'

The butler appeared, made a one-handed sweep, gathered the poodle, and disappeared.

'Damned dog,' said Synat. 'It averages about fifty pounds' worth of damage a month. And who the devil are you, and what's all this about somebody called Scorpio?'

'Not that I like them,' said George, 'but it probably doesn't get enough exercise. And Scorpio – if I have to tell you – is blackmailing a friend of mine, and I think you could be in the same boat. If you're not, I'll apologize and leave you to your coffee.'

Sir Alexander Synat put his cup and saucer down on the table and looked at George. He looked the kind of man, George decided, who somewhere had a complete inventory of the room filed away for insurance purposes but preferred to ignore what he saw. Somewhere upstairs, probably doing her fingernails leisurely in bed, was the poodle's owner and she wouldn't be Lady Synat. No, put a peaked cap on this man and he would be a cargo skipper out for blood if he were kept a day over schedule in port, loading. Short, stocky, with black hair brushed hard back, he was wearing city dress – striped trousers, black coat, grey waistcoat with a gold-fob chain and a cravat that had come up perfectly like a meringue. His mouth was pugnacious and there was a fine veining against his hard brown face.

'You believe in getting to the point, don't you?'

'I'm more interested in getting to Scorpio. In the last twenty-four hours it's become an ambition. With a little more time it could be an obsession – I hope.'

Synat laughed suddenly, exploding the sound into the

room like a liner calling for a tender. 'Sit down,' he said. 'Sit down. I won't offer you coffee. Nobody in this house knows how to make it. Muck.' He pulled a gold cigarette case from his waistcoat pocket and offered it to George. George took one and a lighter was snapped under his nose with a glint of gold.

George said, 'I gather that Scorpio does mean something to you?' He slipped out the Professor's envelope and held it up. He went on, 'A little chap called Fettoni was knocked down by a bus. He had four letters on him. Last night I had a good look around Rix Villa, Fentiman Road.'

'Private detective?'

'No. I'm doing this for a friend.'

Synat stood up and walked to the window. He looked out in silence for a while, then he spun round and said crisply, 'What do you want from me?'

'Information. How long has Scorpio had you on the hook?'

After a long pause, Synat said quietly, 'Too long.'

'You think he's dead? Run over by a bus?'

'For a moment I was fool enough to hope. Oh, yes, I had the police here, waving a letter at me. But one look at Fettoni's house told me that Scorpio would be out of place there on what I pay him alone. Fettoni was just a pawn.'

'Haven't you ever tried to find him?'

'Naturally. When I get hurt I do something. Tried some years ago. Private detective. I had a first-class man on the job for me. A real sticker. Know what happened to him? He took a sleeper on the Paris–Bern train. Don't ask me why he was going to Bern – nothing in his reports about it. He was found in his pyjamas alongside the track – the other side of Troyes, I think it was. And he wasn't the kind to sleep-walk on a train. After that I gave up and went on paying.'

'I must remember not to use sleepers.'

Synat gave his explosive laugh. Then he said, 'You find Scorpio, I'll deal with him. Pay your expenses, first class. Make you a handsome present afterwards.'

'We're rushing things a bit,' said George, 'but I'll keep it in mind. Do you know the four people involved in this?' He waved the Professor's letter again.

'Yes. I'm putting you with Professor Dean. Right?'

'Yes.'

'Then there's the Temple woman and Berney. My God – why didn't you break in on his breakfast?'

'I can't take politicians too early in the morning. Now listen, Sir Alexander – I've met Nadia Temple's daughter. That only leaves Berney. Four people, four lots of facts about the past. That could give us a lead on Scorpio. I'm already pretty sure that the letters were sent to Fettoni from somewhere around St Tropez.'

'Are you? I see. Well, what's the form?'

'I've got Professor Dean's story. I'd want as much as you, Nadia Temple and Berney would be prepared to tell. Somewhere along the line something might crop up. Would you come in on that?'

Synat was silent for a moment, then he nodded.

'Would you do it now?'

'The sooner the better. What is more, I'll get you an introduction to Berney. Where do I begin?'

'There are some questions first. Did you ever go into this question of a straightforward transfer of money to the Scorpio Holdings account in the City?'

'Yes. I've got more banking contacts than most people. Even on the old-boy basis I couldn't get anywhere. I've an idea about it, of course. But Berney should have a better one. Try him.'

'Bianeri. Mean anything?'

'No.'

'Fettoni?'

'Years ago. Used to be a waiter at a restaurant I used, called El Drago. It was bombed to hell in the war. That's where my trouble started. But I'll swear Fettoni didn't know the first thing about it. He was a lackey.'

'And the blackmail business?'

'Yes, that. Well, it's like this. My father came south with

39

his brother just before the First World War and they started a building business in London. My uncle was the brains, the drive, and the business did well. Then he died and it began to go to pot. I came into it around 1930, when I was twenty, and I had to start pulling it together.'

He went on to explain how he had done this. In partnership with a man called Vinescu, who ran a restaurant called El Drago in Soho, he had bought old properties in and around Soho and converted them into flats. Vinescu had the handling of the flats. The two men prospered. In 1937 when his father had died Synat had started to tender for Government and public contracts. Through Vinescu he was shown ways of influencing the placing of contracts with his firm and the business began to boom. However, just before the war, Synat – now big enough to stand on his own – had broken, amicably, his partnership with Vinescu. Chiefly – George could read this between the lines – because he no longer needed to use the methods Vinescu could provide. He took a partner called Lince and by the end of the war Synat was a very wealthy man with his sights set high. During the war Vinescu and his wife were killed in a bomb incident which destroyed El Drago. Synat did not grieve much over this, George gathered. By now he was shortly due to become Master of his Livery Company, and he was a member of the Common Council of London. He had the money, he had the time; eventually he would become an Alderman and after that there was the chance of becoming the Right Honourable the Lord Mayor of London. A great prospect for an ambitious man. But in 1946 he got his first letter from Scorpio. It enclosed photostatic copies of letters between him and Vinescu, copies of cheques, and extracts from rent books and private ledgers – enough evidence, Synat said, to blast all his ambitions sky high if it were made known to the right people. He paid up, put a detective on to Scorpio and, when that failed, went on paying.

He finished, 'I'm not proud of what happened in those

early days. But if you're going to build big . . . well, you can't always be too nice.'

George said, 'What did your detective find out about Vinescu?'

'His parents came from Rumania, ages back. He married a girl called Carla Samuels from Hackney. She was killed with him in 1943. And I thought that bomb had wiped out all his records.'

'Did they have children?'

'No. Mrs Vinescu was rescued from the wreckage and survived him by about two hours. Her will left everything to her sister, a Mrs Grace Pinnock. So she got the lot. My chap went to see her – she lives at a hotel in Tunbridge Wells. He got nothing from her, except that she hadn't taken over any of the Vinescu papers.'

'How well did you know Vinescu?'

'Very well in the early days. He was much older than me, but we were friends. I went to parties in his flat above the restaurant.'

'What about people he knew? His other friends? People close to him who might have got their hands on his papers?'

'He was a pretty close fish. Fettoni was his head waiter, but he was never at the parties. There was a youngish girl he was rather keen on – an Elsie somebody. But his wife – who was very fond of the girl – used to give him hell about that and I don't think it ever became anything serious. Though now I come to mention it, I'll tell you something funny about that. I was in Venice – 1949, I think it was – staying at the Danielli, and one day on the quay outside the hotel I thought I saw this girl getting into a gondola with a man, a tall, fair-haired chap. They moved off before I could get to them. I'm not going to swear it was her, but I've always remembered it. Does any of this tie up with Dean's story?'

'I'm afraid not. But I haven't questioned him closely yet.'

'You want to go on with this?'

'Certainly I do.'

'And you're prepared to tackle Berney?'

'Yes.'

'Wait there.'

Synat went out of the room and closed the door. After a few seconds George heard the poodle whining at it. Ten minutes later Synat came back, heralded by a yelp from the dog outside.

'Berney will see you at eleven. At Queen's Gate. I told him it was important and confidential and you had my full backing for any suggestion you made. All right?'

'Thank you, Sir Alexander. I'll keep in touch with you.'

Synat rang a bell and the butler appeared.

'See Mr Constantine out, Milligan.' He shook George by the hand and, as George left the room, called after him, 'Watch out for that bloody poodle.'

At that moment the butler fielded the dog as it rushed at George. He carried it under his arm to the door.

As he ushered George out, the butler unfroze long enough to say, 'My apologies for the dog, sir. With all due respect, it's a real sod.'

'Don't worry,' said George. 'But if you want any peace, take my advice – a good long run around the park every morning. Do wonders for both of you.'

Berney's secretary took him upstairs, and along a pillar-box-red carpet, with a black stripe down the middle, to a sitting-room door which was white with gold mouldings. Inside was a black carpet with an eight-pointed golden star in the middle. The Right Honourable John Hope Berney was standing in the west quadrant.

The Minister was a tallish, well-made man. He wore a light tweed suit, an MCC tie, and well-polished brown brogues. His face was just short of handsome, lined exactly where it needed to be to suggest strength of character, loyalty and resolution. His brown hair was just a shade full over his ears and his plum-dark eyes had a touch of warm, almost mournful fidelity which, with a slight sag-

42

ging of his lower cheek muscles, gave him an honest, doggy look somewhere between a bloodhound and a spaniel which must have been worth a lot of votes to him.

The secretary left them and George made a mental note to be polite and watch his language. This was no Synat.

Berney said, 'Do sit down, Constantine.' He pulled a watch from his waistcoat pocket. 'I can give you half an hour. I'm just off to the country.' He said it as though somewhere, vaguely out there, the country was waiting for him impatiently. There was no mistaking the voice, manly, ringing with the distant echo of Wales, a voice – George remembered – which some political commentator during the Suez crisis had called, 'the voice that breathed o'er Eden'.

George said, 'It's very kind of you, Minister, to see me. I'll try to be as brief as I can.'

'Do,' Berney smiled. 'It will be a change from the wordy circumlocutions with which many of my colleagues regale me.' As a joke it hit the ground without any crispness, but the Minister smiled an epitaph over it.

'Frankly then, Minister,' George could not resist it, 'a friend of mine is being blackmailed, so is Synat, and I'd like to know whether you are too. Scorpio is the name of the collector.'

Not a muscle changed place on Berney's face. He just looked at George with the dying shades of his smile still intact. Then, very slowly he walked over to a marble-topped sideboard and, as he reached for a decanter, said, 'I don't usually drink before noon, Constantine. But then, I don't usually get such frankness before noon or after. Will you take a brandy with me?'

'No, thank you, sir. I apologize for my directness. If I'm right off the beam, I can find my own way out.'

Berney turned, brandy glass poised, and he poured himself a generous helping. 'On the contrary, Constantine, just go on being frank. Despite what some people say of me, I can be a good listener.'

George gave him then the facts as he had given them to

Synat. He told him how Synat had admitted that he was being blackmailed and was willing that something should be done about it if the other people involved would co-operate. He did not give him the story of Vinescu, but simply pointed out that with four lots of information a lead might be found to Scorpio. And as he spoke the Minister listened and George got the impression that somewhere behind the dark eyes a first-class brain was going into top gear. Whatever public image Berney liked to put across for political purposes, behind it was a man who had come far and fast on his own and didn't want to be slowed down now.

When he had finished, Berney came back to the north-west corner of the star, and said, 'Interesting. And I make now no bones about it. I had a visit from a Deputy Commander of Police and I have made my own inquiries. I must say that it very quickly occurred to me that a Luigi Fettoni of Fentiman Road could never be Scorpio.' He sipped at his brandy, cocked one eyebrow and in a different tone said, 'My secretary, Maurice, is very efficient.' He nodded to a sheet of typed foolscap on the sideboard. 'Since Synat telephoned me, Maurice has produced a fairly comprehensive biography of George Constantine. From it, I should say that you are determined to go through with this thing whether you are to get any co-operation or not from me?'

'I am, sir.'

'Then there's no point in putting difficulties in the way.' He looked at his watch. 'The country will have to wait a little, while I tell you something which I never expected to tell to anyone.'

He told it, laying it out, not like a politician who was after effects, but like the barrister he had once been, interested only in facts.

His father had never had much money. When he – Berney – had come down from Oxford to read for the law he had had to some extent to earn his way. He had become a political journalist, though there had been no thought

44

of a political career in his mind. Money had always been his big problem because he had a natural tendency to live beyond his income, a tendency encouraged because his friends were all considerably wealthier than he. In 1946 a London editor had introduced him to a Swiss international financier named Gustav Aboler. Aboler had a comprehensive network of confidential correspondents in most countries who covered for him the financial, industrial and political scenes. Berney became his London political correspondent at a handsome salary. He interpreted political trends, gave such information as came his way, and – more significantly – wrote detailed reports of his opinion of politicians of all parties. In return Aboler paid him, and advised him on investments. Berney began to build up a reasonable fortune. In 1949 Berney had decided to enter politics. His letters to Aboler had been shrewd, frank, and castigating. He knew that these – if they came to the eyes of the men concerned – were political dynamite. In 1949 he visited Aboler – for the first and only time – at his villa on Lake Geneva in Switzerland and asked, in view of his decision to stand for Parliament, that the letters be destroyed. Aboler said he would do this. Berney won his election in 1949 and his career since then was public knowledge. In 1955 Aboler died. A month after his death Berney received his first letter from Scorpio, enclosing copies of the most pungent and damaging of his letters. Scorpio pointed out that his letters, if made known to the men who were now his colleagues in the party, would put an end to his political career. Berney paid up. At this moment there was an autumn election in the offing. If his party went back in power Berney would have an important Cabinet position and, eventually, the highest plum on the tree waited for him. He had started by paying a thousand pounds a year. He was now paying two thousand.

He finished, 'Perhaps I don't have to tell you of the petty jealousies involved in politics – worse than any girls' school. What I wrote to Aboler years ago in all frankness would make many men my enemies, would destroy me. And frankly, Constantine, I do not mean to be destroyed. I would rather pay. Scorpio, whoever he is, takes his pound of flesh but he is careful that his victim should not bleed to death.'

'Tell me about this Aboler. How often did you see him?'

'Only twice. In London when our arrangement was made. And in Switzerland when I asked for the letters to be destroyed. I met his widow in London in 1956 and asked her about the letters. She told me that she knew nothing about them, except that Aboler – who knew he was dying of cancer – had destroyed all his personal correspondence two months before his death. Only he had access to the private vault in his house where he kept his confidential files.'

'Then someone must have got copies before he died. What about when you visited him in Switzerland? Who was there? I mean could you have been overheard asking for the letters to be destroyed?'

'No – not unless there was a microphone in his study. As for the people – there was a small house party. I don't remember many of them.'

'Who do you remember?'

'Let me see. There was an Italian, middle-aged, tall and fair-haired. I always felt he was one of Aboler's Milan correspondents. I remember him because of his fair hair. I can't recall his name. But he had a woman with him – his mistress, I think, Aboler told me. A Latin-type girl, good looking. I remember her first name clearly because it was Maria which was the name of my mother.'

'And her last name?'

'I don't remember. But with them was another man, a middle-aged, rather bald Jew. I don't remember his name. I think he was something to do with some theatrical venture that Aboler was backing.'

'And the rest of the party?'

'They're very vague. Mostly much younger people, Swiss, maybe French. Aboler liked young people.'

46

'No English girl?'

'I don't think so. I only wish now I had insisted on the letters being destroyed in front of me. But I trusted Aboler. I still think that he did what I asked.' He moved to the sideboard and put his empty brandy glass down.

George said, 'You make your payments to the Scorpio Holdings account in the City?'

'Yes.'

'No comment?'

Berney turned and smiled. 'I've made inquiries in a roundabout way but I got nowhere. Even if I went to the highest security level – which would mean exposing my whole predicament – I still think I might be blocked. Scorpio must have other irons in the fire besides blackmail. Does any of this help?'

'It could do, later.'

'You're determined to go on with this?'

'Yes.'

'Very well. I'll give you any other help I can.' Just for a moment the voice was limp, exhausted, as though the review of past memories had left Berney full of weariness.

George said, 'You've had letters from Scorpio over the years. What kind of impression have you formed of him?'

Berney's shoulders came back as he shook off his fatigue, the dark eyes brightened, and he was in command of the public Berney again.

'I'd say he was a man of the world, intelligent, educated, ruthless within limits which he sets very strictly for himself. I've always had a feeling mine was not a solitary case, that there were others and by that I mean more than just the four we know about. He's running this thing like a business, and there isn't anything he doesn't know about human weakness and ambition. If it were more profitable for him to destroy me rather than bleed me, I don't think he'd hesitate for one second.'

Back at his flat George got on the telephone to Professor Dean. It was a brief conversation and one which he marked up against Scorpio if he should ever get to him. Just the sound of the old boy's voice at the other end when he began to read the score made George's hand tighten hard about the receiver. The Professor's wife was due back that afternoon. George arranged to meet the Professor at six o'clock that evening at the Trout at Godstow. He could tell Lucy that he was going into College.

He then telephoned Nicola and said he was coming round to see her. She said she was washing her hair and he said he didn't care a damn. Anyway he liked girls with damp hair.

3

BEHIND THE villa and on a level with the first-floor bedrooms, where the hillside had been cut back to take the building, was a long terrace of red tiles. At the far end was a small balustrade beyond which could be seen part of the falling hillside, pine- and shrub-covered, and a small blue angle of sea. This end of the terrace was shaded with a striped awning carried from bedroom-window level to two poles slotted into brass sockets sunk in the tiles. Three coloured mattresses were spread in the shade of the awning.

Maria lay on one of them wearing a yellow bikini. She lay on her stomach, reading, the top half of her body in the sun. By raising her head from her book she could look straight through the open french windows of her bedroom. Just inside the room was a small table with a red telephone on it. She lay there reading, her long legs raised behind her, the toes of one foot now and then caressing the sole of the other. On the hillside behind her the cicadas fiddled in the pines and now and again there was the sharp crack of broom pods exploding. From somewhere below the end of the terrace and out of sight came the sound of a hose being used, and now and then a slow, contented phrase of whistling. It was Gian washing the staff car. After a time the sound of hosing ceased. A few minutes later she heard the door of her bedroom open. She looked up from her book to see Gian come out of the darkness of the room and stand in the french windows. He was wearing khaki shorts and nothing else. There were patches of damp on the shorts from washing the car and his copper-coloured hair dripped with water where he had put his head under the hose to cool himself off. The water glistened on the brown skin of his neck and shoulders. He looked at her, smiling; a young man with narrow hips and broad shoulders and a pleasant face.

He had a towel in his hand and came across and squatted beside her, rubbing the back of his head and his neck. Drops of water splattered on to the pages of her book.

'Where have they gone?' he asked.

'Cannes, I think.'

They both spoke in French.

'They'll be late?'

'Could be.'

He dropped the towel and reached out for her cigarettes and lighter. He lit his cigarette and threw his head back slightly to take the first draw. It was a movement that tightened the line of his throat, familiar to her and filling her with a strange physical pleasure.

'Some day,' he said, 'I'd like to go off. For good.'

She smiled. 'Where?'

'Somewhere. Anywhere.'

He put his hand out and drew a forefinger slowly down the shallow valley of her spine, letting it come to rest just above her lower bikini slip.

'Don't do that, Gian.'

'Why not?'

'You know why not. Lodel would kill you.'

'Lodel!' The word was full of contempt. Then, taking his hand away, he dropped full length alongside her, resting on one elbow, not touching, but looking closely into her face. Smiling, he said, 'You love Lodel?'

49

'No.'

'And Bardi?'

'No.'

'You ever love anyone?'

'I forget.'

He blew cigarette smoke gently into her face and they both laughed.

He said, 'You know why I drink too much sometimes?'

'No.'

'Because I love you. When I drink it makes it easier.' He put a hand on her shoulder and moulded the flesh gently in his fingers. 'We could go off together. I could get some money.' He touched the side of her neck gently with his lips.

'No, Gian.' She rolled away from him slowly and sat up.

Calmly, he said, 'You are afraid?'

'Yes. For you.'

At that moment the telephone in her bedroom began to ring. She stood up and walked – tall, brown-bodied – into the room and picked up the receiver.

Gian watched her, heard her say, 'Yes, this is Maria.' He saw her reach for a pencil and a pad and then sit sideways on the table, the receiver cupped between her shoulder and her neck so that her hands were free. He watched her writing; the movement of her hand, the pose of her body and the still concentration of her face made him full of an angry longing to be free.

He got up and walked into the room as she put the receiver back. She dropped the pad and pencil alongside the instrument. As she turned he put his arms around her and kissed her on the mouth. For a moment she resisted him, took her mouth from his and tried to say something, but he kissed her again, his hands moving over her back, and the resistance went from her. He swung one hand down behind her legs and, his mouth still on hers, lifted her and carried her to the bed. He put her on it, breaking their embrace, and she lay there, untouched by him, her eyes wide open. Slowly she put up her hand, caught his arm and pulled him down towards her.

Outside the cicadas called, sun-demented. A small breeze ruffled the scalloped edges of the awning and a stray zephyr idled curiously into the room, gently lifting the edge of the pad on the table by the telephone. On it, in French were a few lines in Maria's neat script. Translated, the words read:

> Bianeri 12 made monthly visit Fettoni yesterday. House locked. Neighbours confirmed Fettoni knocked down, killed by bus five days ago. Entered house. No sign Scorpio letters. All clean any connection Fettoni with Bianeri.

When George got round to the Temple flat he found that not only Nicola was there, but also her mother.

Nadia Temple was a tall, elegant, dark-haired woman whom George liked at once. But he soon realized that under a rather fluttery manner she was a woman very much in command of herself and quick to make up her mind about people and the best way to present herself to them. For George, to begin with, she decided to be a helpless woman. When Nicola explained to George that she had told her mother that Scorpio was probably not dead, Nadia Temple said, 'It's dreadful, isn't it, Mr Constantine? That monster still alive . . . still hanging over my life like an evil cloud . . . For a while I was deliriously happy, imagining myself free. Now, how can I carry on? How can I?'

Nicola said, 'Come off it, Mummy. You've stuck it for years. Anyway, George is going to do something about it. Aren't you, George?'

'But what can one do? The man is so . . . so devious.' Nadia Temple fluttered her hands and settled back into a chair like a butterfly making a delicate landing on a flower.

Nicola said, 'She's not always like this. Stop putting on an act, Mummy. She's as tough as nails, really. She just wants your sympathy, George.'

'I'm hoping to come up with something more than sympathy,' said George, and he told them both about his interviews with Synat and Berney. He went on, 'Miss Temple, would you like to tell me how Scorpio came into your life? It could help.'

'What, go through all the horrible details? Really, I don't know . . .'

'Of course you can tell him,' said Nicola. 'You tell it very well, too.'

Nadia Temple looked at George, appealing to him for sympathy against the forthrightness of Nicola, and George gave it to her in an encouraging smile.

'I'd like to hear,' he said. 'There's no need to tell me anything that will distress you.'

'But everything about it distresses me, Mr Constantine.'

'Then don't leave out any details, Mummy,' said Nicola. 'You tell George, and I'll go and get my hair dry.'

Alone with George, Nadia abandoned her helpless manner and gave her story simply.

In 1932, when she had been seventeen, Nadia had left the Royal Academy of Dramatic Art and got a small part in a comedy at the Haymarket Theatre. Two years later – after a succession of small parts – she married a man called Desmond Keefe. He had three interests in life, drink, gambling and women, and – she soon learned – lived off the last two. Nadia had left him in 1935 and shared a basement flat in Hampstead with another girl. From time to time Keefe appeared, usually drunk and demanding money. One afternoon in 1937 Keefe appeared at the flat about five o'clock and found Nadia alone. She had a good part in a West End play and was on the point of leaving for the theatre. He was drunk, demanded money, and when she refused it became violent and started to strike her. Frantic with the fear of being marked on the face, Nadia picked up a heavy silver hand-mirror and threw it at him. The mirror hit him on the forehead and he fell backwards to the floor and crashed his head against a tiled fire-surround. She went to him and realized that he was dead. At this moment the girl with whom she shared the flat came in with a young man.

'You will understand, Mr Constantine, at that moment I was a frightened, hysterical girl of twenty-two. Thank God Elsie was far more capable than I.'

'Elsie?'

'The girl I shared the flat with. She was very fond of me and knew how terrible Keefe had been. She and the young man just took charge of everything – and I was glad to let them.'

They calmed Nadia down and told her to go off to the theatre and leave things to them. The next morning Keefe's body was found at the bottom of a flight of area steps some doors away up the road. At the inquest it was disclosed that he had been drinking all day and had announced his intention of going to see his wife. That January afternoon had been one of black, freezing rain, and it was presumed that he had drunkenly mistaken the entrance to a flat higher up the road for Nadia's, and had slipped to his death. Nadia testified that he had never called on her and, in view of his character, no suspicion was ever raised that she might have anything to hide. The following summer Nadia's girl friend Elsie had gone abroad and they had lost touch with one another.

By 1940 Nadia Temple was a star, and in that year she married a Battle-of-Britain pilot, Francis Meade. Two months after her marriage she received her first blackmail letter from Scorpio. Enclosed with it was a blown-up photograph of Desmond Keefe lying dead on the floor of her room. Alongside him was the mirror and a folded copy of the *Evening Standard* – which he had brought with him – that gave the date of the day on which she had accidentally killed him. Nadia had confessed the whole matter to her husband. He had agreed that they must keep it from the police and he had paid the demand. At the same time he had engaged a private detective to try and trace Nadia's girl friend and the young man. A month later Francis Meade was shot down in a dog-fight over

Dover and killed. A month later the detective reported that he could not trace the young man or the girl. In February 1941, Nicola had been born and each year from then on Nadia Temple had paid her blackmail money, the amount rising with her own success.

George said, 'What was the last name of your girl friend?'

'O'Neil – at least that was her stage name. Elsie O'Neil.'

'What did she look like?'

'Tall, blonde, very lively. She was a dancer and worked in touring revues mostly. She was wonderful . . . a very good friend to me. I don't believe she would have had anything to do with blackmail.'

'And the young man?'

'She called him Rick. Richard, I think. I can't remember any other name. Elsie had so many boy friends. He was a rather solemn-faced young man – older than Elsie, though. Dark, and always rather flashily dressed. And I believe he was in show business.'

'The photographs were taken in your room – obviously after you left for the theatre and before they carried the body out. Elsie must have had something to do with that.'

'No. She walked down to the bus with me, because I was in such a state. Rick could have taken the photographs then and said nothing to Elsie. Elsie was rather keen on photography. She had a camera in the flat and a flashlight attachment thing.'

'Did this Elsie ever talk about her family?'

'No. Not that I recall . . . But then the whole thing now is like a horrible nightmare to me. I didn't know anything about her background.'

Later, when George was leaving the flat, Nicola came to the lift with him and said, 'Thank you for being so nice to Nadia. She likes you, too. She tries not to show it, but she has had a very unhappy time with this business. You're going to Oxford today, are you?'

'Yes. I think this thing is beginning to add up a bit. We'll have a talk when I get back. Unless you'd like to come up with me now?'

'Can't. Sorry. Dinner date.'

'Pity. You like him?'

'I'm not sure. He's in the Brigade and about seven feet tall, no chin, pots of money and we go back to his flat afterwards and he plays Benjamin Britten records.'

'Sounds like hell.'

'It is vaguely. But he's got a title. A girl will do anything for a title.'

'That so? Well, I'm the blood brother of a king. He's got a nice little place on the Rio Negro. I'm entitled to an equal share in all his wives and cattle.'

They sat out on the long terrace overlooking the river. A chiff-chaff was putting in overtime in one of the willows on the island across the way. Two peacocks came slowly by them, dragging their skirts like hard-up dowagers walking home in the half-light because they hadn't the price of a taxi. From the bar inside there came a lot of hearty laughter from some University types. The trout and dace were rising greedily to a fresh hatch of gnats, and cars went slowly over the bridge, headlights dusting the underside of the tree foliage a pale sulphur colour.

George and the Professor drank whisky and smoked to keep away the midges, and the Professor was showing nothing of what George knew he must feel.

George said, 'I've got two months before I'm away again. It'll be good to have something to do. Something I want to do. Even if it's going to cost money it doesn't matter. Synat's promised to take care of that. The thing is now to get it organized.'

'You're going to put your head down and charge, eh?'

'I want to make sure of the direction first. You've heard what the others had to say. I'd like to know whether any of it rings a bell.'

A swift came shrieking low over the dusk-darkened river, cutting through the gnats.

The Professor took off his glasses and chewed the end of one of the side-pieces thoughtfully.

'Fettoni,' he said. 'He could have been a waiter at Morelli's in Brighton. I seem to remember someone like that about.'

'And this Elsie? Ever come across her?'

'Jane had a friend who came to the cinema with us once or twice. She'd have been about fifteen or sixteen. I thought her name was Maisy or Daisy. The description fits, though. Blonde, lively. I fancy she worked at Morelli's, too.'

'Vinescu?'

'No.'

'This young man, Rick somebody?'

'No.'

'Grace Samuels? Mrs Pinnock?'

'No. I'm sorry, George. It was a long time ago.'

'Never mind. Do you really think this Jane Barnes kept everything to herself?'

'At the time I did. But now, I wouldn't swear. I've learnt that if you've got something on your mind, it's a relief to talk to someone. She might have mentioned it say, to this Maisy or Daisy girl.'

'Who could have been Elsie?'

'Possibly.'

'She seems to run through the whole thing – except the Aboler episode. What about a fair-haired Italian? He'd have been, say, nineteen or twenty if you'd met him in Brighton.'

'No.'

Behind them the University types came out of the bar and began to make rugby passes and rushes up and down the terrace with a chair cushion. It ended as it had to end. The cushion made a slow parabola out over, and then into, the river.

George and the Professor left the party deciding who

was going to strip and swim for the cushion.

'Nothing changes,' said the Professor smiling as they went back to their cars. 'You sure you want to drive back tonight?'

'Yes. I can have a nice long think.'

The Professor looked at him, was about to say something, then changed his mind. He gave George a little nod and then got into his car and drove off.

The nod and the look on the old boy's face turned a screw a few threads tighter in George.

The next morning, while his eggs were frying, he called Synat and got from him the hotel address of Mrs Grace Pinnock in Tunbridge Wells. Over his cigarette and coffee he called the hotel and spoke to Mrs Pinnock and she said she would be glad to see him any time before lunch, but not afterwards as she would be playing bridge. He said he would be there before lunch. From her voice he got the impression that she would play a good hand of bridge.

Before he had finished his coffee there was a knock on the door and Nicola came in.

She said, 'I heard you wanted a woman for washing up and tidying. You can tell me how you got on with the Professor while I'm doing it.'

'Coffee first?'

'No, thank you.'

'I make good coffee, and you might need it. I'm driving you down to Tunbridge Wells.'

'For the mineral waters?'

'To see a Mrs Pinnock. I'll put you in the picture as we drive.' As she began to collect the breakfast crockery, he went on, 'How were the Britten records?'

'Bang on. I was so appreciative he allowed me one Ella Fitzgerald to go home with.'

The Farley Hotel was almost opposite the town hall. It was a solid, stone-built building with a pillared portico and a quiet gloss about the hallway as you entered which said that residential terms for a suite could be anything

57

from twenty-five guineas a week. It was a haven for wealthy old ladies who knew exactly what they wanted and got it.

Constantine and Nicola were shown up to Mrs Pinnock's sitting-room. It was a big, comfortable room with a fire burning although it was June, but the morning outside had turned to drizzle. There was a comfortable settee and two armchairs, a television set, and a Sheraton card-table tucked away in a corner. On a low table by the fire was a copy of *The Times*, folded to the crossword page, and a blue-backed copy of *The Oxford Dictionary of Quotations*. Standing by the fire was Mrs Grace Pinnock. She looked about fifty, but it turned out later that she was seventy. She was alert, bright-eyed, her grey hair tinted with purple and beautifully looked after. She had good legs, a slim figure, and would have made a great many women of forty look like hell. She sat them down, offered them Martinis which they refused, and helped herself to a generous measure of Drambuie while Constantine introduced Nicola as his secretary, Miss Nicholls, and himself as George Conway, a private inquiry agent, who – as he had said over the telephone to her – wished to make some inquiries about the late Anton Vinescu.

Apart from their names, he decided to be frank with Mrs Pinnock.

He said, 'A client of mine is being blackmailed. There is reason to believe that the blackmailing material was obtained from Vinescu. I am not suggesting, of course, that Vinescu while he lived had anything to do with blackmail. This has happened since his death.'

Mrs Pinnock lit a cigarette, and said amiably, 'You needn't try to be too polite, Mr Conway. I only met Vinescu once or twice, but it wouldn't surprise me if he had been a blackmailer. He was most things in his time. I never understood why my sister, Carla, married him. But she did. And frankly, I'm glad now that she did. I inherited a considerable sum from him through her. However, I can't tell you anything about him. Not only did

Vinescu not let his left hand know what his right was doing, he kept it a secret from the left that there was such a thing as a right hand.'

George decided that there was no dividend coming from Mrs Pinnock without frankness. He said, 'I understand all Vinescu's papers were destroyed.'

'They were. It took my lawyers two years to sort out his property and assets and, I may say, all of them were converted into different holdings on my behalf.'

'Although you say you met him very seldom, do you remember any of the people connected with him? For instance – a dark-haired man called Rick? Or a fair-haired young man who might have been Italian?'

'It's an unusual combination. What was his name?'

'I don't know. Then there was a girl called Elsie to whom your sister was very attached. This girl's other name could have been O'Neil.'

Mrs Pinnock nodded and then stood up.

'This Elsie O'Neil, as you call her, had every reason to have Carla's affection. Carla was her aunt. Elsie was one of my daughters. Elsie Pinnock. I also know the two men you mention.'

She said it without emphasis, but it burst in the room like a bombshell. Mrs Pinnock saw the surprise in them and, smiling, she said, 'Perhaps you will change your mind about having a drink? Ah, I'm so glad.'

She went to the sideboard and fixed George a Martini. She looked at Nicola and Nicola said, 'Nothing, thank you.'

Mrs Pinnock came back to her seat and said, 'I seem to have surprised you both. If there's anything you want to know about Elsie, I'll gladly tell you. We were never very close, but I'm sure that she never did a bad thing in her life. Which is more than I can say for her husband. He, I think, must be the fair-haired Italian you speak about. In fact he was British, of Italian descent.'

George put his Martini down. It was a good Martini – just the kind to take the edge off mild shock. Elsie was a very interesting character. She got around. 'Tell me, Mrs Pinnock, did your daughter ever work as a waitress at a restaurant in Brighton called Morelli's?'

'She did. That was where she met Tony Longo – her husband – his father owned the place. Elsie worked there when my husband and I were in summer shows at Brighton. We had an act, singing and dancing. It was good, but never up to topping the bill at the Palladium. Now then, what is it you specifically want to know?'

'Perhaps,' said Constantine, 'you would be kind enough to give us a brief outline of Elsie's life, and also tell us where she is now.'

'I can tell you about her, but not where she is now. I wish I knew. The other man – the dark one – was a Ricardo Cadim. Elsie worked with him on and off for many years.'

Mrs Pinnock went back to the beginning of the Elsie Pinnock story. She and her husband were in vaudeville, and were always travelling. Elsie was born in 1915 and Brighton was a regular date of theirs in the summer. Elsie – even as a schoolgirl – used to work at various summer jobs to fill in the long holiday. Morelli's restaurant was one of the places. Tony Longo was the son of the proprietor and Elsie had met him first in 1931, when she was sixteen and he twenty. They saw each other occasionally up until the time when Elsie went on the stage. They must have kept in touch with one another because, Mrs Pinnock said, in 1939 Elsie – who was touring with a troupe of dancers in France – wrote and told her that she had met Longo in Paris and they had married and were going to live in Switzerland where Longo had a job. The job was not specified and the only address Mrs Pinnock had was a hotel in Bern. She had lost touch with her daughter throughout the war and had not heard from her again until early 1947.

Elsie had written then from a villa on the coast near St Tropez where she said she and Longo were staying. She enclosed some photographs of herself but never gave her address or said whether they owned or rented the villa. In 1950 she had written from an hotel in Milan saying that she had just had a child – a son – and because of Longo's infidelities she was thinking of leaving him and going back to the stage. Mrs Pinnock had written back offering her and the child a home, but the letter had never been answered. Mrs Pinnock had never heard from her or from Longo again. She explained that because of their profession the family had been used to being separated and to long intervals between letters. But she had begun to worry about Elsie and had written to her old theatrical agent in Paris – in 1954 this was – to ask him if he knew where Elsie was. He had replied that she had not been on his books since the end of the war and he knew nothing about her.

George said, 'What was Elsie like to look at?'

'Very beautiful,' said Mrs Pinnock, getting up and going to a small bureau. 'She was tall, a natural blonde – though she often changed the colour of her hair. She was a singer, and reasonably good. I never liked Longo and when I heard she was thinking of leaving him I was glad. Elsie could always get work and knew how to look after herself.' She opened the bureau and began to take some photographs from it. 'Just think, I'm a grandmother and I've never seen my grandchild.' She came back and handed some cabinet stage-photographs to George. 'These are of Elsie, and there's one of her at the St Tropez villa. You can keep them for a while if you wish. But I'd like them back. There's one of her with Ricardo Cadim, too.' She lit a cigarette as George went quickly through the photographs, and then said firmly, 'One thing I can tell you, Mr Conway. I am absolutely certain that Elsie would never have anything to do with blackmail. Longo, Vinescu, or Cadim, maybe – but not Elsie.'

'What about Ricardo Cadim? Did you know him well?'

'Not very. He was a tall, dark, Jewish-looking man, older than Elsie. He was very fond of her, but in a brotherly way. They did an act together for some time, and abroad I think he used the same agent as Elsie – a François Laborde who has an office in the Avenue Marceau. When I inquired about Elsie I also asked about Cadim, but Laborde said he knew nothing of him.'

'What kind of act did he do?'

'He was from a circus family, I fancy. Originally, I think, he was an acrobatic juggler. You know, walking a wire rope, spinning plates and balls. Elsie was his assistant for some time. I don't remember much about him – except that he hated cats. Elsie only brought him home about twice and my husband had to shut our cats away. Cats gave Cadim the most terrible asthma.'

George said, 'How well did you know Longo?'

'Not well.'

'Was he an intelligent man?'

'Like a knife. Intelligent, full of charm and devoted to himself, and he had a tremendous appeal for women.'

'Anything else?'

'No . . . except that he was mad about hunting and shooting. A first-class shot.'

'Elsie would be getting on for fifty now and Longo four years older. Do you think she's still alive?'

'God knows . . .' For a moment the well-kept face was shadowed. 'Yes, I think she is. But I only say it out of instinct. Her boy would be fourteen. And I've never seen him.'

'Maybe we shall find him and her,' said George.

'I hope so. I do hope so . . .' She moved across the room and helped herself to more Drambuie and, without turning, said, 'Is there anything else you would like to know? I am more than anxious to help you.'

George stood up, shuffling the photographs together. Nicola, standing, too, said, 'There's Aboler.'

George nodded. 'Do you remember if Elsie or Longo ever knew a man called Aboler – in Switzerland?'

'Not that I remember.'

'Does the name Fettoni mean anything to you?'

'Yes. He was a waiter at Morelli's. My husband and I

often ate there. Fettoni was a very nice man, I thought.'
She saw the look on George's face and, with a wry smile,
said, 'Do I gather that I was wrong about him?'

'It could be. He's dead anyway. But thank you for your
kindness in talking to us. You've been very helpful and
we appreciate it very much. I'll let you have the photographs back. By the way' – George paused on his way to
the door – 'what was your impression of a Mr Wheeler
who came to see you once, some long time ago? A man in
the same profession as myself?'

Mrs Pinnock looked steadily at him, then dusted a little
cigarette ash from the front of her dress.

'He was a horrid little man. A bully. He asked no questions except about Vinescu.'

'He was killed sometime later by being thrown off a
train in France.'

'Indeed.' She smiled. 'Possibly, he started to bully someone on a train and met his match. No, Mr Conway, he was
no credit to your profession – if it is your profession?' She
laughed. 'Don't worry, Mr Constantine. You see I'm a
great reader and all the Pinnocks have been blessed with
the most phenomenal memories. In my bookshelf there is
a copy of *Amazon Aspects* with rather a bad photograph
of you on the dust cover. Perhaps you'll autograph it for
me before you go?'

4

COMING BACK from Tunbridge Wells George had his
first argument with Nicola. With Wheeler in his mind, he
realized that this search for Scorpio could be dangerous
and he did not want Nicola to come to Paris with him.

She insisted that she was coming – and if necessary she
would go alone. She had a bigger stake in this affair than
he had. Did he think she was a child who couldn't look
after herself?

Against her spirited opposition George could do

nothing. She was coming and that was that. Seeing the look in her blue eyes, the set of her firm chin, George decided that there was no hope of making her change her mind.

They flew over to Paris the following morning. Synat got them their flight-booking through his firm. Synat, too, offered them the use of a car which he kept permanently in Paris for continental use. Synat had said as well that if they kept in touch with him he would pass on any progress to the other three. Synat also arranged a large credit for them at the Banque de France. Synat, in fact, was behind them a hundred per cent.

As a matter of caution it had been decided that all four of them, Synat, Berney, the Professor and Nadia Temple, would make their annual payments to Scorpio. This was unfortunate, but essential. If Scorpio did not get his money and George began to get too close to him, he would know at once for whom George was working. It was vital that Scorpio should have no idea anyone was trying to trace him, or – if he did suspect this – that he should not be able to pinpoint the source. Once he knew that George was backed by the four, he could call the hunt off by threatening to expose the four immediately and he might well do this even though it would mean a loss of income to him. This led to the problem of Nicola's and George's identity. Scorpio might well know that a George Constantine had been brought up by Professor Dean. Equally well, he would know that Nadia Temple's real name was Meade and could connect Nicola with her. It was here that Synat again came to the rescue. He gave them the name and address of a man he knew in Paris who would fix them up with false British passports which would be quite adequate for hotel purposes in France. Business men, he explained, often wished to travel incognito abroad and you could not do it if you had to slap down your real passport when checking into a hotel. The false passports would not stand up to expert scrutiny, but they were adequate enough to satisfy a hotel clerk and the local police.

Just before noon they drove to the address which was just off the Avenue des Ternes and George went in with their real passports, a letter of introduction from Synat and spare passport photographs which they had brought over with them.

He was told to come back at three-thirty. At three-thirty-five he had the false passports of George Conway and Nancy Marden – this last Nicola had spent a lot of time on in the plane because she had her initials on some of her travelling equipment. There was nothing to pay. The account would go to Synat.

At four o'clock they were booked into the Hôtel Sainte-Anne near the Bibliothèque Nationale. At four-thirty George was in the Avenue Marceau. Monsieur François Laborde ran a theatrical agency, three floors up and two rooms. The reception room had a girl behind a typewriter at a desk. The girl wore spectacles so thick that they made her eyes look like streaky agates and she had green card-board cuff-protectors on her wrists: something George had never seen before. She understood his French, which was a point in her favour, asked him to wait a moment, in a voice which he felt might have a German accent, and then disappeared through a door at the side of her desk.

George wandered around the room. Apart from the desk, it had three chairs against one wall, and a long leather bench against another. All the walls of the room were plastered with photographs of clients. Most of them looked as though they had been clients for a long time. George went rapidly through the gallery. He was looking for Elsie. Among the more recent ones were quite a few good-looking girls, but none that could be Elsie.

Miss Spectacles came back at that moment and said Monsieur Laborde would be happy to see Monsieur Conway. George was shown in.

François Laborde was a barrel-shaped man, and had an outsize baby face under a light fuzz of brown hair. An unlit cigar was stuck in the corner of his mouth and there was a flash of gold from his teeth and his right hand.

George, who was glad to have the cover, explained that he was a private detective acting for a Mrs Pinnock in England who was anxious to trace the whereabouts of her daughter Elsie.

'I understand,' he said, 'that many years ago you acted for this Elsie Pinnock, and that some years ago Mrs Pinnock wrote to you about her and a man called Ricardo Cadim.' He dropped a photograph of Elsie on the desk in front of Laborde.

Laborde nodded, picked up the photograph and studied it.

'Good legs. Good figure.' He nodded to himself again. 'Yes, I remember her – and her mother writing. But I know nothing of her now. She was on my books before the war and for a couple of years after. Then – phut!' He handed the photograph back.

'You knew she was married?'

'I seem to remember something about it.'

'Did you know the man?'

'No, monsieur.'

'Would you have any old records, giving her address, maybe?'

'No, monsieur. When a client leaves my book' – he patted a fat, black-covered loose-leaf ledger on his desk – 'the pages go out and into the basket. Otherwise,' he smiled, 'I would need a library as big as the Sûreté's.'

'And this Ricardo Cadim? She worked with him sometimes I believe.'

'Yes, I remember him – but that was before the war also. When I was new in the business. But I have not heard of him for years. I am sorry, monsieur. But in this business people come and go, and when they go they do not keep in touch. Have you been to other agents in Paris?'

'No.'

'Tell me where you stay, I will make inquiries for you.'

'That's good of you. The Hôtel Sainte-Anne. You know it?'

Laborde shrugged his shoulders. 'It is all right, but there is no restaurant.' He pushed his chair back and hoisted himself up. 'I am sorry to be of so little help. But I will make other inquiries and ring you, perhaps. You know' – he put a little extra effort into his smile – 'always I have had a romantic thing about detectives. I read nothing but *romans policiers*. Maybe I would have been good.' He moved to the door as he spoke. 'At least it would have been more exciting than this.' A fat hand looped slowly round the room. 'Comedians, show-girls, acrobats . . . they are very dull, monsieur. You know why? I tell you – because they are egocentric. Egocentric people are always dull, even in bed.'

He opened the door.

George thanked him. The door shut behind him. Miss Spectacles watched him go out and gave a little nod of approval to herself as he shut the door without slamming it.

From the window of his room, a few seconds later, François Laborde watched George come out on to the pavement and begin to look around for a taxi.

Laborde went back to his desk. He thumbed a bell push. Miss Spectacles came in with a notebook.

'Dorothée,' said Laborde, 'where is Cadim this week?'

Dorothée raised her lensed eyes to the ceiling and thought. After a moment she said, 'He's still in Cannes. He was held over for another week.'

'Phone him and give him this message.' He leaned back, put the tips of his fingers together and stared at a Cinzano ashtray on his desk. Dorothée sat down on the chair beyond the desk and balanced her book on her knee.

Laborde began to dictate. His message read:

Visited today by George Conway, British, alleged private detective. Inquiry whereabouts Elsie Pinnock. Lead to me from mother. Will check credentials soonest.

When he had finished, he said, 'I shall be at home all the evening.'

Dorothée nodded and went out.

Laborde pulled the telephone towards him and dialled a Pigalle number. When, after a long interval, it was answered, he said, 'Ernst? François here.' The reply made him smile and then he went on, 'Sometime or other we all get disturbed at that wrong moment. Listen. A Monsieur Conway, British, staying at the Sainte-Anne. Anything you can get. And stay with him. Report to Dorothée.'

He put the receiver back, swivelled his chair and awkwardly lifted his feet to the desk and stared at the door to the reception room. It was a long hard stare that had a lot of probing thought and speculation behind it.

Against some argument from George they went to the Tour d'Argent for dinner that evening.

Nicola said, 'I can't think why you bellyache so. Isn't it enough that I want to go there? Synat's paying. He wouldn't dream of going anywhere else. Anyway, it's part of the agreement.'

'What agreement?'

'That as far as this business is concerned, I'll do exactly as you order when it's work. Out of hours, all the decisions are made in the ordinary way.'

'What way is that?'

'Mine chiefly.'

'I can't think of anything fairer.'

Over dinner Nicola said, 'You don't think you'll get anything from Laborde, do you?'

'No.'

'Why didn't you try him with a few other things? Scorpio, Longo or this Bianeri thing?'

'I was tempted. But I thought that if I did – and if he were in with Scorpio somehow – then it might give too much of a lead back to our four.'

'And if nothing comes from Laborde, what do we do?'

'Go through with what we've planned. Go down to St

68

Tropez. That's where the blackmail letters were posted. Elsie used to stay down there with her husband at a private villa. We've got a photograph of it showing the front. Any agent in St Tropez will be able to tell us where it is. Then we have a look at it and, I hope, the people inside. And I'm hoping one of them will be Scorpio.'

'And when do we go?'

'Midday tomorrow. We'll give Laborde until then to phone.'

George looked across at Nicola and temporarily forgot Scorpio. She was wearing a little black dress that did things for her figure which George found hard to put out of his mind. On it was pinned an orchid which he had presented to her in a cellophane box and which would not be charged to Synat's account.

'You know,' he said, 'one's second thoughts sometimes are the best. After I'd brassed you off for pinching my parking space and you walked away, I told myself that I ought to have asked you out to dinner instead. I didn't think then that I'd get the chance to do it in Paris. Romantic, isn't it?'

'Every girl's dream.'

'And we're staying at the same hotel.'

'Don't worry. I shall lock my door.'

'Sensible. And don't forget to put the orchid in water. I can't afford a fresh one every time we dine.'

Nicola smiled. 'It was rather a nice touch, the orchid. Is that your usual line?'

'Depends. Some girls like a manly directness. Grab and scuffle. I thought you were different.'

'I am. But I should think you were pretty good at grab and scuffle. You've got the build. I bet it went with a swing on the Orinoco.'

'Naturally. It's no good trying orchids there. They're as common as daisies.'

In actual fact, the moment for grab and scuffle came sooner than George expected. After dinner they went to a night club for an hour, discovered they were both bored with it, and decided to call it a day. It was just before midnight when they went up to their rooms. Nicola's room was next to George's and he paused outside to say good night and see her in. She gave him a warm smile, a slight shake of her head as he contemplated prolonging the pause, and then was gone.

He went to his own door, unlocked it, and went in. The light was switched on and a man was bending over his open suitcase by the window. Briefly George saw the open doors of the wardrobe and the drawers of the chest pulled out.

The man dived for the room door, trying to hand George off as he went. It didn't work. George grabbed him by the back of his jacket, swung him round and, as the man tried to kick out at him, he lifted him off his feet and slung him hard across the room. The man thudded against the bed and collapsed to the floor. George picked him up and sat him on a chair and then jerked his head down between his knees which was the only cure he knew for bringing round a man winded in a tackle.

George said, 'Just get your breath back and think up a story.'

He took his hand away from the back of the man's neck and as the other straightened up George slapped at his pockets and went on, 'Just keep your hands nicely out in the open. Otherwise I'll knock you through the window. Do you understand English?'

'Perfectly, monsieur.'

He had a mild voice and a small, pale rabbity face, the likeness accentuated by a nervous twitching of his upper lip. He wore a neat grey suit with a thin red line in it, a red bow-tie, and grey silk socks with red clocks.

'All right. Well, let's have the story.'

The man gave a little shrug of his shoulders, his composure coming back fast. 'There is not much to tell, monsieur. Principally, you returned too soon.' He fanned one hand gently at the room. 'I have taken nothing. Lately, I have been very unlucky.'

70

'You speak English damned well. Who are you?'

'My name is Ernst. I worked in England once in a travel agency.'

'Ernst what?'

'Fragonard.'

'Don't tell me you're a painter as well.'

Ernst smiled without enthusiasm. 'The joke is often made, monsieur. No, I am just an opportunist. I work the hotels. You intend to hand me over to the police?'

George considered this for a moment. Whether he believed Ernst's story was one thing. Handing him over was another. That would mean two complications: a loss of time in Paris, and maybe some awkward questions about his own registration at the hotel under a false name.

George said, 'Stand up.'

Ernst stood up. He winced and rubbed at his left ribs. He said, 'You are very powerful, monsieur.'

George said, 'I want everything out of your pockets and on the bed. Get moving.'

Ernst went to the bed, hesitated, and then began to clear his pockets. As he did so – maybe because he sensed hope in the air – he said, 'If you had been a Frenchman the room by now would have been full. The hotel manager, the staff. I have always admired the British phlegm.'

He put on the bed a wallet, a ball-point pen, a dirty brown envelope, a clean silk handkerchief, a packet of Weekend cigarettes, some loose money, a box of matches, a small screwdriver with a plastic handle, a penknife, a thin torch and a fat bunch of keys.

George went through the wallet, keeping half an eye on Ernst as he did so. It held some notes and an identity card for Ernst Fragonard. George handed it back and Ernst made a little inclination of his head. There was less twitch to his upper lip now and hope was brightening his eyes.

George opened the unsealed brown envelope and took out two well-thumbed photographs. They were of the same girl, a rather fattish brunette who, both photographs taken together, had made no secret of any of her charms. George handed the collection over.

Ernst, rather apologetically, said, 'My fiancée. She is a very intelligent girl.'

George nodded, and said, 'It's about the only thing that doesn't come out well in the photographs.' He handed back everything else except the fat bunch of keys. He knew skeleton keys when he saw them. 'I'll keep these,' he said. 'I might want to go in for your line of business.'

'But monsieur – they are my living.'

'Too bad. But it's part of the bargain. You go free – I keep the keys.'

Ernst considered this and then with a shrug accepted it.

'Very well, monsieur. But could I have the key of my apartment. Otherwise I am free but homeless.'

George handed him the bunch and watched him take a Yale key from it. As the bunch was handed back, George said, 'You ever been in the theatrical business?'

Ernst shook his head. 'No, monsieur.'

George moved quickly, grabbed the front of Ernst's jacket and lifted him until his toes just touched the ground. He shook him. 'Does the name François Laborde mean anything to you?'

Ernst waggled his head, panic chasing hope from his eyes. 'No, monsieur . . .'

'I could bounce you around this room until your girl friend wouldn't recognize you. Think – François Laborde.'

'Monsieur . . . please . . .' It was a thin wail that did nothing to soften George's heart.

'François Laborde. Think!'

Ernst shook his head. 'No, monsieur. I swear. I am as I say . . . Please, monsieur.'

George let him go. He went to the door and opened it. 'Out,' he said, and stood waiting. Ernst hesitated. He had more intelligence than his girl friend probably, but he was not so well protected in the right place as she and he could read George's intention.

Suddenly he made a dart for the open door, but he was

dealing with a man who had been practising the art of kicking ahead from prep-school days. George got him fair and square as he went through the door. There was a wail as Ernst's acceleration increased.

George went carefully through his belongings. Everything was there. He took his and Nicola's real passports from the inside pocket of his jacket and put them under his pillow. Ernst might be a genuine sneakthief, he might not. If he were not then the whole incident was far from amusing.

He went along to Nicola's room. Somewhat suspiciously she let him in. When he had told her what had happened, he went on, 'Now you see why I didn't want you to come to Paris. This might be only the beginning of trouble.'

Sitting on the bed in her dressing-gown, Nicola said firmly, 'Don't let's start that argument again. I'm not some fragile Victorian miss. If Ernst had been in here he would have been put through some judo exercises. So stop fussing.'

'Judo?'

'That's what I said. Do you want a demonstration?'

'No thanks.' George went towards the door. 'But I still think —'

'Go back to bed, George dear. It's nice of you to fuss — but there's no need. Good night.'

She gave him a big smile and closed the door on him. He heard the key turn in the lock.

At ten o'clock the next morning François Laborde came into his office through the private door, hung his tawny-coloured felt hat on the peg behind it, walked to the half-open window, put a cigar in his mouth, and admired the morning with genuine appreciation. It was a morning full of sunshine and the warm smell of croissants and coffee, a morning which put the tails of the Paris sparrows up and an ivory sparkle on the white batons of the traffic police. He watched a dog lift its leg against the side of an advertisement kiosk, a woman shake a duster from an opposite window, and a Facel Vega come down the Avenue making the other cars look like something that had crawled out of the sewer vents.

He rang for Dorothée, who came in and put two messages in front of him, and then, to her greeting, added, 'There are three people waiting to see you. That man from the Bal Tabarin again. A Mlle Liepe, by appointment, the one who was Miss Tractor Queen at Clermont-Ferrand last year. And the Dutch illusionist.'

Laborde picked up the messages. 'Get the illusionist to make them all disappear. I'll ring when I'm ready.'

The first message was from Cannes, and read:

> Conway. Usual arrangements. Have
> Bianeri 12 check his English police
> licence.

The second was from Ernst Fragonard and Laborde didn't have to be told that Dorothée had made a précis of the original telephone message. It read:

> Hôtel Sainte-Anne. George Conway, British passport 3967 checked. Details. Private detective. Born Plymouth, 16.6.1934. Address: Woodbridge, Suffolk. Height 6 ft. Hair, light brown. Eyes, blue. Scar over left ribs. Passport issued, London, 1960. Visa and entry stamps – Italy, France, Spain. Disturbed in room, midnight, held, passed as hotel thief. Pleasant type, but tough. Luggage normal. Could be high-class detective, but query. Kept my keys. Questioned about you. Denied. Query whether believed. Expenses and fee – 70 NF.

Laborde considered the messages for a while and then he picked up the telephone and rang Richelieu 12.56 and asked for Monsieur Conway.

Over the telephone he said, 'Monsier Conway? *Bonjour.* I have made some inquiries for you from other agents, but none of them can help, I regret. However, if you are going to be in Paris, I will make some inquiries also direct at the cabarets and night clubs . . .' He paused, listening and then resumed with a laugh. 'Not at all. I told you this

74

life was dull. I do it willingly. Just for a time it takes me into another world, no?'

When he had finished he rang for Dorothée and gave her two messages.

One was for Ernst Fragonard. It read:

Conway staying Sainte-Anne two more days before leaving for Bern. Check him to train. Expenses and fee first job 65 NF. Deduction for incompetence.

The second was to Albert Larch, Poste Restante, Leicester Square, PO, London. It read:

George Conway, private detective, Woodbridge, Suffolk – maybe London firm – check police licence.

When he had finished dictating these messages, he said, 'Send in Miss Tractor Queen first, and interrupt me with a phone message after five minutes.'

They left the Hôtel Sainte-Anne an hour before noon. At Fountainebleau they went left-handed to take the N6 route. It was the usual business, more and more lorries with trailers on the road, the big radiators roaring past, each one with an orange-tighted skating girl pin-up. The only thing to do was to put your foot down hard, keep your eye off the advertisements and, if you got bored, tell the story of your life to your passenger. George's story lasted the thirty-three kilometres from Fountainebleau to Sens, where they hit the N6 proper. Nicola got hers in between Sens and Auxerre which was fifty-seven kilometres – a discrepancy in time and distance accounted for by the wayward detail she put into her fewer years. At Auxerre they stopped for a drink and some food and then Nicola took over the driving. Much later they turned off the N6 at Tournus and took the N75 to Bourg-en-Bresse. They stayed at the Hôtel France in the Place Bernard, a pleasant square, near enough to the N75 for George to be kept awake most of the night by lorry drivers throwing dustbins off their vehicles as they roared through. He lay awake, convinced he had done a wise thing in letting Laborde think he was still in Paris before going to Bern. Ernst Fragonard had been too good to be true. He awoke the next morning, rather short-tempered and with a touch of indigestion from the *quenelles de brochet* he had had for dinner, and was gratified to find that Nicola was the kind of girl who knew when not to talk. Everything was normal again after a quick coffee stop at Lyon, and after that it was hard driving, made pleasant by Synat's car, which was a low-slung, green Lancia, and a dusty thankfulness when they arrived in St Tropez where they got rooms in a small hotel, without a restaurant, overlooking the port.

At half past six, bathed and changed, George walked into the *Agence des Maures* and found a white-haired estate agent with twinkling blue eyes, and the slowest movements in the world.

George showed him the photograph of Elsie Pinnock taken at the front of the villa in which she had stayed with Longo. It was quite a comprehensive view of the façade, umbrella pines behind and some sea away to the left, taken at an angle. George said he had promised a friend in England to call at the villa, but unfortunately had lost the name and all the directions to find it. Perhaps Monsieur could help him.

The agent took a good look at it and nodded his head slowly.

He said, very deliberately, 'It is not on my books. Another agent in town has it. But I know it. Who could not? It was built just after the war by a builder from Beauvallon. He is good. Always he gives this Spanish look to the patio.' He handed the photograph back and smiled.

'Where is it?' asked George.

'On the cliffs beyond Cap Camarat. It is called Les Roches-Pins. You are thinking of buying around here, monsieur?'

He might have been slow but he hung on and it took George some time to make it clear that he was not buying and to get out of the place with the name of the agent who handled Les Roches-Pins. He went back to the hotel, picked up Nicola and they went to one of the cafés on the Quai J.-Jaurès for a drink. From the café Nicola telephoned the other agent and came back with the news that the agent sometimes had handled the letting of the villa, but not for the last four years – though he had plenty of others as good on his books, if Madame were interested – and that the owner was a Mlle Guntheim, 203 Rue Poliveau, Paris.

'Well, there's nothing to do tonight,' said George. 'We'll leave it all until tomorrow. For the time being, let's relax.'

They sat for some time over their drinks, the evening breeze setting the water slapping gently at the sides of the moored yachts. It was June and the place was filling up but there was nothing like the crowd there would be when the French holidays began.

The following morning George hired a motor boat. He had some difficulty in persuading the boatman that he was quite capable of handling it himself, but clinched it eventually by leaving a large deposit with the man. He took it out of the port with Nicola sitting up in the bows and, keeping as close inshore as possible, rounded first Cap St Pierre and then Cap St Tropez and headed due south towards the lighthouse at Cap Camarat. On their starboard hand was the long low sandy stretch of the Pampelone beaches. Inland the sun was gilding the flanks of the Massif des Maures. It was a calm morning, the sea as smooth as oil. When they had cleared the Camarat headland with its white block of lighthouse buildings, Nicola reached for her field-glasses and began to search the coast. The land curved inwards from the headland, steep pine- and shrub-covered slopes rising for about two or three hundred feet. They kept about five hundred yards out and there was no trouble in spotting the villa Les Roches-Pins. It stood on its own, about two hundred feet above the sea. There was another villa much nearer the headland. Through the pines a road could be seen coming down to Les Roches-Pins and there was a white car parked to the left of the house. A small path zig-zagged down the slope from the villa to the sea. A yellow dinghy was drawn up on a flat rock, clear of the water. There was no sign of life from the villa. George eased the motor down so that they only just had way on them, and took the glasses from Nicola.

'Perhaps they're late risers,' she said.

George ran the glasses slowly over the place. There was no mistake about it. There was the long run of terrace and patio with steps going up to it, the arched lower-roof supports, the tumbling bougainvillaea and coloured splotches of geranium and petunias. The white car was a Mercedes. He handed the glasses back to Nicola, opened up the engine, and they went fast down the coast, the flank of the cliffs blocking off their view of the villa.

They went down almost as far as the next headland and then came idling back, George watching the cliffside closely. For the moment, if anyone were watching from the villa, he wanted it to seem as if they were just a couple of holiday people taking an innocent trip. He surveyed the steeply-rising ground, taking in its general lay-out, knowing that the picture would stay in his mind and serve him even in the dark if necessary.

Nicola said, 'What do we do?' She lit two cigarettes and tossed him one. He caught it in his palm and right-ended it before it could burn his skin.

'Go back. We don't want to draw attention to ourselves. We'll have a look at it from the land side and then decide.'

Two hours later they were in the Lancia, Nicola driving and George with the Michelin Sheet 84 on his knees. Once out of St Tropez the road dropped to the flat land behind the Pampelone beaches, olive groves, fields of maize and tomatoes and, nearer the sea, long thickets of bamboo growths. They passed a couple of ox-carts looking like something from the Middle Ages. A lorry overtook them in a cloud of dust and a blue-jeaned boy in the back stuck his thumb up in derision. Some two kilometres before Ramatuel they swung left-handed on to a side-road leading

78

up to the lighthouse. The ground rose and they were in pine trees. The road began to snake in sharp curves, as though it hated the climb and was trying to avoid it. Half way up, as they approached a corner, there was a blare of horns ahead and a white car came sweeping into sight. Nicola pulled over hard to the right and the car went by them in a cloud of red dust. It was a white Mercedes. George had a glimpse of a sandy-haired young man at the wheel and a rather stiff-faced, dark-haired man in a white shirt sitting alongside him. He turned but was too late to get the number, though he did see the CH touring plate.

'Swiss,' he said.

'Road hog,' said Nicola.

George smiled. 'Pull in where you can. We'll walk. We must be close.'

Nicola pulled off the road between some pines and, as she cut the engine, the noise of the cicadas came up loud and insistent. A hundred yards farther up the hill there was a rough driveway opening on the right. The gate was drawn back and had a board on it marked, *Les Roches-Pins*. Another sign on the roadside said, *Propriété Privée. Entrée Interdite*. And another sign, nailed to a pine tree, said, *Chasse Privée. No Camping*.

'Whoever lives here,' said George, 'believes in privacy.'

'Good luck to them,' said Nicola. 'From what I know of the French they'll camp and hunt just where they want to. Do we go down and try and get a subscription for the parish magazine?'

George, who was looking at a barred grille let into the road between the gate-posts to keep cattle from passing over it, said, 'No. They'd know we were coming. Look.'

He pointed to a thin cable that came out of the ground to the left of the grille and ran down the driveway fastened about a foot high to small posts. 'Put your weight on the grille and it goes down half an inch and makes a contact. Somewhere down there a bell would ring. They like to know what's coming. Not that I'd call it unusual. Land-owners everywhere are touchy.'

'What do we do then?'

'Well, we know the lay-out. I suggest we have a drink somewhere and decide. We don't want to be caught loafing around here.'

They went back to the car and then drove down the hill and on to Ramatuel. They had a drink in a café whose forecourt was shaded by a gigantic elm and there, over beer and grenadine, they came to a decision.

The blackmailing letters had been posted recently from St Tropez. Their only other connection with St Tropez was this villa where Elsie had stayed with her husband, Longo. It might well have changed hands since then. The Longos might only have rented it for a short period, but if Longo still had an interest in it, still came here – and if he was anything to do with Scorpio, or even Scorpio himself – then the letters might well have been typed at the villa. In that case, in the villa somewhere there might be stationery that matched the envelope and writing-paper used, and there might be a typewriter whose type would match the type of the letters. Before they could do anything about Scorpio they had to identify him. The first step seemed to be to get into the villa and to see what could be found. If they could prove the letters had been written there, they were well on their road to Scorpio.

'So you're going to break in?'

George nodded. 'There were two men in that car that passed us. I've got to find a place where I can watch the villa. When the car goes out with them – I go in.'

'But there may be other people there still.'

'Of course. I'm going to have to make certain of that first. It's just a question of watching and making sure before I move. And it may take a few days. I'd be crazy to go in at night. The place is probably stiff with alarms.'

'And what do I do?'

'Exactly what I tell you.'

'Masterful, eh?'

George frowned. Then he said, 'Let's be straight about this. All right, it's the South of France, sunshine and beach umbrellas. But a man called Wheeler was thrown to his death off a train. Four people, at least, are being blackmailed. Scorpio doesn't fool around. Neither do we. Besides,' he smiled, 'I'm beginning to get fond of you – even though you keep your hotel door locked – and I don't want you hurt.'

5

AN HOUR after lunch, while she was working in her office, Maria heard the Mercedes drive off. She worked for another ten minutes, then tidied her desk and went out, locking the door of the room. She went through the back of the house and looked into the kitchen. Lodel had left it, as always, clean and with everything in its place. She smiled to herself. For all his hardness there was something of a woman in Lodel. Maybe of any room in a house, the kitchen was the place where he was happiest . . . cooking, in command. Once, a long time ago, she thought, she had come near to loving him but at some point the emotion had shredded away in her. It was her fault, the capacity for love wasn't in her. Maybe it was because of all the others, each new one making the one thing desired farther away.

She went to the refrigerator and poured a glass of orange juice. She went upstairs to her room. The red-tiled terrace outside was swamped with sunlight and there was not enough breeze to move the scalloped edges of the awning.

She slipped off her dress, unhooked her brassière and pulled on a thin silk dressing-gown. She stood at the window for a moment, sipping at the glass of orange juice, feeling the heat of the air on her skin. Then she lay down on her bed, feeling sleep and contentment in her.

She heard Gian come into the room but she kept her eyes closed. He lay down beside her and for a moment his lips touched hers gently. He put his hand on her stomach and it was cool against the warmth of her own skin.

'Where has Lodel gone?' His hand slid upwards cupping one of her breasts.

'The bank. St Tropez.'

'It's true – we move tomorrow?'

'Yes.' Bardi had gone the day before, driven to the airport by Gian.

The hand moved to her throat and one finger followed the line of her chin. 'If I had money – they could go one way, we another.'

'If you had money.'

'Real money.' He laughed and his hand was gone. 'Where does one get real money?'

'Some people do.'

'Bardi does.' He laughed again and his hand came back. 'Maybe I should ask him. Would you come, if I had it?'

She opened her eyes and saw his close to hers. She nodded. He kissed her gently and, as his lips came away from hers, he said, 'Somehow, I will arrange it. Not soon, maybe. But somehow, sometime. Can you wait?'

She nodded again, smiling. 'For the money, for the time to go . . . but for nothing else. Gian . . .' She closed her eyes and felt him move, felt him close to her and, suddenly, there was no thought in her except the nearness and the urgency of his body.

George had found a place southward along the cliffside from the villa. He lay at the edge of a small plantation of pines, screened by clumps of sharp, sword-leaved cactus and the straggling branch of an arbutus. He had been there since ten o'clock that morning and there was a lot more patience in him yet. They had come out in the boat from St Tropez that morning and, out of sight of the villa, well down towards Cap Taillat, Nicola had put him ashore. Their arrangement was simple. She could spend the day as she wished – she had food and drink, fishing gear and a book to read – but she would come back to the place where she had landed him every three hours until dusk.

During the morning there had not been a lot to see. A copper-haired young man had washed the Mercedes down at this end of the villa. He had been joined once by a tallish, dark-haired man with a white apron over dark trousers who carried a tray. They had drunk together and, through his glasses, George had watched them. They were, he felt sure, the two who had been in the Mercedes. He had seen no other sign of movement until some time after lunch when the copper-haired young man had brought the Mercedes to the front of the house. The dark-haired man had come out and got into the driving seat. The car had driven off and copper-head had spent half an hour watering the flower beds around the house with a hose. A job, George thought, which ought to have been done in the cool of the evening. Then copper-head had gone into the house to take, no doubt, a not very hardly earned siesta.

It was nearly four o'clock and George was beginning to think he would get no opportunity to enter the house that day when copper-head came out on to the terrace, wearing red bathing trunks and carrying a towel. He came down the steps into the sun, flexed his arms, and took the cliff path down to the sea. George watched him until he was half way down and the twisting path took him out of sight. He decided that if there was going to be a moment today, this was it.

He went up the hill through the pines and then worked swiftly across the slope towards the house, watching the ground for the dead branches of pine that might snap under his feet. At the side of the villa was a small green door. He went quickly over to it.

The doorway led into a small corridor and then to a kitchen, spotless and tidy. Beyond the kitchen was another corridor with two doors. One door opened on a shower and toilet room, black-tiled with silver dolphins. The other was locked and George left it for the moment. A curtained archway at the end of the corridor took him into a large room that ran, blue-and-white-tiled, across to the patio. Away to the right was the doorway to another room. George tried the handle gently, eased the door open a fraction and listened. There was no sound from the room. He slipped in. Facing him was a desk with a pale golden leather top, a couple of chairs in the same colour leather, and behind the desk a wall safe.

George went to the desk and pulled open the drawers. Most of them were empty. One had a collection of oddly shaped pebbles and sea-shells, another a few boxes of ·22 ammunition. There was no sign of any envelopes or stationery. He got out Ernst's keys and tried the safe. To his surprise, one of the keys fitted the old-fashioned lock. There was nothing in the safe except the dried corpse of a butterfly which had chosen the wrong place to hibernate.

George went back to the main room, skirted a settee, and tried a door behind it. It was a man's bedroom. He went through it quickly. The suits and shirts were hand-made but, curiously, there wasn't a maker's label on any of them. There was not one personal touch to be found anywhere. The whole lot could have been packed in a large case in five minutes.

George went back to the curtained archway, Ernst's keys in his hand, to try the locked door down the corridor. He was about to pull back the curtain when a voice from behind him said, 'Stay exactly where you are and turn slowly.'

George turned very slowly.

Near the door to the bedroom a wall tapestry had been half pulled back, revealing a flight of stairs going to the upper part of the house. A woman stood on the lowest step, one hand holding back the curtain, the other pointing a small gun at George. Her dark hair was untidy and her eyes a little baggy from sleep. A silk dressing-gown was belted loosely at her waist and her feet were bare, the toe-nails painted red.

George smiled, but was careful not to move. In English

with the same deliberation as she had shown, he said, 'I ran out of petrol on the way to the lighthouse. I was looking for someone. You know, to borrow some petrol.'

For a moment he thought that she had not understood him. Her eyes went over him carefully. She had a striking face, strong and well shaped.

She came down a step and said in good English, 'You need keys when you come for petrol?'

George looked down at his left hand. He was holding Ernst's keys which he had got out for the door down the corridor.

'Car keys and others. Got to carry them. There's a hole in my pocket.'

She ignored this and said, 'Just go over and sit there.' She let go of the curtain edge with her left hand and motioned to the settee. 'Slowly,' she added.

'Look,' said George, 'you've got this all wrong and —'

She moved her right hand this time, jerking the gun up. George went slowly to the settee and half turned to sit down. As he did so he whipped out his right hand and grabbed at a loose cushion, intending to sling it at her and go for the gun in the moment of surprise.

The surprise was the other way round. Almost before he had his hand on the cushion, she fired. The bullet hit the wooden, carved rail at the top of the settee upholstery a foot from George's head and sent a great splinter of wood buzzing past his face. He sat down quickly.

For the first time she smiled, but it was not meant to encourage anyone. She said, 'Don't mess around again. The next time I'll put it in your leg.'

George said, 'Your English is good. So is your shooting.' He glanced at the splintered settee rail. Mlle Guntheim would want at least fifty francs in damages for that.

She said nothing. Holding the gun on him she backed towards the wall by the door that led to the room with the desk. When she reached it she slipped her left hand behind her. Distantly George heard a bell ringing through the still afternoon. Copper-head was being called up from his swim.

She came back to the middle of the room and stood looking at him thoughtfully.

She said, 'Open your shirt-front.'

'Look,' protested George, 'what is this strip-tease act? I just wanted some petrol —'

'Open it. Wide.'

Slowly George undid his shirt front and pulled it back. She came forward three feet and looked at his brown chest. Across his left ribs ran a long scar which never took tan.

At that moment a voice called from the lower steps of the terrace, 'Maria!'

Without turning her head she said, '*Son qui, Gian.*'

Gian, the copper-head, came up the stairs three at a time and across the terrace. When he saw George he pulled up sharply. The sweat was running over his broad shoulders from his hurried climb. When the bell went three times in the way Maria had pressed it, it was obviously an emergency signal.

Gian came into the room and said something very rapidly to Maria in an Italian which George had no hope of following. Maria answered him in the same language and, with a look of curiosity at George, he went through the curtained archway. He was gone about half a minute. When he came back he had two lengths of rope in his hands.

Maria said, 'Stand up.'

George did as he was told. He was getting used to being obedient now. Like Pavlov's dogs, he thought, he was a fast conditioner.

'Turn round.' George turned facing the settee. He heard Gian come up behind him and then his hands were pulled backwards and the ropework started. For a moment he debated starting something with Gian as a shield. Only for a moment, though.

Gian tied his wrists and then his ankles, and then gave

him a half turn and push. George dropped awkwardly to the settee.

Maria said something else in Italian, tossed her gun to Gian and went quickly across the room, through the curtain and up the stairs.

George studied Gian. He was a well-built young man, a lot of shoulder, little hip, and as brown as a locust bean. He had a pleasant enough face and there was a look to his eyes which did not seem to preclude reasonable conversation.

George said, 'You speak English, or French?'

Gian nodded, hoisted himself half on a small table, laid down the gun and helped himself to a cigarette from a jade box.

George said, 'What's the form? This is getting beyond a bloody joke!'

Gian shrugged his shoulders and blew some cigarette smoke idly into the air. Outside the cicadas fiddled away, a couple of butterflies drifted along the terrace petunias and there was the sound of sparrows quarrelling as they dust-bathed on the driveway. Without wanting to, George suddenly remembered how Wheeler had been thrown off a train. Gian, he thought, would have been little more than a boy then.

'What's Maria doing?' asked George. 'Telephoning for orders?'

Gian shrugged again.

This annoyed George. He said with real anger, 'All right, don't damned well talk.'

Gian smiled. Then he slid off the table and dropped into an armchair, sprawling his legs out, the gun in one hand.

George said, 'You wouldn't flop around like that if the boss were about.'

Gian considered this for a while. Then unexpectedly he said, 'You from London?'

'Could be.'

Gian got up and came over to the settee but he kept his distance. He looked George over carefully.

'Good shirt, nice trousers, expensive watch. You are rich?'

'I get by.'

'Please?'

'No. Not rich.'

'*Dommage.*' Gian went back and flipped into the chair. 'Why?'

Gian tossed up the gun and caught it.

'I wait for someone rich,' he said.

'Why do you wait for someone rich?'

Gian grinned and showed the whites of his eyes.

'To make some money, of course.' He sounded offended by George's simpleness.

'How much money?'

Gian considered and said, '*Vingt mille francs . . .*'

'That's a lot of money.'

'Yes, a lot.' Gian nodded dreamily. 'You have that much money?'

'If I had?'

'I let you go free.'

'Only that?'

'You want something else?' He laughed and it was not pleasant. 'You don't know what's coming to you.'

'I can guess,' said George. 'But I'd still want more – even if I had the money.'

'What more?'

'Some questions answered.'

'I don't like questions.'

'Try.'

Gian considered this. Then he shook his head. 'No money. No questions. *Dommage.*'

After that, for a good fifteen minutes, Gian said nothing. He smoked and ignored George. Then high up in the corner of the room a bell rang briefly and, distantly, there was the sound of a car.

Gian got up and stood by the table.

A car drew up quickly in front of the villa. The dark-haired man, whom George had seen that morning, came into the room.

There was a rapid Italian conversation between him and Gian and then the dark-haired man went up the stairs. Gian was left alone with George. But it was a different Gian. He stood with his back to the terrace and said nothing, looking thoughtful and occasionally rubbing the point of his chin with his fingertips. Overhead George heard voices and the movement of feet. It sounded as though two people were arguing, almost quarrelling. He had a feeling that the subject under discussion was himself.

Ten minutes later the dark-haired man came down into the room. With him was Maria. She had a white dress on, her hair was tidy, and she was frowning and looked bad-tempered as a woman might who had lost an argument. The dark-haired man nodded to Gian and held out his hand for the gun. Gian gave it to him and went out through the curtained archway.

The man came over to the settee and looked at George, whistling very gently to himself. The temperature around the settee seemed to drop sharply as he considered George. Suddenly he whipped out his right hand and smashed the fist against George's face, jerking the movement so that the ring on his finger cut the skin of George's cheek. George went backwards hard against the back of the settee.

'Lodel!' Maria's voice came sharply across the room. Lodel took no notice of her. He stood back and let George recover. Then he said, 'Who are you?'

'You could have asked first and saved the knuckle work.' It was George's first experience of being struck without the chance of hitting back, and he hoped his blood pressure would take it.

'Who are you?'

George lurching up to a sitting position, got his hands on the hard upholstery and shoved himself off violently, kicking up his feet and driving them from flexed knees into the man's groin. Lodel fell backwards, crashed against a table and was on his feet in a flash, gun still in his hand, before George could follow up any advantage there might be in it. He stood there, breathing heavily, and if he felt any pain he let it freeze slowly within him. Behind Lodel, Maria laughed gently.

George elbowed himself back on to the settee and said, 'Now we're quits. What was the question you asked me?'

For a moment he thought Lodel was coming for him again, but the slight movement hardened up.

The man said, 'Who are you?'

'Conway. George.'

'What are you doing here?'

'My car ran out of —'

'Stick to the truth.' His English was good. 'Why do you come here?'

'Not for the friendly welcome. I'm looking for a woman. A Mrs Elsie Longo, maiden name Pinnock. She stayed here some time ago.'

'Why do you want her?'

'Her mother wants to know where she is. She hasn't heard from her for years.'

'I don't believe it. Who are you really working for?'

'Her mother.'

'No.' The man shook his head. 'You would have come openly if so. Who is it?'

George shook his head. 'You are hard to convince.'

Lodel said, 'You say who it is and nothing happens to you. But stubborn —' he shrugged his shoulders.

George shook his head. He waited for the blow. It did not come.

Lodel said, 'Think it over. If you don't talk you will be picked up dead on a beach tomorrow morning.' He came round the back of the settee and his hands caught George around the neck. He held him, tightening up the pressure expertly and at the right moment throwing George sideways on to the settee. As he walked away, George through a red mist heard his voice say, 'Think it over for a while.'

Dimly George was conscious of someone else coming

into the room. Ten minutes later he saw that it was Gian who had taken up guard duty. The other two had gone.

Just before dusk Lodel came back and joined Gian. There was a discussion in Italian between them and then Gian came over and took the rope from George's ankles.

He was jerked to his feet and pushed towards the terrace. They went down the steps and across the drive to the small path that led down the cliffside. For a moment George considered staging a sit-down strike, but he realized that it would be asking for a crack over the head.

They went down to the water, halting on a flat rock platform. Gian stood behind him with the gun while Lodel hauled in the dinghy. He got into it and lowered an outboard motor over the stern. He looked up and signalled to George to get into the boat. He was manœuvred on to the central thwart and Lodel said, 'If you feel like answering my question we will go back to the house. Something could be arranged.'

George shook his head.

Gian stepped into the bows of the boat.

Lodel said, 'Don't try going over the side. You'll only get a few bullets in you to make you sink quicker.'

He started the motor and the dinghy moved away from the little inlet and, in the purpling dusk, headed northwards towards the headland where the lighthouse stood. They kept well in to the shore. There was a chilly little breeze coming in from the sea now that the sun had gone. The lighthouse beam probed the growing darkness.

They were a tidy lot, thought George. They didn't want any corpses making their front drive look unkempt. Probably they were going to take him round the headland to the Pampelone beaches. There were two or three miles of them, cut into dunes and backed by tall bamboo growths. At this time of the year nobody would be on the beach so late. He worked again at his wrist bonds but he could do nothing with them. Gian must have seen the movement from behind him, and he felt the gun tap him on the shoulder warningly.

The breeze had beaten the sea up a little now and he could see the white wash against the cliff foot as they rounded the point below the lighthouse.

He was right about the Pampelone beach. They came in close, so close that he could see the long foaming inward sweep of the breaking waves sliding up the sands. They went a quarter of a mile along it to avoid the few chalets and bungalows at the lighthouse end and then the dinghy was turned inwards and run fast ashore, grounding on the sands. Gian jumped out and, with the next wave, ran the dinghy a little higher.

Lodel motioned to George to get out. The water came swirling up around his ankles as he did so. In a few seconds the dinghy was pulled above the water line and George was being marched up the sand slope with the two men at his side. They crested a sand dune, dropped down the other side and splashed through a narrow stream. Beyond the stream the wind was raising a myriad thin, rustling noises in a bank of bamboos. A small path led through them. After five yards it opened out to a patch of sand and scrub about the size of a tennis court, fringed on all sides by the tall feathery growths that fretted noisily in the sea wind.

Lodel put out a hand and spun George round. For a moment George saw Gian's young face watching him, deep-shadowed in the starlight.

'Who is employing you?' Lodel spoke without emphasis.

George said, 'You're wasting your time.'

It began then. A hard fist driven straight at his face, driven with science, with a nice precision that sent him staggering backwards to be caught and steadied by Gian behind him.

'You have only to speak when you are ready,' said Lodel and the fist came at George again. This time it was just above the heart and Gian again caught and held him upright.

Lodel, his face a pale grey loom in the night, struck again, and slowly the night began to dissolve around George. There came a time when even Gian could not hold him, and then it was a boot that struck and, shortly after that, the dissolution of the night was complete and he seemed to be sliding down some rough tunnel, fast, faster every moment, with his body being slung cruelly from one wall to another. Suddenly the tunnel journey came to an abrupt end. He came out into the open, his body slamming to a stop against something, and there was a moment of intense, pain-filled clarity.

Over him he saw the two men.

A voice said, 'Finish him. We are wasting time.' It was Gian's voice and he sounded bored, as though the performance had been nothing like as good as he had expected.

Against the star-pierced sky an arm stretched down and the hand at the end held something black and awkward-looking.

Then there was the shot. One. Then two more rapidly, and then another two. George lay there, counting them stupidly in his fading clarity. There was another shot and he gave up counting and let himself slide away completely.

After that, but how long after he had no idea, the thing was like a crazy film which annoyed him because he had not enough concentration to make sense of it.

He was being hauled about. There was water over his feet. A woman was cursing him with a queer kind of anguish in her voice. There was a brief smell of 'Miss Dior'. More water, all over him, soaking into his shirt, the salt biting hard at the cuts on his face. Then came the cursing again and, after that, a long, long period when there was only the sound of an engine bubbling away. That was the best period and he was unhappy when it ended. And it ended with a quarrel somewhere . . . some man shouting in French about his boat. Then the voice changed, was suddenly sympathetic, almost fatherly, and

George knew that he was walking, someone on either side of him.

He woke at three o'clock in the morning. He knew that it was three because, the light being on, he looked automatically at his watch. The glass was cracked but the second-hand moved steadily.

He was in his bed at his hotel and the light was on over the dressing-table. His body was so stiff that he felt that if he moved something would crack. Standing at the end of the bed was Nicola in a dressing-gown. Seeing his eyes open, she came to him quickly.

'George. Oh, George. . . . My God, I thought you'd never come round.'

To his surprise she bent down, put her hands, warm and soft, on each side of his bruised face, and kissed him.

He shut his eyes, relaxing, and said, 'I like that. What happened?'

'Never mind for the moment.' The hands left his face.

He opened his eyes and smiled. The muscle movement made his face feel brittle as though it were made of spun sugar.

He said, 'Perhaps a drink would help.'

Nicola said, 'You've had a lot of brandy already.'

'Give me another then. Maybe I'll remember this one.'

She brought him a drink and sat on the bed, one arm behind his shoulders to help him drink. The drink did something for him, softening up the spun-sugar feeling to his face, waking his body to a few more aches and pains.

He said, 'Who was the bloke who did all the arguing?'

'The boatman. He was furious about his boat being out so late. But he calmed down and helped me here with you.'

'And the shots. Hell' – he sat up sharply – 'was that you?'

'With Nadia's gun. Relax.' Her hand pushed him back to the pillow. He shut his eyes.

'You had ammunition?'

'I thought it might be useful.'

'What was the damage?'

'I think I hit one. He shouted. But it was all very confused. Now forget about it until the morning. Do you think anything's broken?'

He shook his head wearily. 'I'll be all right. It's not much worse than a Twickenham match.'

'You get some sleep.'

He drifted off, but a few moments later opened his eyes. She was sitting in an armchair by the dressing-table with her feet up on another chair, a blanket over her knees.

She said, 'You're supposed to be sleeping.'

He smiled and it was not so bad this time. 'How the hell did you get that gun through customs?'

'In my handbag, of course.'

'Good Lord. . . .'

6

IT WAS raining outside: June rain, straight and steady with no wind behind it, and in some ways François Laborde found it as pleasing as sunshine. It put a different set of highlights on familiar things and suddenly made this well-known street look different. The rain-slicked sides of the tall buildings opposite reminded him waywardly of the tall cliffs along the north coast of the Quiberon peninsula. He had been born in Quiberon, and hoped one day to go back and settle there. *Crêpes* and fresh sardines. *Crêpes* with Armagnac. The thought made him feel hungry although it was not long past breakfast. Big tall cliffs with heavy seas crashing at them, and the straight, straight rain without wind that made the rocks like black marble.

Dorothée came in and gave him, '*Bonjour.*' He went and sat at his desk and stared at her as she put a sheet of paper in front of him. If he had had any choice in the matter he would never have chosen a secretary like

Dorothée. As a secretary, of course, she could not be faulted. Perfection. But a secretary, too, should be worth looking at. Stripped, her figure wouldn't be too bad, but her face . . . she was plain in a way that was worse than being ugly. He didn't, he supposed, really look at Dorothée more than two or three times a year: white blouse, those terrible cardboard cuff things, grey skirt, sensible shoes and no emotion ever allowed to filter past her thick-lensed spectacles.

She said, 'There has been some trouble. Lodel telephoned my flat late last night. It's there.' She nodded at the sheet of paper.

The message from Lodel read:

> George Conway at St Tropez. Caught Les Roches-Pins, pm. Inquiring Elsie Longo. Refused disclose name of employer. Unfortunately persuasive methods and disposal interrupted. Girl with him. Why not informed this? Villa closed this night.

Laborde considered this for a while and then said, 'Where's Bardi?'

'Switzerland.'

'You'd better let him know.'

'Lodel will have done that.'

'You do it as well. Why did the fools try to kill him?'

'Lodel probably panicked without Bardi there.'

'He won't be pleased about this.'

Laborde stared at the ceiling for a while. Then, frowning, he went on, 'How the hell could I know Conway was going to St Tropez?'

'You couldn't,' said Dorothée. 'The point is now – will Conway make a fuss about the villa?'

'Only if he's prepared to go to the police. And if he does it won't help him.' He smiled grimly. 'He didn't waste time, did he, this Conway? It must have been quite a shock when they found him in the villa. I wonder how he got on to that?'

Dorothée said nothing.

That morning George woke at eight. Nicola was no longer in his room. His mind was clear now, and there was a driving urgency in him that got him out of bed. For a moment he stood on the carpet feeling about seventy and wondering if he should dare to straighten up. He hobbled to the bathroom and took a shower. It was a minor kind of agony, but his stiff muscles slowly thawed out. He came back to his room and dressed. His face in the mirror was unfamiliar, bruised and cut, like a bad Press photograph of a heavyweight wondering what had taken him in the tenth round.

As he put on his jacket Nicola came into the room.

Gloomily, George said, 'Well, I made a mess of that all right, didn't I? Blundering straight into them like a bull in a china shop. I should be kicked around the room for not using my head.'

'I don't know. It could have turned out differently.'

'The point is – what do we do now?'

'I've already done something. I've telephoned the villa twice this morning – and there was no reply. I think they've cleared out. Before we can decide what to do we'll have to make sure about that.'

'We? I'm not letting you go near that place. Hell, they thought nothing of deciding to kill me. That's a very uncomfortable thought.'

'You're not going to bring up that old business of me staying with you.'

'I am. I think you should go back to London and stay there. As for me, perhaps I should consult Synat and see what he has to suggest.'

'But you can't do that until you know whether they are still in the villa. The phone might not have been answered because they were all taking an early morning swim. Though my bet is that they've gone. And as for my going back to London, I'd like to point out that you would have been killed if I hadn't been around. Though' – Nicola's face became serious – 'I take your point about the future.

97

We know what they're like now. You'll have to cut out this Rugby football, head-down-and-charge-in stuff.'

'Once bitten, twice shy. But you're not coming near the place. And when we know whether they've gone or not . . . well, then we can argue about your going back to London.'

'It won't do you any good. Nothing is going to make me pull out now. But I'll be a good girl this morning and wait for you at Ramatuel while you have a look at the place. I'll get the car round for you.' She came over and kissed him lightly on the cheek. 'Poor George . . . Here, you'd better have this in case of another emergency.' She handed him the ·22 Walther.

Fifteen minutes later they were driving out to Ramatuel where George was to leave Nicola. It was a beautiful morning, high white clouds like the lightest dumplings, and the sun warm on the pink-and-white farm buildings. It would be a good morning, George thought, to feel absolutely fit and to have half an hour alone with Gian or Lodel.

He left Nicola at the café in Ramatuel and then went on alone. He parked the car past the villa entrance, well up towards the lighthouse, and walked back. Although there was a quiet undercurrent of anger running in him, he decided that he was not going to take any more chances.

The gate across the top of Les Roches-Pins' drive was locked. George climbed the fence and circled down towards the villa through the pine trees. He watched the place for a while. There was no sign of life and there were no cars standing outside of it. All the windows and doors were shut which would have been unusual on a hot morning if the house had anyone in it.

Five minutes later he broke the glass of a back window, slipped the catch, and climbed in.

The place was empty. It had been cleared completely, and he had the feeling as he went through the villa that these people were used to moving out suddenly. Even the last of the kitchen refuse had been carried out to the incinerator. There wasn't a scrap of paper, an unemptied ashtray or an untidy room. The beds had been stripped and sheets and blankets folded and piled. The study desk was cleared even of the pebbles, shells and ·22 ammunition. The only sign of his visit was the smashed rail at the back of the settee.

George went back to the car and then drove on to Ramatuel where they had a late breakfast, sitting out in the open under the elm. Over the last of their coffee and a cigarette George laid out the position as he saw it and Nicola made notes for the report – their first – which they had promised to send back to Synat for distribution to the others.

Roughly the position was:

1. Since they didn't want to be involved with the police – not yet, anyway – they had to accept that there was nothing more to be gained by staying in St Tropez. If he had been there, Scorpio had done a flit, and so had the others.

2. There were two lines of investigation away from the villa. One was through the owner, Mlle Guntheim, in Paris, who could tell them to whom she had let the place; and the other was through Laborde.

3. Laborde clearly was connected with the people in the villa because they had identified George, knew that he had a scar under his ribs. This last argued that someone had checked his false passport details. That – possibly – linked Ernst to Laborde.

'Where does that take us?' asked Nicola.

'Back to Paris. First the Guntheim woman, and then Laborde and Ernst.'

'Mr Laborde, I imagine, will find some answer, not necessarily a truthful one. Paris – that's a hell of a trudge.'

'We can take it easy, and it's on the way to London for you.'

'You can forget that.'

George gave her a look, decided not to push the point at that moment, and said, 'Their car had a Swiss touring plate. I wonder if they've gone back there? You really think you hit one of the men?'

'I think so. It was all a bit confused. Frankly I was in something of a panic. I'd never fired a gun in anger before. I saw the dinghy go off with you in it. At least, through the glasses, I thought it was you. So I followed. I lost them round the point but I kept well in and spotted the dinghy beached so I ran ashore lower down and came back.'

'Thank God you did. Sometime – if you give me the chance – I'll think up a really nice thank-you.'

'I can see you're recovering fast.'

'It's the coffee and the fresh air. All right – so it's Paris. But I think we'd better get that report off to Synat first. If he wants to, he can write to us at the office of his Paris agent.'

They started for Paris after lunch, and they got there late in the evening of the following day, which was a Saturday. They avoided the Sainte-Anne this time and stayed at a small hotel on the left bank near the Quai St Bernard. The chief thing in its favour, George found on consulting a street guide, was that the Rue Poliveau where Mademoiselle Guntheim lived was only a short walk away, through the Jardin des Plantes. On the way back to Paris, George brought up the question of Nicola staying with him. She was quite adamant about it. She was personally more involved in this affair than he was and she stubbornly refused to pull out, and he had no way of forcing her. In the end he gave way – but both of them now accepted that they must take no stupid risks. Scorpio and the people with him were dangerous and not likely to turn gentlemanly because of Nicola.

The next morning George walked leisurely through the Sunday morning parade in the Jardin of young men and girls, strolling in the sun, children shouting to be bought balloons and old men and women sitting on seats wondering just exactly where and when it was that life had got away from them. Normally he would have been hard put not to dawdle. But today there was no room for botany in his mind. He was on a different hunt. A man hunt.

The Rue Poliveau was a turning to the right, some way down the Boulevard de l'Hôpital from the Gare d'Orléans, and number 203 was almost on the corner, a tall apartment building with a door at the side of a *boulangerie* from which women were coming carrying long loaves of bread. The door of the house was open on to a steep run of stairs. There was no *concierge*'s office, but on the wall was a small board with grubby rows of visiting cards slipped into brass frames. Mademoiselle Guntheim had the fourth floor.

George began to climb the stairs and hoped that she was in. If he had been able to find her name in the book he would have telephoned for an appointment. He stood aside for a moment on the second landing to let a woman coming down pass him. She was a happy-looking, plump woman in a tight costume, her head covered in close blonde curls topped by a scrap of lace and velvet that saucily called itself a hat. She gave George a wink, maybe because it was a fine summer morning and the hat was new, and passed him leaving a fall-out of some strong scent. On the third landing an apartment door was partly open and great gusts of the Symphonie Pastorale swirled out. On the fourth floor there was one door with a card stuck into a brass holder reading, *D. Guntheim.* Below it was a small brass figure of a winged cherub. It was a few seconds before George discovered that by pressing the cherub's stomach a bell rang in the flat.

He had to ring twice before he heard a movement inside the door. It opened about a foot and a woman's head appeared. The head was a surprise to George. The hair had obviously just been washed and a small pink towel had been wound around it turban fashion. A few escaping rat-tails of brown hung over the woman's ears. The face was pink, bath-fresh, and the eyes distorted behind thick-lensed glasses. George recognized it at once.

George got his foot in the door just as it began to slam and took most of the pressure with his left shoulder. For a moment the woman persisted and then she gave up. She stepped back and George moved through the doorway, closing it behind him but being careful to face the woman all the time. He wasn't taking any more chances with anyone connected with *Laborde et Cie.*

He said, 'Good morning, Miss Guntheim. It's very nice of you to ask me in.'

Some kind of look formed behind the glasses but he could not put a name to it. She turned and walked away from him, down a narrow hallway.

George followed her into a large sitting-room overlooking the street. There were a lot of books in shelves against one wall, a row of brass figurines on the mantelshelf of the fireplace which housed a mica-windowed stove. One of the figures was Rodin's *The Thinker.* There were a couple of armchairs, a big sofa and a narrow table with a green chenille cloth and a bowl of mimosa bloom. Dorothée stood in the window and looked at him.

He said, 'I just want a little information. I won't keep you long.'

For the first time she spoke and her voice was rather prim. 'You have no right to force your way in here. I should call the police.'

'Go ahead.' He sat down on the edge of the sofa and gave her a friendly smile.

She considered this for a while. Then to his surprise she pulled cigarettes and matches from the pocket of her dressing-gown and lit herself a cigarette. George had the impression that under the gown she wore only a skirt and a brassière. On her feet she had pink, fluffy slippers with black Pierrot buttons on them. She was an odd mixture: prim, myopic, cardboard cuffs to keep her blouse clean, neat, efficient, and unattractive – and then fluffy pink slippers that matched her turbaned towel and a room that had the comfort of a bachelor apartment.

George lit himself a cigarette and said, 'That's better. Now let's get down to the questions. You are, I understand, the owner of a villa near St Tropez called Les

Roches-Pins. It's a nice villa, too, though I'm a bit puzzled to know how you could buy it out of the salary Laborde pays you?'

Quite calmly she said, 'It's no business of yours but I don't get any salary from Laborde. I own a fifty per cent. share in his business. And, if you want some very sound advice, I should suggest you get a plane back to London as soon as you can.'

'Leave Paris on a day like this? Be reasonable. No – let's stick to the villa. I'd like to know who the present tenant is? In case you don't know, he left a few days ago, hurriedly. Even so everything was spotless and tidy – except for a shattered bit of wood-carving on the settee in the main room. You'll have to claim damages for that.'

She moved slowly towards the fireplace and tipped the ash from her cigarette neatly into a brass ashtray shaped like a fish.

'I'm not interested in the damages, nor in the villa, and I certainly can't tell you who was renting it.'

'I think you can.'

'No, monsieur, I can't.'

George nodded towards a little secretaire which stood to one side of the fireplace. 'You're a methodical girl. I could go through your desk and find your records – with your permission, of course.'

'It wouldn't help you.' She was completely in control of herself. 'I don't know where you got your information about the villa, but it's out of date. I sold it some years ago to a man in South America. He's a Señor Carapiotti and he lives in Brasilia. Why don't you go, you're spoiling my Sunday morning?' There was an edge of hardening impatience in her voice.

'Don't let's rush things. I'll give you that you don't now own the villa. I don't suppose you ever did. You were just a nominee – like Señor Carapiotti is now. But, while you had it, you let it. Particularly you let it to a man called Longo and his wife Elsie. All I want from you is the address he gave you when you let it.'

'I know of no one called Longo.'

'And you've never heard of Elsie Pinnock or O'Neil?'

She shook her head. The sureness in her began to touch George and he felt his temper rising.

'Look, Miss Guntheim, a few nights ago – in the course of my professional inquiries – I was in that villa and I had a very unpleasant time one way and another. I don't mean to drop this business. I'd like to conduct it in a gentlemanly way. But there comes a point when I say to hell with etiquette.'

'There comes a point, too, monsieur, when I wish more than ever to be left alone here.'

'Then, for both our sakes, I suggest we make a compromise.'

'Indeed?'

'You go and finish your dressing and I'll take a look round here, particularly in the little desk, and see what I can find. I'll leave it all neat and tidy and then walk out. Fair enough?'

George stood up and stubbed his cigarette in a duck-shaped brass ashtray on the table. At the movement she backed away from the fireplace towards the window. He saw that in her right hand she now held the brass figure of Rodin's *Thinker*.

She said, 'It will spoil my Sunday morning, but don't think that I will not do what I say or that I have anything to lose from any story you may tell the police.'

George frowned. 'I'm not with you. What's this about?'

She did not answer right away. Instead, she put the brass figure down on the back of an armchair, within easy reach, and then she slipped off her gown. George had been right about the brassière, but wrong about the skirt. She wore rather brief pants, and there was nothing wrong with her figure. She tossed the gown on to the chair and picked up the statuette.

'I'm giving you exactly one minute to get out,' she said evenly. 'If you don't go, I shall throw this ornament through the window, scream, and go on screaming while

I tear my clothes.' She backed closer to the window, the top of which was open, and went on, 'You have now rather more than thirty seconds if you want to avoid a charge of attempted rape.'

George considered this. She meant it. There was no doubt of that, and it was a move to which he had no answer. There wasn't a French jury that wouldn't be solidly on her side against *le monstre anglais . . . la bête de la Rue Poliveau.* He gave way with good grace. She was obviously tied in somewhere with the real beast, Scorpio, but there was something likeable about her and she was certainly no fool.

He said, 'All right. Put your dressing-gown on. You'll catch a cold from the open window.'

He turned and left the room. When he got to the apartment door he looked back. She had come to the sitting-room door and was watching him, her dressing-gown draped across one arm. It was a pity, he thought, about her face and those ghastly glasses because her figure was good. He raised a hand in farewell and went out and down the stairs to the street.

Back in the apartment Dorothée threw the bolt across her door and went back to the sitting-room. She sat down on the edge of the settee and fumbled in her dressing-gown pocket for her cigarettes and matches. She lit the cigarette, and then looked down at her right hand. It was trembling and to stop the shake she caught hold of the flesh of her knee, pressing her fingers hard against the skin.

It was eleven o'clock when George got back to the hotel. He told Nicola what had happened and, following the plan they had already agreed, they got the Lancia and drove to the Avenue Marceau.

On the way George said, 'Short of putting the police on to her there's nothing else we could get from Dorothée – unless I went back and gagged her before she could scream.'

'You're not going back there,' said Nicola. 'According to

you her figure's too good and she might not scream. For all I know you might have a thing for girls with glasses.'

'You may have a point there. Anyway, I have a feeling that Scorpio's advance guards only know just enough to let them function efficiently. We'll test it after lunch. Right now I want another look at Laborde's place.'

'You're really having a wonderful Sunday morning, aren't you? Attempted rape and now housebreaking. You'd be blackballed from the Travellers' Club.'

They parked the Lancia in the Rue Boccador and walked round the corner into the Avenue. The building in which Laborde had his office served apartments as well as business premises and the street door was open. George and Nicola went up to the office floor. The door was locked. George took out Ernst's bunch of keys which the villa people had not thought important enough to take away. The old-fashioned lock gave no trouble.

They went in. Dorothée's desk was neat and tidy. The green cardboard cuffs were in the empty OUT tray, and there was a brass pen- and pencil-holder shaped like a swan. She was a great girl for brassware, thought George; and he remembered her standing at the window half-naked, the Rodin figure poised. They went through her desk, which was a model of neatness and would have gladdened the heart of the principal of any secretarial training college.

In the top left-hand drawer was a bulky loose-leaf book with alphabetical tags sticking out from the leading edge.

'Look at this,' said Nicola, flipping over the pages.

It was a home-made Spotlight of all Laborde's clients and it must have given Dorothée hours of quiet pleasure with glue-pot and scissors. Carefully pasted in the book were professional photographs of Laborde's clients and on the facing page details of their names, addresses, style of act, fee required and a space for comments. Some of the comments were obviously not intended for the clients to see. The first photograph in the book was of a wet-eyed brunette called Clea Albertine and the comment: *Cabaret singer. No good straight theatre. Unreliable. Drinks. Popular with men. Not particular.*

'Not particular about what?' asked George.

Nicola sighed. 'Just keep to the business in hand, shall we?'

'All right.' George pulled out the small cabinet photographs of Elsie and Ricardo Cadim from his pocket. 'Let's go right through the lot and see what we can find.'

They went through the book. They found no trace of anyone at all like Elsie but they found Ricardo Cadim almost at once, listed under his own name. His photograph stared up from the page at them. It was a much later photograph than Mrs Pinnock's. He had a long, smooth, whitish face, a high forehead moving to baldness with wings of dark hair above his ears, brilliantined tight and glossy to his skull. The nose was a little hooked and the mouth intelligent, expressive. It was almost an intellectual face and there was a suggestion of quiet humour in it.

The page opposite the photograph gave very few particulars.

Name.

Ricardo Cadim.
Billing. Monsieur Magique.

Address.

Agencie Laborde, Paris.

Act.

High-class cabaret. Conjuring.
Leger-de-main. No film, television
or theatre.

Fee.

By arrangement. Minimum weekly
800 francs.

Comment.

Speaks English, German, French, Italian,
Spanish. No engagements England or outside
Europe. Fee includes own assistant.

George straightened up and slid the book back into the drawer. 'No English engagements – that's interesting.'

'The thing is,' said Nicola, 'where is he now?'

'I think we can find that out. When I asked Laborde about Elsie, he referred to a black book on his desk. That will have all the real details, engagements and fees. And that bastard Laborde said he knew nothing about him. You know ... I get a feeling that we're running up against the advance posts of some pretty considerable organization.'

The door to Laborde's office was locked but Ernst's keys provided the answer to that. And Ernst again provided the answer to a locked lower drawer of the desk in which George found the black register. With the register in the drawer was a faded sprig of white heather, a bottle of Black and White whisky and a plastic tumbler.

'Secret drinker,' said Nicola. 'Probably gets sloshed and then maudlin over some ancient trip to the Highlands.'

'It's not Highland heather. It's a piece of *Erica arborea* – the Mediterranean stuff. Now let's see what we have about Mr Magic.'

He flipped the pages out of the register and found that Cadim was there – just a name at the top of a page and then a list of bookings with the fees paid carried over into the right-hand column. He had for a long time been in steady work all over the place from Stockholm to Naples and the money he made must have kept his tax accountant busy. All his payments were well above the minimum eight hundred new francs. For the last two weeks he had been working at Cannes; that was until the previous day. His next booking showed him as due at the Hôtel de l'Empire, Annecy, where he was due to start on the Saturday of the coming week for two weeks. After that he was booked solidly at places as far apart as Italy and Spain, until the middle of September.

George dropped the register back into the drawer, decided it was too early for whisky, and said to Nicola, 'I think when we've finished our next bit of business we could think about a trip to Annecy at the end of the week.

All we have to do now is to leave everything neat and tidy so that Laborde won't know he's had visitors.'

George took a quick look through the rest of the drawers which were unlocked. There was nothing in them which seemed as though it would help him.

Before he left the office he looked up Ernst Fragonard on the offchance in the telephone directory. He was listed at the same address which George now remembered from his identity card.

They drove up the Avenue, partly around the Place de l'Étoile and down the Avenue Wagram to the Place des Ternes. Ernst lived conveniently close to Laborde. The address in the Rue des Ternes was set back in a little courtyard, with a strip of garden that boasted a tulip tree and a little coop which held three bantam fowls which an old man was feeding with hard crusts of bread.

In reply to George's question, he said, 'First floor,' and his eyes never left the bantams.

Nicola said, 'What fine birds.'

The old man, with only the briefest look at her, said, 'I have lived in the city most of my life, mademoiselle, but my heart is in the country. I look at my birds and they take me there.'

They went up a flight of stairs to a landing with two doors. One was marked Trempaud and the other Fragonard. George knocked on Fragonard and, after an interval, a voice from within called '*Entrez!*'

They went in and found themselves immediately in a large bed-sitting-room with two doors opening from it. Most of the room was taken up by the large iron-framed bed which was made up with a red woollen covering. There was a blue-and-white plaster Madonna on the wall behind it. Ernst was sitting in a cane chair at the window, his feet up on the open ledge. He was in his shirt sleeves, a green bow-tie at his throat and the sheets of a Sunday newspaper on the floor at his side. He looked round at them without surprise.

'Don't get up,' said George. 'This is a very informal visit.'

Ernst nodded, slewed his feet off the window ledge and swung his chair round to face them. 'I saw you come across the courtyard.' He studied George's face and went on, 'You have been fighting, monsieur?'

'It became necessary.'

'I hope it won't be so here.'

'That depends on you.'

Ernst smiled. 'Then there will be no need.' He looked at Nicola, the smile widening appreciably. 'You would be Miss Nancy Marden. I got into some trouble with Monsieur Laborde for not realizing that you were also staying at the Sainte-Anne with monsieur.'

'You told me that you didn't know Laborde,' said George.

'Naturally. At that time I had to protect my employer. You would have done the same.'

'And now? What's changed you?'

'Circumstances, monsieur. There is no point in persisting with a lie when you know that someone is ready to beat the truth out of you. So – for my own protection – I become an honest man.'

'So you work for Laborde?'

'Occasionally, if he wants information about someone. I get it the best way I can. He doesn't pay very well, I may say.'

George said, 'He wanted to know about us?'

'You first. I checked your passport at the hotel and gave him the details. Then when you disappeared from the hotel he was angry. A few days ago he asked me to check on mademoiselle. I did this from the hotel records.'

'And that's all?'

'Absolutely, monsieur.'

'Why should Laborde be so interested in us?'

Ernst shrugged his shoulders. 'I don't know, and I don't ask. I work for other people besides him.'

'What is Laborde besides a theatrical agent?'

'Nothing, so far as I know. He has been in the business many years.'

'Dorothée Guntheim – what do you know about her?'

'The secretary? Nothing, except that she lives alone, naturalized French woman. No lovers. No nothing. But then —'

'All right. Try a few names. Elsie O'Neil or Pinnock?'

'No.'

'A man called Longo?'

'No, monsieur.'

'He's not going to be of any help,' said Nicola.

As a parting shot George tried him with one last question.

'Does the word "Bianeri" mean anything to you?'

'Bianeri?' Ernst rolled it over his tongue and then sadly shook his head.

George said, 'All right – but if you could find anyone who could answer them I'd pay a thousand francs, maybe more.'

Just for a moment there was a sharp gleam in Ernst's eyes, then the brightness dulled and his head shook sadly again. 'I am sorry, monsieur.'

He came with them to the door and stepped outside with them, half closing the door behind him. In a quick whisper he said to George, 'Listen – a thousand francs for some answers, yes?' He jerked his hand warningly back over his shoulder. 'Guntheim is in there. She came to warn me you might come.'

George nodded.

Ernst, his voice low, said, 'Here. This evening at eight.' Then, his voice rising to its natural pitch, he said, 'I am sorry I can't help you more, monsieur. *Au revoir* . . . mademoiselle, monsieur.'

He slipped back into the room and George heard the bolt go over.

George shook his head warningly at Nicola as she was about to speak. They went down the stairs together. The old man had disappeared from the courtyard.

Back in the room Ernst went over to the window, swung his chair round to face the courtyard and took up his position, feet on the window ledge. He watched George and Nicola cross the yard and turn down the street towards the Place des Ternes.

He gave them a few moments and then, without turning his head, said, 'They've gone.'

A door on the far side of the bed which had been slightly ajar opened and Dorothée Guntheim came into the room. She wore a brown beret and a rather severe brown suit, with a large handbag looped over her arm.

Ernst dropped his feet to the floor and lit a cigarette, looking up at her.

'He has a good memory. He remembered my address from my identity card. Only a professional, surely, would do that?'

'Maybe.'

'What made you think he would come here?'

'He came to see me. He wouldn't miss anything.'

'How did I do?'

'Very well. You earned your money.'

She clicked her bag open and burrowed into it. She dropped two notes into his hand. Ernst pocketed them and slewed back towards the window, putting his feet up and blowing a lazy smoke-ring.

She stood close behind him, looking over his shoulder at the courtyard. The tulip tree was noisy with the courting quarrels of sparrows.

Her voice a little distant she said, 'So, Dorothée Guntheim lives alone. No lovers. No nothing . . .'

'You told me to be natural, truthful. He would have made trouble. Could have searched the place.'

'You did well. I watched. Yes, very well.'

'Where do you think he picked up that "Bianeri" stuff?'

'I wish I knew.'

Ernst blew another smoke-ring. 'He's got money. A thousand for answering a few questions.' He laughed gently. 'A thousand . . . The old man down there dreams of the country. But me, always I dream of money and it is never more than a dream.'

Dorothée closed her bag with a slight click of the fastener. Her voice even more distant, but now faintly touched with a breath of exaltation, said, 'I have my dreams . . . Now and again, even now, they become real. But it is safer to keep to the dream, perhaps.'

Ernst shook his head. 'A dream is only a dream. You can't live with it all your life.'

Dorothée gave a wry little laugh. 'For a thousand francs you would sell your mother, would you not, Ernst?'

Ernst chuckled. 'Maybe. If there were a market. And you? For a few favours from Bardi, Longo or Scorpio, call him what you will . . . what would you do? I love money. You love a man. Shall we ever get enough of the thing we want?'

'I wonder.' The words came from her with a faint sigh. Her right hand which had been burrowing in the bag moved upwards. A long blade caught the sunlight from the window and then the hand came down, vigorously, surely. Ernst never moved, made no sound.

After a few moments Dorothée drew her hand back. For a while she stood behind Ernst, her eyes closed, her body trembling. Then she turned slowly and went across the room and opened the second door. From inside, there was the sound of running water. Then she came back into the room, closing her handbag.

She looked across at Ernst, his feet still up on the window ledge: Ernst who had now come to the end of his shabby dream; Ernst who had said, 'Shall we ever get enough of the thing we want?' Ernst who had been judged even before he had said it. She shrugged her shoulders, refusing to think any more about him and went out, leaving the door unlocked, and down the back stairs so that she would not have to pass the old man in the garden who dreamed of the country.

At eight o'clock that evening George found Ernst still

sitting in his chair, the evening air moving a little freshly into the room. *Rigor mortis* had set in, and there was surprisingly little blood from the dagger wound in the side of his neck. He just sat there, a stiff little man with the edges of a dream cold about his lips, a cigarette burnt to dead ash between his fingers, and the penalty paid for showing too clearly that he was tired of waiting for dreams to become reality.

George pulled on his driving gloves and then eased over the thick window curtains. He switched on the room light. As he did so a small light came on above the Madonna on the wall above the bed. He went through Ernst's pockets, not liking himself much for doing it, but forcing himself to it, thinking of the beating-up he had taken on the Pampelone beach, thinking of the Professor, Nadia Temple and the others, and of Longo who might be Scorpio . . . and of Dorothée Guntheim who might be a murderess, and wondering what influence there could be behind her to force her hand to it.

There was little else in Ernst's pockets which he had not already seen once at the Hôtel Sainte-Anne. But in the hip pocket of his trousers there was a small silver cigarette-case which he had not produced at the hotel, maybe had not carried then. In it were five cigarettes without a brand name. George sniffed them and knew hemp when he found it. Behind the cigarettes was a dirty, edge-worn visiting card. Printed on it in running script was the word 'BIANERI' and then, inked in under the word, the number 37. On the back of the card Ernst or someone had written in pencil, *Café J. César, Quai de la Râpée. Wednesday.*

George kept the card and put the rest of the stuff back into Ernst's pockets. Fettoni had had a 'Bianeri' card. This one might come in useful.

George went through the rest of the room and the other two rooms. There was no desk, no sign of personal papers. Ernst had had little else in the world except his clothes and his dreams.

George went out, wiping the door handle he had marked

on entry, switched off the light and tip-toed past the old man who was sleeping in the *concierge*'s office, and joined Nicola who was waiting in the Lancia parked down the road.

7

DOROTHÉE GUNTHEIM lay back, watching Antonio Bardi. He stood at the end of the bed wearing a green dressing-gown, a white silk scarf at his neck, a glass of whisky and soda in his hand. There were little silver gleams in his whitish hair under the bright chandelier. The blue eyes smiled at her and she knew that as long as she lived she would never be able to convince herself that there was nothing behind the smile. For this man – though there were moments when he was far from her, when she could find the strength to hate him – she knew that she would do anything. She was the girl who had killed Ernst because he had said it was necessary.

He had used her, used his wife, used Maria, Cadim . . . so many others. Bardi, Longo, Scorpio . . . the names altered, the shape and feeling of him remained, and when he smiled at her there was no will in her except his. Would she, she wondered, one day find a will to oppose his? One day, her use would be finished and then she would have the choice . . . to make it like Maria, content to be passed on, or to make it like his wife and find herself destroyed.

She smiled back at him through her spectacles and he raised the glass slowly to her; yet, while she longed for him to come to her, she knew that she meant nothing to him. In a little while he would finish his drink and, putting out the light, come to her. . . . Always in darkness he came and then the tenderness and the passion in him would make her forget everything except the will to please him. . . .

He said gently, 'In a little while you will forget Ernst. You know you will because you have forgotten others.'

She nodded. 'I shall forget. Yes.'

He turned away, walking slowly to the curtained window. 'The thing has been badly handled. Lodel should never have panicked. Maria should have accepted the man's story about petrol and let him go. By opposing him, we gave him proof. He should have been left to run around beating his head against walls without doors.'

'You believe he comes from Mrs Pinnock?'

'No. But even if he did he is now just as dangerous.' He turned and the smile was still on his broad face. 'Has Laborde still got records of Elsie?'

'No.'

'Of Cadim? Is he still on the books?'

'Yes.'

For a moment the smile faded and his voice came crisply, 'Then tomorrow tell the fool to destroy them. Where is Cadim?'

'He was at Cannes. He opens in Annecy at the end of this week. You want me to let him know that this man may be looking for him?'

'Yes. And tell Cadim I am coming to see him at Annecy. And I want every Bianeri to be warned about this man. I want to know where he goes and what he does.' He drained the glass and put it down.

Sitting on the edge of the bed, he laid his hand on her thigh. She closed her eyes momentarily. The touch sent a slow fire through her body.

'You remember when we first met?' The change in his voice told her that the discussion was over.

'I remember.' It had been in Hamburg where she had been an accounts clerk in an hotel where he was staying with his wife. She had been summoned over some query on his bill and had gone up to his room – his wife was out shopping. The thing had happened like some dream. She, never looked at by men, shy, her face like an ugly banner, suddenly felt his hands on her arms; suddenly, brutally she was on the bed, and enslaved for ever. Lying there, remembering, she saw him slip off his gown. He reached out his hand and took off her glasses. She shut her eyes and heard the click of the light switch, and suddenly felt him beside her, his hard body against her softness, his passion mastering the anguish in her while a voice in her mind, distant, so remote that it was almost unheard, cried for release.

On Monday morning George and Nicola drove from Paris down to Orleans for the day. They kept their room on at the Paris hotel. Before they left George had a telephone conversation with Berney and then with Synat. With the death of Ernst they had been left without any direct lines of approach except Dorothée Guntheim and Laborde. They were not likely to get anything from them and, in view of the drastic measures taken against Ernst, George was not at all anxious to let them know where he was. Somewhere behind them was Scorpio and until Saturday, when they could come up with Ricardo Cadim at Annecy, they were left with time on their hands. Time on George's hands was like itching-powder at this particular moment. So, remembering that Berney had said that Madame Aboler had left Switzerland and had retired to a château in France, he got from him her address. Any information about the past they could get might be helpful. Madame Aboler lived beyond Orleans near a village on the Loire called Beaugency.

To Synat, George gave a report of all that had happened so far and then – remembering Ernst, and to insure himself against the future if the occasion should arise – asked him how much he could spend if the chance came to buy information.

Synat had said, 'I'll back anything you think is reasonable.'

They reached the Château Albris just after two o'clock. It was a turreted, blue-slate-roofed château, with a broad water meadow lined with elms and limes running down to the river. The driveway was closed by large ironwork gates, to one side of which was a small lodge. George got out of the car and knocked on the door of the lodge. An oldish man came out. He was in shirt sleeves with a green baize apron and a black beret and he needed a shave.

George gave his real name and said that he would like to see Madame Aboler if she were in. He was about to tell the man to inform her that he was a friend of Berney when the old man nodded and said, 'Monsieur Constantine, yes? Madame is expecting you.' He stepped inside the lodge door, picked up a telephone and at the same time pushed a button which caused the large gates to swing open. He waved George back to the car.

As George drove up the driveway, he said, 'Berney must have telephoned her. I wonder how much he told her?'

They had the answer in a very few minutes from Madame Aboler herself. They were shown through the great hall of the château to a lofty conservatory which overlooked the river and the meadows. The conservatory would hardly have been out of place at Kew Gardens. It was a green, humid world, luxuriant with plants that at any other time George would have been happy to spend a lot of time examining. In the centre of the floor was a large pool, the surface almost entirely covered with water-lilies and other aquatic plants, and in the depths the movement of fish.

Madame Aboler was sitting in a wheel chair, smoking a long thin cigar. As the footman announced them she pointed the end of the cigar at a low stone bench at the edge of the pool near her chair. 'Do be seated,' she said in unaccented English. 'Berney telephoned and I have been expecting you. I hope the heat in here won't distress you. Or my cigar.' She smiled at Nicola. 'While my husband was alive I smoked them in secret. He hated to see me with one. Now he is dead I smoke when I like. Somewhere, no doubt, he is scolding over my naughtiness. Men are such fussers, and greedy – they want to keep all the pleasant bad habits to themselves. Berney didn't say so, but from the way he spoke I imagine he's in some kind of trouble. If I can help I should like to. I should warn you that I am a very talk-

118

ative old woman but I don't mind at all being interrupted. In fact, you will probably have to do just that to keep me to the point. You see while Abby was alive he did all the talking. Just like the cigars. I now indulge myself.'

For a while George and Nicola just let this torrent wash over them. She sat in her wheel chair, talking now from behind a thin blue haze of cigar smoke, a frail-looking old lady who could have been eighty, ninety or a hundred, a thin, fragile creature with a powder-white face, white hair piled in old-fashioned buns behind her ears, and a great rope of pearls hanging from her thin neck and looping into the lap of her long black tea-gown. She had big grey eyes and her face was a long, wrinkled oval. Once, Berney had said, she had been a great beauty. All that remained now were the large grey eyes which were as alive and expressive as a girl's.

George, a little bemused, cut into a remark she was making about her pearls and how she always wore them in here because they loved the heat just as she did, and said, 'It's quite true that Berney is in some kind of trouble and we are trying to help him.'

She nodded her head and said, 'Tell me how I can help you.' She raised the loop of pearls with one hand and then let it drop. 'Abby gave me jewels, of course. Oh, so many. But never pearls. He didn't like pearls. He was a curious man. So many funny little dislikes. I bought these myself – and no doubt I was cheated. But there, what is the good of having —'

'What I would really like to know,' said George ruthlessly, 'is whether up to the time of your husband's death – and particularly when you were living in Switzerland – you had any servants whom you distrusted or even had to dismiss for dishonesty or other unusual causes.'

'Why do you ask that?' For a moment her voice sharpened. Then suddenly she smiled, 'No, no, I apologize. It is, of course, a natural asperity. A criticism of one's household arrangements. But, of course Abby engaged all the servants. Even my maid, and he was most particular. A man in his position just had to be.'

George felt a trickle of sweat roll between his shoulder-blades and he glanced at the pool, envious of the fish in the cool depths.

'But did you?' he insisted. 'Berney's trouble stems from a breach of confidence which would have been unthinkable in your husband. It could have come from someone employed and highly trusted by him. Also – and I know it's a long time ago – would you conceivably remember any of the other people who were house-guests on the only occasion that Berney visited your husband in your Swiss home?'

For a moment she was silent and the silence in the conservatory was complete. It was like the passing of a cool breeze. Then she smiled and nodded encouragingly. 'I like you. You want something. You go ahead. Please smoke if you want to.' She stubbed out her cigar-end in a silver tray attached to the chair, then, with a deft movement of her hands, rolled the chair backwards a yard, picked up a silver-knobbed ebony stick from the rest against her legs and levelled it, *épée*-wise, at one of the near-by conservatory columns. With a little jerk of her hand she thrust it forward and held it against a bellpush set into the column. Almost, it seemed, while the stick was still on the bellpush, a footman came into the conservatory. He was tall and dark, dressed in black and white with tight knee-breeches, and only needed a buckled black hat to look like a Pilgrim Father.

'Lambiel, get the guest book for 1949. And a tray of drinks.'

Lambiel departed without a word.

'Lambiel,' she said engagingly, wheeling her chair back to the pool, 'gives me the creeps. But under a clause of Abby's will I am not allowed to get rid of any of the servants – except for misdemeanours – until they are of age to be pensioned. Lambiel was Abby's chauffeur once, but he has had his licence taken away for drunken driving.

However, the incident occurred while he was on holiday so I could not fairly say he had misbehaved himself while in my service. None of the other servants like him either.'

'What servants have been dismissed for misbehaviour?' asked George.

'Only one. I was going to tell you about him. He was Abby's valet. An oldish man. Italian. He married a French cook we had. Abby liked him, trusted him, but after his death the man simply went to pieces. He drank and he stole, quite blatantly, and then he seduced two of the maids – not one, but two – in the same week, apparently. One of them had a child later. I dismissed him and pensioned off his wife, dear Rosa. Andrea Palloti. That was his name. And he is the only one who ever gave trouble.'

'Do you know where he is now?'

'No, but his wife lives not far from here with her son. You could talk to her. Maybe she knows where he is, though I doubt it because after the affair with the maids she renounced him. Her own word, renounced. I remember because it seemed so biblical and yet so right. Dear Rosa. I am still so fond of her.' She paused, opened the lid of a silver box on the right arm of her chair and took out a fresh cigar. She lit it from a lighter concealed in the silver knob of her cane.

Inwardly George groaned, caught Nicola's eye in sympathy, and at that moment Lambiel came back with a large leather-covered volume under one arm and a tray of drinks in his hands which he put on a small table by the pool.

Madame Aboler said to Nicola, 'Perhaps, my dear, you will help yourself? That's all, Lambiel.'

As Lambiel withdrew and Nicola began to fix long drinks, George handed Madame Aboler the black book. She rested it on her knees and began to turn the pages over, saying, 'I have a very good memory. Abby always said so. And I remember Berney very well. I thought he was a little like the young Lloyd George, though much taller. I'm English, you know, and I met Lloyd George once or twice. English, yes. Though I don't ever go back. It's so cold. So changed, too. I can't stand cold or change. Ah, here it is.'

She raised the book near her face, studying it without the benefit of glasses.

George took the photographs of Elsie and Cadim from his pocket and handed them to her. 'Do you remember either of these two as your guests?'

Madame Aboler lowered the book and studied the photographs. Then she handed them back and nodded. 'Yes, the man. He was at the house party. Let me see' – she referred to the book. 'He was called Ricardo Cadim, and he had something to do with the entertainment side of a new hotel my husband was going to help finance. I don't think it ever came to anything. Abby would suddenly go cold on a project and I would never know why. And I remember the girl – but she was not a guest at the time Berney visited us. She visited us the previous year with her husband. I remember him particularly.'

'Why?'

'Because he was a guest also when Berney was here, and he brought with him another woman. His mistress.' She raised the book close to her eyes. 'That's right. She was a dark, Spanish-looking creature, and she was called Maria Vendez. I didn't care for her much. I'm a little old-fashioned, you know, about marriage and fidelity, but Abby used to tell me that if he refused to do business with a man because of his morals he would have no business.'

'And the man she was with, the husband of this woman?' George held up Elsie's photograph. 'Who was he? A tallish, well-built, fair-haired man? Called Longo?'

Madame Aboler studied the book again. 'Your description is right, but the name is wrong. He was called Antonio Bardi.'

'Bardi?' George frowned. 'Are you sure?'

Her head came up a little sharply. 'Of course I'm sure, monsieur. I have a good memory, and anyway Bardi for a while was quite a frequent visitor. In fact, I think Abby met him during the war and, although he never said so, I fancy this man had something to do with Intelligence work. Abby, because of his important international position, was somewhat involved in that. Why? Does his being called Bardi upset you?'

'No. But I happen to know that the blonde girl in this photograph married a man called Antonio Longo who fits the description of Bardi.'

'Then they are probably both the same. It is not difficult to change a name.'

'Does your book say where these people came from, give any addresses?'

'No. It is just a guest list with a note of all the menus that were served. Abby insisted on this. He was a nuisance over details like that.'

'Who were the other people present, may I ask?'

The book was studied again. 'Two of my sisters with their children, quite grown up, of course. Then there was Abby's German representative and his wife. The Strossbergs, but both of them are now dead. They were killed in an air crash near Mexico City some years ago. You know Abby was scared of flying. He flew everywhere himself, but would never let me. It was very inconvenient at times because I hate trains.' She looked at Nicola, smiling. 'Help yourself to another drink, my dear. You look terribly hot.'

George, to the sound of ice clinking in the drinks Nicola made, said, 'Could I ask what business connections Bardi had with your husband?'

'Of course. Originally, as I said, I think they met during the war. But at this time I think Bardi was interested in the hotel project which Abby finally dropped. Anyway, he never came to the house again and Abby never spoke of him.'

'Did you,' said George, 'ever hear your husband speak of something called the Bianeri?'

'Bianeri?'

'Yes.'

'No. I've never heard the word before.'

Ten minutes later they were out of the château. All the windows of the Lancia were down and George kept his foot hard on the accelerator pedal. The air came sweeping in to them in a long, steady, cooling stream.

'I wonder,' said Nicola, 'she doesn't melt away.' She undid the top buttons of her blouse and held the material away from her and sighed.

George grinned. 'We could find a way down to the river and swim.'

'Just keep driving,' said Nicola. 'We've got to talk to dear Rosa.' Then, lying back against the seat, letting the cool air beat over her, eyes shut, she said, 'So now we know, don't we? Elsie married Longo. Longo changes his name – and he could have plenty of reasons for doing that. In 1949 he's carrying on with Maria Vendez —'

'Who could be the dark-haired, gun-happy girl in the villa.'

'And in 1950 – according to Mrs Pinnock – Elsie more or less decides to leave Longo and take the new-born child with her. What happens after that? Where did Elsie go? And what about the child?'

'I'd like to know. Abby seems a shrewd number. He didn't apparently buy the project which Cadim and Bardi were putting up to him. But he'd worked with, or accepted help from Bardi during the war. Bardi-Longo could have set up an organization for intelligence deals in Switzerland. He probably sold to the highest bidder. That would explain an account in London which still exists and is still respected by our Security people. They probably don't know anything about blackmail, but maybe he still is useful to them in other ways. After all, if you blackmail on a big scale, you must pick up other information about people and affairs which, while not blackmail material, is still worth money in the right market.'

Nicola nodded. 'I've a feeling that Ricardo Cadim is the man you want to get talking.'

'So do I. But first of all we'll try Rosa.'

Madame Aboler had given them Rosa Palloti's address

and a letter of introduction to her. Rosa and her son had a small farm – bought for them on Rosa's retirement by Madame Aboler – near a village called Voves off the Orleans-Chartres road. With the letter Madame Aboler had also given them a basket for Rosa which held a couple of bottles of champagne, a leg of pork, and a carton of Chesterfield cigarettes – all of which, she said, Rosa loved. She had explained that Aboler would never have pork served at his table, and thought that champagne was a poor drink. Driving hard, George felt himself fantasy-bound as he thought of Madame Aboler who had obviously loved her husband dearly but now indulged herself with all the things he had forbidden, cigars, champagne, pork, pearls and, no doubt, air travel.

The Palloti farm was a couple of miles outside Voves, down a long cart-track fringed with poplars. A wide expanse of beet and cornfields spread to the horizon.

The farm buildings consisted of a long, slate-roofed, monastic-looking barn with a small house tucked on the end. There was a stable under the house which was on the first-floor level. A run of wooden steps went up to a small wooden balcony lined with old tins in which little clumps of snapdragons and tobacco plants struggled to make a brave show. A few bantam hens foraged around the dusty yard. There was a strong ammonia smell from a dung pile against the barn wall. A black-and-white mongrel bitch was fastened to a chain at the foot of the steps and took no notice of them until they were half way up the flight; then it stirred and gave one long howl which brought Rosa to the balcony. She stood just inside the door, and, as George handed her Madame Aboler's letter and the basket of gifts, he wondered whether she ever came out of the door. She was one of the biggest women he had ever seen, and she had one of the roundest, reddest faces he had ever seen, and she looked completely happy. At a pinch, he told himself, if she turned sideways, she could just manage to pass the door.

She read the letter, nodding her head, then bent a little forward and eyed the basket and nodded her head more. For a moment George thought that the weight of her breasts and the big nodding head would topple her forward. However, she kept her feet and asked them in.

The room was dark and cool and a cloth-covered table in the centre took up most of the space. An oil-lamp hung from the ceiling and there was a fireplace blocked with a large fan of pink crinkled paper. A door at the back of the room was open, giving a glimpse of a kitchen and another run of wooden stairs, presumably to a couple of bedrooms. Rosa, who spoke reasonably good English, offered them wine, bringing out the bottle and the glasses before they could refuse. The champagne she was obviously keeping for a quiet celebration on her own. It was a rough red wine with a strong metallic flavour and George grinned as he saw Nicola wrinkle up her nose when she tasted it.

Rosa said, 'Madame says you want to know about my Andrea?'

'That's right,' said George. 'He was Italian, wasn't he?'

'From Milan. But I meet him in Switzerland. Before he came to the house he was a waiter all over: France, Italy, Germany. He liked to travel. There were too many things he liked. Young girls, the maids mostly.' She laughed without concern. 'I say to him before I renounce him – before marriage a man is free to get in any bed. Nobody cares. But after marriage – then a man must be discreet and not dishonour his wife by letting everyone know it is not her bed alone he shares. Andrea is not discreet – so I kick him out.'

George nodded. A kick from Rosa would be quite something. 'Where is he now?'

'I should not know. We have no communication. Somewhere he works, somewhere he drinks too much, somewhere there is some fool girl who catches his eye.'

From outside came the sound of a tractor driving into the yard. Rosa said, 'That is my son, Pierre. I insist on the French name for him. He is good farmer. When it is dark he comes in to eat and sleep; when it is light again he goes out. It is hard here, but we are happy.'

Through the open doorway George saw the tractor pass out of the yard into a field, a trailer of dung being drawn behind. A thickset man was driving it.

He said, 'Your only son?'

Rosa shook her head. 'No. I have a much younger son, but don't ask me where he is. He is like his father. One place, one woman, is no good for him. He goes like a bird. He comes back, says hello, and then is gone again. This is him.'

She levered herself up from the table and rolled towards the shelf over the fireplace and reached for a photograph in a small velvet frame. She came back and laid it before George.

'He is good-looking – not like Pierre. Like his father.'

George raised the photograph towards the light. He was looking at a young man of about twenty, stripped to the waist, one foot up on a fallen tree-trunk, one hand resting on an axe. The face, turned slightly back over the broad shoulder, was familiar, unmistakable.

'Gian,' sighed Rosa. 'He and his father are from the same mould.'

George handed the photograph to Nicola. He said, 'Gian is very much like a young man I met once in the South of France. A young man with reddish hair.'

Rosa nodded. 'Gian has that colour hair. Like his father. Only Pierre is from my side. Tell me, monsieur, why are you so interested in my Andrea?'

George was silent for a moment. It was a good question. Why? Because at the moment he was interested in anything to do with Scorpio, Longo, Bardi – call him what you like. Andrea Palloti was Gian's father. Both rolling stones. Both bad eggs. What did he say to this fat, simple woman who lived happily here with a dour, hard-working son who would never give her any trouble?

He said, hesitating, 'Well . . . it's difficult to explain,

madame. I am looking for something, for some information and I don't know quite —'

'Madame Palloti,' Nicola interrupted him, 'did your husband ever belong to something which is called the Bianeri?'

'The Bianeri?' Rosa said it without surprise. 'You are interested in that?'

Nicola nodded. 'It would help us to know what it is. You see, what we are trying to do is to help someone who was a friend of Monsieur Aboler. We can't tell you what it is. But it is very important.'

'Monsieur Aboler? What could the Bianeri have to do with Monsieur Aboler, rest his soul?'

'Nothing probably,' said George. 'But what do you know about the Bianeri?'

Rosa shook her head. 'Nothing, monsieur. I just know there is such a thing. Once, when Andrea was very drunk, he mentioned it.'

'What did he say?'

'Say? Not very much. It is many years ago now. For the winter we are at the Paris house and one night Andrea comes back late and very drunk. I think he has been with a woman. I put him to bed and he swears he has not been with a woman. He swears it – and all I can get from him is that he has been to a club drinking. What club, I ask? And he says the Bianeri. I say, what is this? A club called the Bianeri? He says it is a club; he drinks, plays billiards there, that is all, once a week – every Wednesday. And then he goes off to sleep and I can get no more from him, naturally.'

'Until the next morning,' suggested George.

Rosa smiled. 'Ah, that is why I remember. When he is sober and I say what is this Bianeri club, he just says what do I talk about? He knows no club called that. He has been drinking in a bistro.'

'And you know no more about the Bianeri than that?'

'No, monsieur. No more. You would like some more wine, mademoiselle?' She put her hand to the bottle.

'No thank you, madame.' Nicola shook her head quickly.

George said, 'Has Gian ever mentioned the Bianeri to you?'

'Gian? Since he was sixteen I have seen Gian about four times. All I hear from Gian is about the fine life he leads because he is chauffeur to some rich man.'

'What rich man?'

Rosa wobbled her head sadly. 'Possibly no rich man, monsieur. Gian is also a liar like his father. He dreams of a rich life. But if the truth is known he probably drives a truck somewhere.'

Nicola said, 'Are you sure it was a Wednesday night on which your husband got drunk at the club? It is so long ago, how could you remember?'

Rosa smiled, filled her own glass with wine, and then ran a large hand over her chins. 'Because, mademoiselle, it was a cheese-soufflé night. Always, every Wednesday evening, Monsieur Aboler insisted on cheese soufflé. Madame and myself were always so concerned about it. Just so, it must be. It was not often that the soufflé went wrong. But this evening, it is wrong, for I remember thinking when Andrea came in, "Ah, what a life, the cheese soufflé goes wrong, and this pig of a husband is drunk again." But no more, mademoiselle. I have a good son, we live, we have peace and now and then Madame sends cigarettes and champagne.'

The light was going from the sky as they left the farm, and as they drove out of the yard they saw the tractor, hull down across the fields, a figure hunched over the wheel. Honest, solid Pierre, thought George, the support of his mother. How much loyalty and villainy tied people to one another, how intricately the web was woven, how impossible it seemed at first to hope to find a way to the centre. But if one kept on probing the thing began to make sense slowly, one path led to another, one person revealed a link with another. No act or individual existed in a vacuum. Honest Rosa had mothered a man who

129

would have helped kill him in the Pampelone bamboos, and Madame Aboler had turned up her nose at Antonio Bardi bringing a mistress to her house where his wife had once been welcomed – had it been that which had privately made Aboler turn down the hotel project? Andrea Palloti, going to the bad after the death of Aboler, had he been the one who had somehow got his hands on Berney's letters?

Roaring along the straight to Chartres, headlights on now, Nicola who was driving said, 'Whatever it is, somewhere at the back of all this I have a feeling is this Bianeri thing. Fettoni, Andrea Palloti and Ernst – they were all members.'

'Members of what? A club?'

'I don't know. But there's an address on the back of Ernst's card. Maybe that is the place in Paris.'

'You mean I've got a membership card – why don't I pay it a visit?'

'Why not? You could try it this Wednesday, before we go to Annecy.'

'You mean stick my head in the lion's mouth, maybe, just to see if he has any teeth?'

'How else can you find out? I'd do it myself, but I have a feeling that women probably aren't admitted to membership.'

Twin horns blaring, she pulled out quickly around a lorry, flicked the headlights down and up, and then began to laugh.

'What's so funny?' asked George.

'I was thinking of Rosa and cheese-soufflé night. I'll bet Madame Aboler indulges herself over that one. She probably has it on Sundays for lunch now just to make old Abby angry wherever he is.'

'It's a pity he's dead,' said George, watching the tail-light of a motor-cyclist coming up and waiting for the swerve, the horns and the headlights, trying not to notice that the speedometer needle was steady at ninety-five miles an hour. 'I've a feeling he could have helped us a lot. As a matter of fact, if you go on driving like this we've a good chance of having a word with him very soon.'

'Stop fussing. I can't stand men who drive fast themselves and won't let their women do the same.'

'Oh!' The exclamation was for the swerve, the horns and the headlights down and then up, and the implied relationship between them.

'And you can go back to base on what you're thinking. It was only a form of speech. I'm not your woman.'

'There's always hope – if we get through Chartres without knocking the cathedral down.'

'Don't worry,' said Nicola. 'Just light a cigarette for me. It's sixty odd kilometres to Paris, and I'm longing for a bath and then a very expensive dinner.' She turned and winked at him.

'For God's sake,' said George, 'keep your eye on the road.'

8

THE CAFÉ J. César on the Quai de la Râpée was on the right bank of the Seine in the Reuilly *arrondissement*. From the pavement there were a few steps down to the entrance which was flanked by two sorry-looking bay trees in tubs. There was a long, low, half-curtained window to the right of the door with the name *Café J. César* painted in black-and-gold letters across the glass above the curtain. In brass holders on either side of the door were handwritten in purple ink a list of *consommations* and the *plat du jour*. It looked a quiet working-man's sort of place, no frills, no nonsense.

George and Nicola looked it over on the Monday, going inside for a quick drink, and on the Tuesday George spent a couple of hours from six o'clock until eight o'clock in the evening watching the kind of people who went in. It was used by some of the bargees from the river boats, families with children, working men on their own, a few couples . . . altogether a quiet, undistinguished set of people. Somehow he didn't see it as the kind of place where Andrea Palloti would go roistering or where Ernst would go to buy a few hemp cigarettes.

On Wednesday George bought himself a pair of second-hand black trousers from a slop shop, a well-worn imitation leather windbreaker, a pair of black shoes with pointed toes that gave his feet hell, and a brown woollen jersey that buttoned close up to his neck. Dressed in these he looked fairly like some of the single young men he had seen go into the place. Nicola bought some hair tint that toned his sandy hair down to dark brown.

He was sitting in the café now at a quarter to eight. He had been there for half an hour and drunk one beer and one pernod. Nicola had been left at the hotel with the promise that he wouldn't go out of his way to look for trouble and that he would telephone her as soon as he left the place.

There was a long, curved, zinc-topped bar that ran from the window down the right-hand side of the room, and chairs and tables down the other side, leaving an open gangway that ran to a bead-curtained doorway leading into a small dining-room. To the left of the doorway was a twisting run of stairs covered with a shabby red carpet. In the half hour in which George had been sitting over his drinks, he had seen about six men come in, go to the bar, stand there and have a drink, talking to a plump, dark-haired girl behind the bar, and then move over to the stairway and disappear up it.

Although these men were a mixed lot, some old, some young, some well dressed, others shabby, there was a curious suggestion of similarity of manner and bearing about them all. George kept feeling that he had seen them all somewhere before.

There was a man at the bar now who he was prepared to bet was shortly going to disappear quietly up the stairs. He was a hunched-up man of about sixty, a grey velour pushed slightly to the back of his head, little wings of grey hair escaping from it over his ears. He wore black trousers, a shabby jacket from some suit which had never belonged to him, the edges of the jacket flapping too long over his thighs, and he held a Malacca cane with a horn handle. He had a long white face with very dark, button-bright eyes and he had a habit of pushing his lower lip up over his top lip after every drink he took. He did it often because he drank fast, taking two glasses of vermouth-cassis at the bar within five minutes. While he drank he rested one arm on the bar and looked round at the room, occasionally puffing out his old cheeks and making little explosive noises with his lips, as though he were carrying on some inner conversation with himself and exploding contemptuously at the stupidity of some of his own remarks. Quite clearly, too, he had had plenty to drink before he entered the café.

He finished his drink now, turned, pushed some money across the bar to the girl and said something which made her raise her eyes humorously and then shake her head. He raised his stick, laughed – a dry croak of a laugh – and then tapped her gently on her head and turned away towards the stairs.

George got up and followed the old man. The stairs took a double twist and ended in a landing from which a narrow passageway ran to the left. The old man, breathing hard, turned and stared at George. The landing was suddenly heavy with the reek of garlic and cassis.

The old man looked him over in silence for a while and then said in French, 'I haven't seen you before?'

George said, 'It's my first time here.' He spoke French.

The old man made a couple of puffing noises with his cheeks and said, in English, 'You're English?'

'Yes.'

'Just passing through?'

George nodded. 'That's it. Just passing through. My first night in Paris.'

The old man said, 'At your age, I'd have found myself

a girl. Not wasted my time here.' His English was good, but the accent was there. 'Go back and arrange it with Renée at the bar. She likes them your age and can be very entertaining.'

'I'd rather come up here.'

The old man shrugged his shoulders. 'Missed opportunities. You'll regret them later. Look at me. All I get from them now is a laugh and a mouthful of sauce. But there was a time when a word, a wink, a look, would have made them jump out of their skirts. Golden times. Golden girls.' He turned and said over his shoulder, 'Come along, then.'

He went slowly down the corridor to a door outside which was a small table with a man sitting behind it. He was old, too, and bald; he wore a yellow linen jacket and a black bow-tie over a not-too-clean shirt. He looked as though he had been sitting at the table for some years and the dust had begun to settle thickly on him so that there was no shine to his eyes, no colour to his face, and an accumulation of greyish fuzz over his bald head. Before him on the table was an open exercise book, a bottle of gin, a glass and a carafe of water. He had a pipe in his mouth with a bowl so big that it threatened to pull his teeth out. The effort of holding it gave him a wolfish, dusty grimace.

George's old man knocked the head of his stick on the table sharply and said, '*Ça va, Marc?*'

The other looked up and said, '*Votre nom, monsieur?*'

George's old man turned to him and winked and for a moment he swayed a little on his feet. 'Marc,' he explained, 'is a great one for rules. It is best to humour him.' He put his hand in his inner pocket and pulled out a card which he dropped in front of Marc.

George saw that it was a printed Bianeri card.

Marc pulled it towards him and very laboriously entered the number on it in his exercise book while at the same time George's old man, with another wink at him, recited solemnly, 'Général de Gaulle, Palais Royal.'

Marc looked up frowning, '*Sois sérieux, mon cher.*'

George's old man winked again and then said, 'Aristide Acard, night porter, Hôtel Gildas. Hôtel did I say? Let us be frank. It is little more than a whorehouse. Me, night-porter to a lot of *poules*, who was once head-waiter at —'

'*Pas des histoires,*' said Marc sharply. Against Aristide's number he wrote the name of his hotel and his occupation and then passed his Bianeri card back to him. He looked up at George then and said, '*Monsieur?*'

George took out Ernst Fragonard's Bianeri card. He was glad now that he had added a figure one in front of the 37 on the card on the off-chance that he might have to use it.

Marc looked at the card and then entered the number below Aristide's. '*Votre nom, monsieur?*'

George said, 'Ernest Smith, kitchen hand, Savoy Hotel, London.' God knew what he was getting into, but whatever it was he had to play it by ear and if Aristide worked in a hotel then there was no reason why he shouldn't do the same.

Marc nodded and wrote down the particulars.

While he did so Aristide, waiting for George, said, 'The Savoy? Once I was in London, too. For ten years. Another golden time. Missed opportunities . . . not all, but some. Ah, the golden times, the golden nights in Hyde Park, the golden girls. . . .'

Marc pushed George's card back and said, '*C'est qui à Londres?*'

George looked blank. Who was it in London? What did the man want?

Seeing his look, Aristide said, 'You do not understand?'

'No, I don't.'

'Who told you in London? Who gave you this address? Marc will not let you in unless you have a sponsor.'

For a moment George, understanding now, hesitated, and then he said to Marc, 'Luigi Fettoni.'

The name produced an explosion from Aristide alongside him. He put one arm round George's neck, breathed a great gust of garlic at him, and cried, 'Luigi Fettoni – my old friend! No, no, it is not possible! Dear old Luigi.' He began to pump George by the hand, swaying even more.

Marc wrote down Fettoni's name and then said to George, '*Quel numéro pour Fettoni?*'

'*Quel numéro?*' roared Aristide. '*Je le sais bien. C'est le numéro six.*' He turned to George. 'Right. Am I right? I have a memory like an elephant. Would to God I had the vigour!'

'Six is right,' said George.

Marc, unmoved, wrote the number down, and then leaned back and opened a drawer in the table and pulled out a fat ledger. He flipped the pages over, pages that George could see were thick with names and addresses, and ran his thin finger down them. After a time his finger paused and he said solemnly, '*Six. Oui, c'est vrai.*'

He closed the book, put it back into the drawer, closed the drawer and then nodded his head towards the door. Taking no notice of them he began to fill his glass with gin and water.

Aristide, one arm linked in George's, moving him to the door, said, 'How seriously Marc takes it all. One must forgive him. Myself, I have begun to tire of it all. Yes, I have tired because it is not as it was in the old days of the war. Now, I come from habit. But tonight is different. For Luigi's sake I welcome you as a friend. You shall drink with me and afterwards, if you wish, I shall fix you up with Renée. Her husband is a good friend of mine. I will arrange it for the whole night . . . a whole golden night.'

He pushed open the door and George followed him in and something told him that while this night might be golden he didn't think it was going to have anything to do with Renée. What the hell was this Bianeri lark?

The room was a surprise to him. It was very large and the ceiling was low. A run of close-curtained windows at the far end looked out over the Seine and the quay, he guessed. By the windows was a snooker-table with four men playing and a row of men sitting on benches under the windows watching, their faces showing whitely beyond the fringe of the great lamps that hung over the green baize. From the door, running at an angle to the snooker-table section, was a large space filled with card-tables, most of them occupied. Beyond the tables was a bar against the wall with a young man in a white jacket serving drinks.

Aristide, acknowledging greetings as he went, steered George past the tables to a little alcove with a marble-topped table. He motioned George to sit down and then ambled off to the bar, returning with a couple of glasses and a bottle of white wine.

As he set them down, he said in English, 'It is the custom always to drink white wine. That is the reason most of us stop to have a couple of stiffeners at the bar. Marc outside is allowed his gin – but only outside. It was so during the war when wine was all we could easily get. It is so now.'

He pulled a small corkscrew from his pocket and opened the bottle expertly.

George said, 'I haven't been a Bianeri long. There's a lot I don't know.'

'Why should you know the French custom, my friend? Everywhere it varies. Italy – it is always Chianti. England – ah, things are better there – whisky or gin. The times I used to get drunk with Fettoni. Tell me, is the old man well?'

'He doesn't complain,' said George.

Aristide nodded, and filled their glasses. They drank, and Aristide, pushing up his lower lip, exploded gently and said, 'But it is not as it was during the war. We were Resistance then – there was a real purpose. I could tell you a few things that went on in this room. I've seen a German major lying stripped on that table, shouting every secret he knew just out of fear of what might happen to him. They knew about us, of course. But they never knew where to find us – the Bianeri.' He raised his glass and drank and then refilled it.

George said, 'But now – the war is over.'

Aristide nodded, 'Thank God. Though it was better then. At least we waiters and hotel people were doing a job, a good job. Now it has mostly gone back to the old business.'

'The old dirty business, eh?' George lit a cigarette and looked around the room. From under the snooker lights came the sharp click of balls, the quiet murmur of voices. Now and again at a card-table, a voice would exclaim briefly at the turn of a card, but this and the other noises were only infrequent moments of emphasis in the quiet, subdued room. And now, he was beginning to understand more. He knew now why all the men had seemed to have something in common. They were all waiters, hotel workers or people in domestic service as Andrea Palloti had been. And the thing they had in common was this subdued, anonymous kind of personality. You saw them, and yet you didn't see them. They served you at table, brought breakfast to your room, quiet, efficient, never obtruding, passing to and fro without comment, and there must be many things they saw and heard which could be useful to a man like Scorpio.

Aristide refilled his glass with wine. 'Yes, the old dirty business. But people ask for it, you know. You're young. You aren't bitter yet. But wait until you get out of the kitchen, wait until you are on room service. You walk into a bedroom and some fool with more money than sense sits up alongside a girl who isn't his wife and doesn't really see you because you're a waiter and his mind is on one thing. Then you get bitter. Then you pick up a nice bit of information to sell. I've done it . . . in the past, I've done it. Yes, it's the old dirty business again now. I don't have anything to do with that. I just come out of habit. Anyway, once in – there's no leaving is there?'

'That's true.'

'It certainly is . . . *i bianchi e neri*, that's what we are – the Bianeri, the black and whites. You know Italy?' Without waiting for a reply, Aristide went on, 'You should go to Italy . . . golden Italy. I was two years in Portofino once, and nearly married one of the chamber-maids. What a girl . . . a great brown, warm-skinned creature who could have stripped and been a ship's figure-head. For breasts, undoubtedly, the Italians are su-preme . . .' He shook his head, heavy with rich recollections and finished his glass.

Bianeri. Black and white. Waiters. A tight organization within the great framework of hotels and restaurants all over Europe. What a set-up for a man like Scorpio! In wartime he used it for intelligence work, and now for blackmail, for buying and selling every kind of informa-tion. People took no notice of waiters. They were like G. K. Chesterton's postman, they moved without being seen. How many indiscretions a week did the average hotel mark up? Men staying with other men's wives. Politicians, actors, industrialists, relying on an incognito that hid nothing. Tongues that loosened up at the bar. Stock-exchange talk. Racing talk. Women talk. Political scandal. And – apart from the famous – there were always the small, ordinary people making the one slip of their lives. The housewife alone in a hotel lounge, bored, lonely . . . the young man or the elderly fool away from home suddenly stepping right outside true character for once, for that fatal once which sent some waiter with information to sell to the Bianeri.

Quite bluntly George said, 'Who started it all? And when?'

'Who?' Aristide looked at him owlishly. 'Who starts anything? Nobody knows. And nobody tries to find out. Don't you be curious, *mon ami*. It's still just as it was during the war. You know the man above and the man below and that is enough. If you got caught then you could not have much to tell.' He tapped George's glass, 'Drink. And I will fetch another bottle.'

Aristide got up and began to weave gently across to the bar. As he did so the main door to the room opened and Marc came in, carrying his exercise book under his arm.

Behind him were two other people. For a moment or two George could not see them very well as they moved across the room. Then they came out of the shadows by the table into the light from the wall brackets behind the bar. He slid back into his seat and dropped his head, putting a hand over his lower face. With Marc were Dorothée Guntheim and François Laborde.

Dorothée wore a brown beret and a loose brown coat and the wall lights made little circles of reflection on her thick glasses. Laborde wore a green pork-pie hat that seemed too small for his large head, a loose-fitting grey suit with a little flick of white silk handkerchief at the breast pocket, and he was smoking a cigar. The three of them went to the bar and the young man behind it began to serve them with drinks. They stood with their backs to the room and no one took any notice of them.

Aristide came back with another bottle, deftly pulled the cork, and smiled a happy, chiding smile as George put his hand over the top of his glass.

'Maybe you are wise,' said Aristide. 'A young man should be careful. Too much wine robs him of his power in bed. But me, what have I to lose?' He filled his glass to the brim and sat down.

George said, 'Maybe you were right, too. Why should I waste my time here? Maybe I should go down and see Renée.'

Aristide chuckled. 'Ah, all this time you have been sitting there, thinking about her. Why not? She has plenty for a man to think about. But there is no hurry. In a moment I will come down with you.' He put out a hand as George began to rise. 'Patience. One more glass and we will arrange it.'

George sat back in his chair and let Aristide fill his glass. He had to get out of this room without drawing attention to himself. He had learned more than he had ever expected to learn. Every moment he stayed now was loaded with possible trouble.

But, even as he thought it, he saw the three at the bar turn towards the room. Marc opened his exercise book and handed it to Dorothée Guntheim.

Laborde tapped his glass on the bar top and said loudly, *'Messieurs!'*

The players at the snooker-table straightened up, leaning on their cues, the talk at the card-tables was suddenly killed. Everyone was looking at the group by the bar.

Slowly, deliberately, so that George had no trouble in following his French, Laborde said, 'Gentlemen, I am sorry to disturb your evening without notice, but there are two matters of some urgency which must be made known. So, with your indulgence, we will go into committee for the briefest of sessions. Agreed?'

A murmur of agreement came from the room and, with it, George leaned over to Aristide, caught his arm and held it firmly. 'Listen,' he whispered, 'if there is trouble do one thing for me. Go to a Mademoiselle Nancy Marden and tell her. Here' – he tore off a strip from his cigarette packet and as Laborde went on talking, he wrote down Nicola's assumed name and their hotel, and then pushed the scrap of cardboard towards Aristide.

Watching the old man's puzzled face, seeing the veined old hand poke at the cardboard strip curiously, he heard Laborde saying, 'The first item concerns a fellow member of ours who unfortunately has been the victim —'

Laborde broke off as Marc's mumbling voice interrupted him saying something which George could not catch. Out of the corner of his eye George saw Marc lean towards Dorothée and stab his finger at an open page of the exercise book. Then his eyes went to Aristide who now held the piece of cardboard gingerly as though one end of it were alight and he knew that if he did not drop it soon it would burn his fingers.

'One thing for me – to wipe out all the dirty things,' whispered George.

And then clear and sharp there came the voice of Dorothée Guntheim, 'Before we go any farther, it is pointed out that we have a guest from London present. Under the rules, of course, he is not permitted to be present during a committee meeting. Would the gentleman in question be kind enough to leave us for a few minutes?'

Aristide said, 'That's you. You understand? What is this?' He waved the piece of cardboard stupidly and made a puffing sound with his lips.

Dorothée Guntheim's voice came again, as she read from the book, 'One three seven, Ernest Smith, kitchen hand, Savoy Hotel, London . . . Would the gentleman please leave?' Her head turned round the room, the thick glasses glinting.

Slowly George stood up, one hand over his mouth, made an inclination of his head towards the bar, and then turned away, making for the door. He had about fifteen paces to go, threading his way through the card-tables. The men at the tables looked up at him, grinned, nodded, commiserating with the interruption of his evening. George, keeping his head turned from the bar, shrugged his shoulder and nodded back to the men. Six paces gone. The door was close ahead of him. He wanted to run, whip it open and be gone, but he forced himself to walk casually. Three paces. He was at the door. He put out his hand and caught the knob and twisted it. The door refused to open.

Behind him suddenly there was a burst of laughter, and Laborde's voice, full of good-humour, said, 'Ah, our careful Marc and his rules. All committee meetings will be held behind locked doors. One moment, *monsieur*.'

George stood at the door and turned slightly. With luck it would be Marc who came to open the door. He stood there, waiting, not daring to turn full round and see who was coming. Footsteps came across the room, some of the men began to talk among themselves, and he heard the clink of glasses, as the barman tidied his counter.

Then a man was at his side, moving by him, a key in his hand. He put his free hand with a friendly gesture on

George's shoulder and began to bend forward to unlock the door. The key was in the lock and he was about to turn it when he looked up, smiling, at George.

George was staring straight into Laborde's face. Slowly he saw the movement of puzzlement over the broad face, then the frown and suddenly the bright look of recognition. Laborde's hand began to come back, withdrawing the key, and George made a grab at it. Laborde swung away from him, jerking his left elbow into George's side, jumping clear and shouting.

The shout brought the whole room alive. There was the scrape of tables going back, Laborde's face, white and bland, mouth open, shouting in rapid French. Desperately George jumped for him, hoping to get the key. Then three of the nearest men closed in on him and he had his back to the door. Suddenly all noise and movement ceased and George was staring at the three men, seeing beyond them Aristide watching stupidly, half-drunk, from the alcove table, Dorothée Guntheim at the bar, one hand holding a small gun, Marc peering forward, his exercise book raised, just touching his mouth, his head shaking disapprovingly. Then Laborde was saying calmly, smiling as he spoke, 'Ernest Smith of the Savoy Hotel? I think, Mr Smith, you have some explaining to do.'

In the sitting-room of his hotel suite Antonio Bardi was writing a letter to his son. The boy had been at an English public school now for over a year. If Bardi had any real affection for anyone it was for the boy. He wanted him to have all the things which he had lacked. His father had been a restaurant proprietor in Brighton and at an early age he had worked in the kitchen after school. After leaving school he had become a waiter for some years. Those were the years which had made him what he had now become and, if he no longer considered with any feeling what he was, he was determined that his son should never be able to blame him for not giving him every opportunity. Other people paid for it, the money was dirty, but the boy would never know and money, as it moved, carried no history with it.

He wrote easily, a good father's letter, and as he wrote he could picture the boy and his surroundings . . . the boy would never know the things he had known, the dirtiness of people, the arrogance of people . . . the smell and heat of a kitchen, with all the tables full in the restaurant and the cook bad-tempered, and quick to bring the flat of his hand across one's face . . . the waiting in hotels later when one could go into a bedroom and some bookmaker or city councillor would roll off the belly of a girl and look straight through one, never remotely considering that this black-and-white creature had any feelings. . . . So many things, and none of them for his son, thank God.

He paused, almost at the end of the letter, considering now how he should finish. Always he liked to finish his letters, the news and chat exhausted, with something which he felt would make the boy think.

He wrote, 'Try to train yourself to make not just quick judgements of other people, but quick and accurate judgements. This is difficult but it can be done. It's not what people say which tells you what they are. It's the small things about them. Look at the boys around you, you know them by now. You know the greedy ones, the lazy ones, the clever ones, the kind, the bullying — Now, what is it, if you were meeting them for the first time, that should tell you what they are? I think you might be surprised how obvious their qualities are from just running your eye over them. Dirty finger-nails, untidy clothes, the way they walk, the tone of voice, the way they sit at a desk, the way they say "Yes, sir" or "No, sir." All these things —'

The telephone rang, interrupting him. He picked it up, said 'Yes', and then, nodding slightly to himself listened. A woman was speaking at the other end. He let her finish and then said, 'What has he got on him?'

Dorothée Guntheim's voice at the other end of the line said, 'Nothing, except some money. And his card.'

'Whose card was it?'

'Fragonard's. He'd altered the number. He gave Fettoni in London as a sponsor.'

'Fettoni's dead. Maybe it's as well. He was getting too old. Wheeler came through him . . .' He paused, reached out for a cigarette and lit it. Then he went on, 'What does Laborde think?'

'He doesn't want to waste time with him. He's not the kind who's likely to speak – unless we take a lot of trouble.'

'It's not worth it. Tell Laborde to go ahead. He knows. He can use the Café César outlet. He used it enough times during the war.'

'And the girl – if we can find her?'

'Find her and then we'll decide. All right?'

'If you say so.'

'I do.'

'Shall I report later to you, when it's done?'

'No. I am busy all this evening.'

'I see.'

He smiled to himself at the tone of her voice and then put the receiver down.

He got up, fixed himself a whisky and soda, and picked up the letter, reading it through as far as he had got. Then he sat down and went on writing.

They had tied his hands behind him and brought him down to this cellar by a set of back stairs. He was alone now with Dorothée Guntheim, Laborde and Marc.

The place smelt of wine and stagnant water. There were two unshaded electric light bulbs hanging from the single roof beam. The ceiling was of stone and the walls were hidden with wine racks. The floor was of large slate slabs, between the cracks of which water seeped gently in one corner.

He was sitting on a chair whose back had broken away, a small marble-topped table almost touching his knees. On the table was a glass and a bottle of brandy, now half empty. Aristide would have appreciated the brandy and so would he – under different circumstances. Thirty minutes ago Laborde had taken the bottle of Remy Martin from one of the racks and uncorked it, saying, 'We only serve the best to our customers.' Since then the ritual of forcing him to drink had gone on steadily and already his head was beginning to swim.

None of them wasted much time on conversation. They all acted as though they knew exactly what was to be done, had done it before, and were anxious to have it over.

Marc stood behind him and Laborde sat on the edge of the table, his hand on the shoulder of the brandy bottle, his eyes on George. George watched his hand, waiting for it to move, for the bottle to be lifted and the glass filled.

Marc shuffled a little behind him, Dorothée Guntheim stared at the far wall, and then Laborde's hand moved and the bottle was lifted.

'Another, my friend? Why not? You're doing well. Most people fall off the chair after half a bottle.'

Laborde reached forward and filled the tumbler with brandy. As the bottle tipped back and its glass rang on the marble top George felt Marc's old hands grasp the back of his neck in a vicious grip. At first he had struggled against this, but Marc, surprisingly strong, had merely pinned him to the chair and Laborde had administered the dose, half the brandy going down his throat, the rest spilling over his face. After the third time he had sat on his backless chair and tried to shut his throat against the dose. But their familiarity with the ritual had defeated this. Dorothée Guntheim had stepped forward and clamped his nostrils in her strong fingers. The physical indignity which made him swallow had also made him hate her and now, somewhere in his growing intoxication, he was sorry about the hatred . . . somewhere deep in his consciousness he knew that Dorothée Guntheim was someone to be pitied, not hated. Laborde you could hate and old Marc, so pedantic about his rules and his exercise book, but not Dorothée. She might not, he thought hazily now, be one of Aristide's golden girls . . . though her figure was undeniably good. But let's face it, she wasn't any golden

Portofino girl. Where was Aristide now? Where? Something he had told him to do. What was it? He tried to force himself to think clearly. His eyes caught the glare of the electric lights, and he swayed suddenly and, for a moment, had to fight to keep his balance.

Laborde's hand came up with the glass. George tried to turn his head from it but Marc held him and Laborde's free hand dug at his jaw, fingers biting into his flesh until his mouth opened. Brandy poured over his tongue and Marc held his head back, one hand slipping round and over his mouth, throttling him until for relief he had to swallow the liquid. The moment he did so all pressure came off him. Marc stepped away. Laborde settled back on the table corner. Through the tears that hazed his vision George saw the figure of Dorothée begin to swing and waver, and he thought that she was going to fall. Then he realized that it was he who was swaying. He made an effort, caught his balance and laughed with a short croak of open delight at the control he still had left.

Brightly, a voice from inside him said, 'What the hell!'

Laborde smiled, beaming approval.

'What indeed, my friend? Better men than you have said it sitting in that chair. I remember a very tough Panzer captain, right through Africa and a spell in Russia. Hard as leather. He said it. He said many things. In a way, you're an exception. We don't ask you to say anything.' He pulled a fresh cigar from his case and began to light it. When it was drawing nicely he set it down on the table edge and said, 'Another, my friend?'

The whole choking, vertiginous ritual began again. And when it was finished George's head dropped forward, his breathing deep and noisy. Aristide, he kept thinking to himself. What was it about Aristide? Something he might or might not do. Something he wanted him to do. Général de Gaulle, Palais Royal. *Sois sérieux . . . Renée . . .* the golden girls . . . Then his head came up, a moment of clearness, like a blue streak in clouds, opening for him. Looking straight at Laborde, he said, 'You bastard!'

147

Laborde chuckled. 'In front of Mademoiselle, too.' He shook his head chidingly.

Dorothée said, 'How much longer?'

'Not long,' said Laborde. He began to fill the glass.

The break of blue in the sky clouded over. George felt fingers grip his neck. He smelt the brandy, felt the hard rim of the glass against his lips, and suddenly his head began to throb as though someone were using it as a drum. He heard the empty glass ring against the marble, then there was a hand on each of his elbows. He was forced up from the seat and it was kicked away from him.

He stood swaying, eyes half shut, and then suddenly the floor began to tilt upwards in front of him until he felt that all the bottles must slide forward from their racks.

He staggered backwards, lost his balance, and crashed into the wall behind him. He lay flat on the floor and Laborde came over to him with another glass of brandy. From miles away he heard the man saying, 'A last one to keep out the cold.'

Laborde bent down and George lost sight of him. The brandy flooded his throat and he choked. He lay there suddenly content, wanting nothing else than to be allowed to rest on these hard, wet flagstones for the rest of his life. And, like a child, held still in some wide-eyed dream, he saw the movement of the three people about the cellar, a cellar whose walls seemed to contract and expand, tip and tilt, while above him whirled a myriad of light bulbs.

Laborde went to one of the racks and, with the help of Marc, he pulled it forward. It came out like a door and the smell of stagnant water was stronger than ever. George watched them with a remote curiosity. They came back and hauled him to his feet. But when they took their hands off him he collapsed to the floor. He was angry at his own weakness. A man should be able to take a bottle of brandy without falling all over the place. Hold his drink. A man should hold his drink. They picked him up again.

Laborde said, 'He's ready.'

George nodded drunkenly. Of course he was ready.

Must be something wrong with the brandy. That was it. Drugged brandy. Never mind. Put me on my feet, point me towards home, and I'll make it.

They steered him to the opening which the outswinging rack section had revealed. A long steep slope about three feet wide fell away at an angle in front of him. It was a stone slope, covered with green slime. George tried to back away, and would have fallen if they had not held him.

'Don't worry,' said Laborde. 'You'll go down like a seal. A free ride to the Seine and you'll never come up for long enough to do you any good.'

Something crashed into George's back and he was pitched head first into the chute. His shoulder smashed against one of the walls. He rolled, his body thudding on to the slippery slope, and then he was sliding fast into darkness, his hands, cut loose by Marc before the push, coming up, covering his face instinctively to protect himself against the hard friction of the stonework.

He slammed into water, went under into blackness, and from that moment was aware of nothing except that he was alone in a curious oblivion that was like the quick flipping of pages in some picture book – a corner of sky with a building briefly silhouetted, an iron ring held in the mouth of a lion's head, darkness shot with the fireworks of some fantastic pressure inside his head, and water choking him, dragging him down, until slowly there was nothing at all, nothing except a long grey dream, a dream with nothing to mark its greyness and in which he was content to dwell for ever.

9

HE CAME out of the blackness briefly to feel hands upon him. There was the flash of a white face before him and the sound of someone breathing heavily. He drifted away down the black stream and then consciousness, distorted, shot with odd details, came back again. Another face peered into his and there was the strong smell of garlic and wine, and the sound of oars in rowlocks. Somewhere high and to the right was a long row of lighted windows and distantly a car's horn blared. He dropped away again but this time the blackness was mingled with a dream that kept coming and going. He could feel the motion of a car and against his closed eyelids was the recurring flare and death of lights. Someone close to him said, 'The second turning on the right, mademoiselle.' Then he was lying on grass, his shoulders half supported by someone. Then the someone became Nicola, her fair hair wet and rat-tailed across the side of her face. Above her he could see a man smoking and beyond him the branches of a tree and stars.

After a while they had him on his feet between them and walked him up and down. Somewhere a small night-bird cried plaintively at their presence, and Nicola kept talking to him and his head felt as though it were made of lead, and all he wanted to do was sleep. Then slowly, as he stood on his feet between them, sleep came and he gave up all curiosity.

When he came round, head throbbing but his senses back with him, he was lying on a strange bed in his pyjamas. Beyond the bed was a window with small bottle panes of glass and by it stood Nicola. The window was partly open and the sound of children shouting came into the room. To the left of the window a small gas stove stood against a wall and he could see steam coming from a coffee percolator.

He sat up slowly. Nicola turned.

'Where the hell am I? And what's happened?' he asked crossly, his forehead throbbing.

'Aristide's room,' she said, and went to the stove. She came back carrying a mug of coffee. It was black, strong and hot. He sipped at it and shuddered.

'Why?'

She took the mug from him and smiled, leaning forward

and kissing him lightly on the cheek. 'Take it easy – you're coming out of the biggest hangover you've ever had.'

He took the mug and drank some more coffee.

'Aristide wouldn't let me take you back to the hotel. We walked you around some park near Vincennes and then we brought you here. I got our stuff and paid the hotel bill this morning.'

'Why?' He could hear the crossness still in his voice.

'Because Aristide said it wasn't safe for us to stay there. One of the waiters is a Bianeri. He was at the meeting and he would have seen you. Aristide's been very good.' She sat down on the bed by him and held one of his hands. 'But we've got to get out of here before he comes back. He's gone off to work.'

'Did he pull me out of the river?'

She shook her head.

'You?'

She nodded. 'He knew what was going to happen and he came for me. Thank God he did. We waited and you came up . . . just once and then went under again.'

'And you went in?'

'Yes . . .'

He put his arm round her. 'Bless you. God, I was loaded with brandy —'

She looked up at him tenderly, 'You smell of it now.'

'Do you mind?'

'No.'

He bent forward and kissed her and the kiss which was warm and grateful slowly gathered strength and changed its nature. After a time she pulled back from him.

'We've got to get moving. You can sleep in the car and when you feel yourself you can fill me in, though I know most of it from Aristide.'

'Good old Aristide. . . .'

'He's frightened. He wants us away before he comes back. We must do that. And he says that we must stay away from hotels in big towns – stick to the country places.'

'I ought to go straight to the police about Laborde and

Guntheim. My God, I'd like a few moments with Laborde.'

'It wouldn't do any good – not to my mother and the others. They'd deny everything, or just disappear. I don't even know that we ought to go on with all this —'

'What!'

She stood up. 'Sorry – but let's face it, you were damned near drowned.'

Slowly George slipped his legs to the ground and stood up and moved to the window. His joints felt as though they were made of wood and lacked lubrication. 'Maybe you should go back. Perhaps I ought to make you. But I'm hanging on. I'm beginning to get the form now. Besides I'm developing a very unchristian attitude. I'm not turning any cheek. I just want to get to the bottom of all this and to get my hands on a few people, Scorpio particularly. And there's a chance now. Aristide won't say anything about us for his own sake. They think I'm dead, drowned. All right, let 'em wait for a few days for my body to come up. In the meantime, I'm going to have a crack at Ricardo Cadim. They've no idea I know anything about him. They're just sitting back, congratulating themselves on having got rid of me.'

Nicola refilled the coffee mug, and then with a shrug of her shoulders, said, 'If you're going to Annecy, so am I.' She held out the mug to him and with a smile said, 'Would you like a shot of brandy in it?'

George grinned, caught her by the shoulders, and said, 'For that you get punished.' He pulled her towards him.

'Mind the mug, you fool!'

He held her to him and kissed her and for a second or two coffee was spilled on to the floor. Then she was very still, tight in his arms, her mouth soft and passionate against his.

It was just after eleven on the Thursday morning when they left Paris. They went down towards Dijon and stayed the night at a small *relais de campagne* just outside. George did a good deal of sleeping on the trip, but he was awake as they passed through Troyes, which reminded him of Wheeler who had been thrown from a train near by. He remembered Laborde and Dorothée Guntheim, could see her agate eyes swimming behind her thick glasses and Laborde smiling, plump, assured, forcing more brandy on him and talking about the Resistance days. Dorothée would have been too young for that business, but she had the right qualities. She had a quick brain and went into action without messing around with preliminaries. Where did she fit in with Scorpio-Longo-Bardi or whatever his blasted name might be now? How could he claim such drastic loyalty from her? There was Maria Vendez, too. Women didn't usually think about money – Laborde and the other men would – but there would be something else that held them, and it didn't take a mindreader to work that one out. Where along the line, he wondered, had Elsie come unstuck? What had happened to her when she wanted to leave her husband? Maybe Ricardo Cadim would have the answer to that.

Over dinner that night, George laid out the facts as he thought they stood at this moment, and later he telephoned Synat to give them to him. It was no good overlooking the possibility that something might happen to him, and in that case it would be an advantage for Synat to be completely abreast of developments.

The main points George made were these:

1. It seemed certain that Scorpio, Longo and Bardi were one and the same.
2. Except for Les Roches-Pins – which Bardi would certainly not use again – they had no idea where he lived permanently.
3. The Bianeri was an organization of hotel workers for collecting blackmail information. During the war it had switched to intelligence and Resistance work. It clearly still did some intelligence work – which explained the Scorpio Holdings account in London. The Security people wouldn't let anyone investigate that.
4. Laborde and Guntheim ran the Paris branch of the

Bianeri. Bianeri members only knew the people directly above or below them.

5. The people – excluding Laborde and Guntheim – who had connections with Bardi were:
   a. Ricardo Cadim, who had been with him at the Aboler house.
   b. Gian Palloti, who was the son of Andrea Palloti, who had been a valet to Aboler.
   c. Maria Vendez, who, presumably, had become Bardi's mistress about the time that Elsie decided to leave him.
   d. The other man at Les Roches-Pins – Lodel.
   e. Elsie, of whom it was not known now whether she was dead or alive.
   and f. Elsie's son.

Synat when he heard all this and what had happened to George reacted very much as Nicola had done.

'You've done damn well. But you don't have to go on sticking your neck out. From here I could put a professional man on who is paid to take the risks.'

'And get the real fun? Listen, I want to meet Bardi.'

'But what about Nicola? She ought not to stay with you.'

'You try telling her that. I have and I've got nowhere. She won't listen.'

'Well, for God's sake be careful. I don't know, maybe I ought to insist —'

'Forget it.' George rang off before the man could marshal any second thoughts.

The next day – Friday, the day before Ricardo Cadim was due to open at the Hôtel de l'Empire – they went on to Annecy. Remembering Aristide's warning about staying in hotels in the large towns, George sent Nicola to an estate agent, and fed the swans at the lakeside for an hour while she made a quick tour of chalets and bungalows for rent around the lake.

Most of the places were already let and of the few left Nicola took for a fortnight the one she considered the most suitable. They drove out to it in the late afternoon.

It was about two miles down the west side of the lake, and had been described by the agent as having a *jardin fleuri et une belle vue sur le lac*. It was a shabby four-roomed bungalow, screened from the lake by a belt of trees through which a rough path ran to the water's edge, where – another feature of the agent's description – a small rowing boat was pulled up on to the gravel for the use of occupants. There was no garden, but a growth of tall brooms and self-sown tree seedlings that grew right up to the windows of the place. Behind the house was a garage and a rough track that led up to the lakeside road about two hundred yards away. When they opened the door they were greeted with a smell of cheap scent and fennel and, wherever they moved, there was the teeth-edging grit of sand under their feet.

George said, 'It will do as base. We can eat out.'

'We'll have to,' said Nicola. 'Come and look at the kitchen.' She opened the door and they both shuddered gently. Withdrawing, she said, 'I've hogged the best bedroom. I hope you don't mind.' She opened the door for him to inspect it.

It had a brass bed, blankets and grey-looking sheets and pillows piled on it, a coloured print of Dante and Beatrice, a hideous yellow wardrobe, a matching dressing-table, and a chair with a hole in its cane seat. Somebody had left a collection of picture cards given away in chocolate packets on the dressing-table and a paperback copy of Moravia's *Woman of Rome*. But that didn't make it a room where you could lie luxuriously in bed nibbling chocolate and reading sexy literature.

George said, 'If this is the best, I don't want to see mine. I'll share this with you.'

Nicola shook her head. 'You'll notice that the door has a key in the lock. That was one of the reasons why I chose it.'

'A gentle kick on the door can fix that.'

'You keep your mind on Ricardo Cadim.'

He grabbed her and kissed her and, after a moment, she

155

said, 'And your hands above the Plimsoll line. Why do you always want to rush things? Let's go and see if this boat holds water and you can row me down to the Hôtel de l'Empire for a drink.'

The boat didn't hold water. It began to leak fast when they were ten yards out and they just made the return trip before it was half full. George left it lying in the water so that the boards would swell up and close the leaks and they called the Hôtel de l'Empire trip off until the next day. They walked a mile along the lake side to a restaurant where they dined off *omble chevalier du lac* which Nicola said was trout and George said wasn't. It was *salmo salvelinus*, or otherwise char. And after the argument was over and they were walking back to the bungalow George said, 'Since you've asked me to keep my mind on Ricardo Cadim, I've done just that. We've got to get hold of him and make him talk. That isn't always very easy – to make a man talk. But something I saw in the restaurant gave me an idea. We've got a nice, quiet bungalow. We can get Cadim and we can make him talk. And the sooner the better. I don't see why we shouldn't do it tomorrow night, after he's finished his show. But first of all you're going to have a busy time tomorrow morning on your own, while I have a look over that hotel.'

He began to tell her exactly what he wanted her to do.

At nine o'clock the next morning Nicola went off in the Lancia on her own. George went down to the boat, hauled it out of the lake and tipped it free of water. He pushed it back into the lake and was glad to see that it was now making very little water. He got in and began to row down the lake.

The Hôtel de l'Empire was just outside the town on the east shore of the lake. It was a long, low Colonial-looking building with a large garden that ran down to the hotel's private beach. In the grounds of the garden were half a dozen chalets that supplemented the hotel accommodation. It was a quiet, well-groomed, expensive-looking place. George ran his boat ashore and went up to the main building for a drink at the bar. He was not very happy about going into hotels now, but the risk had to be taken. He wore sunglasses and a rather worn Panama hat which he had found in the coat cupboard at the bungalow. The bar, crescent-shaped, was walled with black nylon fur, had red furniture and silver fittings, and the price of a gin and tonic made him blink. He was served by a tall young man, wearing a tight-fitting red coat with silver buttons, who gave one look at the Panama as he took it off and clearly disapproved.

George left him a large tip when he paid for his drink and the young man thawed enough to push a plate of olives over the bar to him.

On a large easel near the door was a deep placard announcing the hotel cabaret. Most of it was taken up with a photograph of Monsieur Magique. George, holding his drink, strolled over to it. The photograph showed a tall, slim man with the smooth, whitish face and high forehead he had seen in Laborde's office, the wings of dark hair spread glossily on either side of his bald head. George remembered the Laborde dossier . . . fee includes own assistant. He went through the names of the other artists. Perhaps Clea Albertine would be here – *Unreliable. Drinks. Popular with men. Not particular.* . . . But he was disappointed. A pity. He was sure she would have qualified as one of Aristide's golden girls.

He went back to the bar, finished his drink, bought another, repeated the tip to the barman, and said, in French, 'Monsieur Magique? Is he good?'

The barman nodded, began to polish a glass, and said in English, 'Fabulous, monsieur.'

'Is there a chance of getting a table for tonight?'

'Certainly – if you book it now. See the restaurant manager as you go out.'

'Does Monsieur Magique stay here?'

'Yes, monsieur.'

George pulled out his cigarette case and the barman

took one and flashed a lighter for George's cigarette. He blew the flame out, and then snapped the lighter afresh for his own cigarette.

The barman said, unprompted, 'He stays in one of the garden chalets. The one near the beach. But his assistant has a room in the hotel. A little blonde.' He winked at George, humanity breaking through, and added, 'Each time he comes he has a different one. I think maybe he has a high casualty rate and some do actually get sawn in half.' He smiled and showed two gold teeth.

George, careless with Synat's money, ordered another gin and tonic and a drink for the barman. The barman fixed himself a large gin and Campari and, with the tip, George had just enough money on him to pay. But the drink kept the barman talking.

Monsieur Magique drove a Bentley. Very successful man. There was always the joke about his assistant, but he, the barman, did not think there was anything in it. You understand, monsieur. If so, why did she stay in the hotel? And anyway, Monsieur Magique, he was sure, was like that. One could tell.

George left him and, on his way out, booked a table at the back of the dining-room for two under a false name. Walking back to the beach and his boat he picked out the chalet. It was on one floor, surrounded by a small box hedge, the main windows overlooking the lake. A concrete driveway ran up to a car port at the side of the chalet. From the open doorway of the car port the big snout of a grey Bentley protruded like the head of a Moray eel dozing between meals.

George rowed away, watching the chalet and the movement of children and bathers on the bright umbrella-mushroomed beach. A beach instructor was putting some young people through a series of exercises that made George feel faintly ill.

When he got back to the bungalow it was to find Nicola waiting for him. She had bought a bottle of wine, some cold meat and French bread for lunch and had set it up on a card-table just above the lake water.

'Did you get them?' asked George.

'Did I? The bloody things. There are six in the kitchen and I know where I can get a couple more this afternoon. What a morning! What about you?'

'Oh, I had a pleasant time over two or three gin-and-tonics with the barman at the hotel. Very pleasant.'

'Well, that's good, isn't it. I suppose you've lived so long amongst aborigines that you think women should do all the heavy work?'

'There's a lot to be said for it. Anyway, when you've got the other two this afternoon you can relax and I'll take you out to dinner tonight – on one condition.'

'What's that?'

'That you bring the Walther ·22 with you.'

Half an hour after George had left the Hôtel de l'Empire, a white Mercedes drove into the forecourt of the hotel with Gian at the wheel and Antonio Bardi sitting in the back. Gian parked the car and then got out, smart in green breeches and jacket, his peaked cap tilted to a jaunty angle, and opened the door for Bardi. Bardi, hatless, wearing a white silk suit and carrying an ebony cane, got out.

'One drink, Gian, in the staff quarters and then back here.'

He walked off, round the side of the hotel, towards the gardens. Gian watched him go, fattened his lips momentarily with dislike, and then moved away.

Bardi went round the side of the hotel and along a concrete path to Cadim's chalet. Bougainvillaea mixed with plumbago tumbled over the porchway of the chalet. Bardi snapped a sprig of the blue plumbago off and threaded it into his buttonhole. He pushed the door open and went in.

There was a small hallway with three doors. He opened the door at the far end of the hall and went into the main lounge whose windows overlooked the beach and the lake. A girl of about twenty-three was sitting on the large divan reading a copy of *Harper's Bazaar*. She was pretty, except for a squat little nose that showed too much of her nostrils, wore a lot of make-up, and her finger- and toe-nails were painted with a pearly-lustre. Her hair was piled, blonde and thick, in a slightly Grecian way on top of her head. She wore a low-cut, green summer dress that showed a lot of flesh from bare arms and legs and shoulders, and she jumped to her feet rather like a servant caught by her mistress taking it easy in the drawing-room.

Bardi placed his stick carefully on a sideboard studded with bottles and glasses and said, 'Tina. Nice to see you again. Is the *maestro* in?'

'But, of course, monsieur. He's resting.'

'Then tell him I'm here and then, little Tina' – he caught her by the arm gently – 'you take a walk in the garden for a while, eh?'

Tina smiled and nodded, and then the smile became a giggle as Bardi's arm went round her and he kissed her gently.

'Monsieur . . . please.'

Bardi released her, smiling. There was a certain coarseness in her voice which he liked: something damp, echoing distantly of slums and tenements. Some time, he thought, he must make an opportunity to know her better, but it would have to be without Ricardo's knowledge. Ricardo got so cross if he took any notice of his assistants. He was like an old hen with them.

Bardi patted her on the bottom and said, 'Go and tell him. And sometime you and I . . . maybe we will have a little time together for dinner one evening. Yes?'

'Maybe, monsieur.' She wrinkled her nose at him and he wished she hadn't. Her nose was her worst feature.

She went and he fixed himself an Americano from the bottles on the sideboard while he waited for Ricardo.

After a few moments Ricardo came in, frowning. He wore light-blue linen trousers and a yellow shirt with the corner of a black handkerchief sticking out of the pocket; his feet were in open-work leather sandals. He was just like his photographs except that he looked a shade older and his shoulders, when he forgot to hold them well, sagged forward a little as though someone had just struck him lightly on the chest.

In a high, almost petulant voice, he said, 'Bardi, you've been at that girl of mine. Oh, I know you've had it in mind for a long time, but I forbid it. Absolutely.'

Bardi shook his head. 'I didn't touch her. I swear.' He smiled.

Ricardo pursed his mouth chidingly. 'Her lipstick was smudged – I can't bear a woman with untidy lipstick. And you've got some on your own mouth. You look quite ridiculous. And anyway, what the hell are you doing here?'

'Business,' said Bardi, and suddenly his tone was changed. 'Sit down and stop bubbling about that little assistant of yours. If you don't want her in bed with other people you should let her get into yours.'

'Bardi – enough of that. What do you want?' Ricardo sat down on the settee and absently tidied the cushions alongside him. Bardi lit a cigar and Ricardo frowned a little at the smell of the smoke.

Bardi said, 'You know I'm having trouble with some client of mine, of course.'

'Yes. Laborde has been in touch with me. The young man and the girl.'

'That's it. They came to Laborde making inquiries for Elsie and for you.'

'Who is the client? If you find that out, my dear Bardi, you can stop the thing at once.'

'I don't know who it is. And I don't think now that it is necessary to know. The young man, I hope, has been dealt with. He was caught at the Café César this week and, like many others before him, he finished up in the Seine.'

Ricardo waved a thin hand. 'Don't give me any details. I've always hated that side of it. Poor young man.'

'A very obstinate young man – and no fool. He got as far as a Bianeri meeting. That was serious.'

'Surely not now?'

'Well . . .' Bardi strolled to the window. The sunlight was bright on the lake. Three young boys were rocking together in one of the hotel canoes so that it slowly filled with water. The canoe sank under them and the air rang with their laughter.

'What's worrying you, Bardi?'

'Nothing, really. But you know I'm a cautious man. I have to be. We all have to be. The young man has been dealt with, but I'm a little puzzled by the action of the girl he was with. She's disappeared.'

'What did you expect her to do? Poor child, she's probably scared out of her wits.'

Bardi laughed briefly. 'You've got these people wrong, Ricardo. She's not a poor child. She's competent and she keeps her head. She rescued the young man on the Pampelone beach and didn't hesitate to fire at Gian. Gian by the way is getting restless, and I think something is going to have to be done about him. There's going to be trouble over Maria.'

'How very tiresome! But what about the girl?'

'Just this. Normally I would have expected her to stay on at her hotel, waiting for the young man to turn up. We know which hotel it was now. She left very early in the morning after the young man was dealt with. And, as far as Laborde has been able to find out, she hasn't gone to the police to report him missing. What do you make of that?'

'Quite a few things. If he were a private detective and she his assistant – then she may have referred to her agency for instructions. She couldn't go to the police without authority from their client. Meantime, she's wisely changed her hotel. Or —' he paused, looking up at Bardi.

'Or?' Bardi blew a fat cigar smoke-ring which began to sink heavily floorwards and then was dissipated in a draught from the window.

'Or, my dear Bardi – something went wrong with the Café César technique. He went into the Seine and came out. So he's still a potential danger.'

'It could be. So nothing must be overlooked. I just want you to keep your eyes open. You've had a description of them. Nancy Marden and George Conway. English. And, so far as we can find out, he doesn't hold a police licence as a detective. I think the names are false.'

Ricardo laughed gently. 'You have a thing about names, Bardi. You have so many yourself. All right, I will watch.'

'You must. You could be their one direct link with Elsie.'

'Ah, Elsie . . . yes.' Ricardo slipped out the black hand-kerchief and just touched his lips. 'She was the one woman who escaped you. It is no good looking stern, my dear Bardi. Only I can say this to you. We both loved her in our different ways. You love her still, though you hate to admit it.'

'And you?'

'I don't think about her. Otherwise I might hate you. Everything you did had to be done – but it was your tragedy, not mine. No other woman has ever meant any-thing to you. And you destroyed her because she would have destroyed you. Not one of the others you take, and you are like a pike amongst minnows, Bardi, means a thing. Am I right?'

'Maybe. What a fool she was . . . a fool to have such virtues, to be so splendid!' Bardi turned and picked up his stick from the sideboard. He held it for a moment with the silver head near his mouth, and then with a sudden shrug of his shoulders, he said, 'I have lost something. But I have a great deal still, and I live in the way I long ago decided to live. Only with you for a few moments, Ricardo, do I allow myself to be sentimental. Will you have dinner with me after your show tonight?'

Ricardo stood up, his shoulders hunching for a moment. 'No, my dear Bardi, you know I won't. After the show I am completely exhausted and I want no more than to come back here and listen to a little music before I sleep. But – since I can see what kind of a mood you are in – you may have Tina to dine with you. But Bardi' – his voice was suddenly, surprisingly adamant – 'only to dine. I don't want her getting ideas, and I don't want to have to get a new assistant yet. You know what a bother it is training the stupid little things. Promise?'

Bardi nodded and smiled. 'You're a bully, Ricardo.'

'With you, sometimes I have to be. Tomorrow we will have lunch together and talk business. I've got quite a few things for you that I've collected in the last three weeks. Such sordid, disgusting things.'

'But profitable?'

Ricardo splayed out his hands and the right one, deftly, miraculously it seemed, suddenly held a red rosebud. He laughed at the sudden pleasure on Bardi's face, and said, 'How you love these tricks! Take it, Bardi, my friend, and wear it instead of that common little sprig of plumbago which matches your eyes most vulgarly.'

10

THERE WERE two cabaret shows at the hotel during the evening. George and Nicola rowed down the lake in time to dine and catch the last show. It was dark when they arrived. George beached the rowing boat alongside the hotel canoes which were drawn up on the *plage* in neat lines.

There was a light showing from the main window of Cadim's chalet, but the curtains were drawn. They went into the hotel through the garden entrance. The dining-room was large and circular in shape with a coloured glass cupola in the roof which was flooded with a sequence of soft, changing lights. Each table had a small, red-shaded light. The place gave the impression of a lofty, red, plush-lined cave full of dark, moving shadows, pricked by the silver of the tableware, cut with the movement of white shirt fronts, friendly with the murmur of voices, and heavy with the smoke-laden atmosphere of high life, the holiday dream of tourists. Hôtel de l'Empire – *Ses bars. Son cabaret. Sa cuisine. Sa plage. Son cadre féerique. Son golf miniature.*

They had a table, deliberately chosen by George, well at the back of the room, away from the stage at the other end, and partly in a small alcove by a window. They chose their meal from two menu cards, each almost as big as the table top. Around the sides of them they consulted one another and then, because they were both far from a mood for eating much, settled for smoked salmon and a cold chicken salad which gave the waiter no joy whatever since he had had orders to try and get rid of the *brochette de rognons grillés à la provençale*.

They were still eating when the cabaret started. It was a good cabaret: a troupe of five dancing girls who stripped down to a final *tableau vivant*; a polyglot comedian with political and *risqué* jokes; a thin, vibrant negress with a voice that made the cupola shake; and then, to top the bill, Monsieur Magique with a small, jolly-breasted blonde girl assistant who postured around him with exaggerated gestures, and never for once let her glamorous smile slip.

Ricardo Cadim, tall, willowy in tails, black wings of hair sleeked away from his bald head, was first class, his hands alive, independent, spreading out to reveal a fan of smoking cigarettes, plucking delicately at the air in front of him to draw skein after skein of silk handkerchiefs from nowhere. The long evening cane was gracefully tossed above his head to disappear and then be plucked deftly from the front of the low-cut bodice of his blonde assistant; wine was poured from a carafe into a glass, pouring and pouring, the carafe never emptying and the glass never filling – then, with a widespread movement of his hands, carafe and glass were thrown to the winds to become two white doves that flew down the room and came back to settle obediently on the blonde girl's shoulders. For his final piece he put the girl in a tall, coffin-shaped box, her hands tied above her head, her ankles tied together. A member of the audience was allowed to test the knots and was rewarded with a kiss from the girl; the door of the box was shut and then the box was spun. Monsieur Magique lifted a trap at the top of the box, dipped his hand inside and whipped out for all to see the white evening gown she had been wearing. Then he opened the box and showed the girl still wearing the gown. The manœuvre was repeated again and again and each time from the trap some article of clothing was whipped away – brassière, panties, stockings – and each time the door of the box was opened and the girl was standing there, fully dressed, hands and ankles tied. Then, with the last thing taken from her, a great band of slave bracelets which she had been wearing, the door was opened to a blare of chords from the band and the girl was revealed, hands and ankles free, naked except for three black-centred, gold-petalled sunflowers in three places where modesty demanded they should be.

As the act finished, George thought grimly: this was the man who helped Nadia Temple in Hampstead and then took photographs of the dead husband, this was Elsie's friend, this was a man deep in blackmail, and this was the man who might know where Elsie was, where Bardi was . . . this man with magic in his hands. He dropped his own hand and felt the bulk of the ·22 Walther in his dinner-jacket pocket. His fingers tightened on it as he remembered the Pampelone beaches and Laborde with the Remy Martin bottle in his hand, and he told himself that Monsieur Magique would have to invent some new trick if he were to escape what was planned for him.

The cabaret ended, George called his waiter and paid his bill and he and Nicola left the room and went out into the garden. They went down the pathway to the beach and sat on the edge of their boat, watching the dark windows of Monsieur Magique's chalet.

Nicola said, 'Why should a man with so much talent have got mixed up in a thing like blackmail?'

George shrugged his shoulders. 'God knows.'

'You think the plan will work?'

'I'm relying on Mrs Pinnock.'

A few moments later a light came on behind the curtains of the chalet window.

George said, 'This is it. You come, too. The girl might be there and you can handle her.'

'Don't you want to do that?'

'There's a time for everything. Come on.'

They went up to the chalet, skirted the garage and walked over the grass to the porch. A dim light burned over it and a few moths fluttered about the bulb. The door was unlocked and George pushed it open gently and slid in, followed by Nicola. At the far end of the hallway a door was slightly open with light showing through the crack. George took out his pistol and went up to the door.

A man's voice from within the room was saying, 'Now, my dear, you know how to fix it. A large tumbler, three fingers of Noilly Prat, four lumps of ice, a dash of angostura and then fill it up with soda. When you've done that you can run off to your dinner party . . . Oh dear, how tired I am! You were good, Tina. You were good. As ever. But do try to cut down the smile a little. Just a little. How was I?'

There was the sound of a siphon going and then a girl's voice said, almost breathlessly, 'Oh, *maestro* . . . *magnifique.*'

'Good . . . good . . .' The sound was like the cooing of a dove.

George pushed the door open and stepped in, holding the pistol.

Ricardo Cadim was reclining on the settee. He had changed into a gold-coloured, quilted smoking-jacket. Tina was standing by the sideboard with a large glass in her hand. At George's appearance, Nicola behind him, she dropped it, and the drink splashed high over the hem of her white evening dress.

George said, 'When Monsieur Magique gets back, you can fix him another. Stand up, monsieur.'

Very slowly Ricardo Cadim stood up, his eyes narrowing momentarily; then a hint of a smile touched his lips.

'Oh dear!' he said quietly. 'I think I understand.'

'Good,' said George. 'Then we won't bother with introductions or waste any time. Are you going to come quietly or do I have to be rough?'

'Not that, I hope.'

Nicola said firmly, 'Tina, turn round.'

Tina hesitated and Ricardo Cadim said, 'Do as Mademoiselle orders, Tina. You're not going to be hurt. Is that so?' He looked at George.

'That's so.'

Nicola stepped forward as Tina, confused, turned her back to her. In her hand Nicola had two lengths of rope which she had brought from the boat.

'Hands behind you,' she said. Tina obediently put her hands behind her and Nicola began to tie her wrists.

'She's terribly good at knots,' said Cadim.

'Maybe,' said George. 'But we only need a little time for a row up the lake. I'm going to gag you. You'll understand the necessity.'

Ricardo Cadim shrugged his shoulders and said, 'You're wasting your time. But I see I can't convince you of that.'

George picked up the man's evening scarf from the settee, moved him round with the muzzle of the pistol and then waited for Nicola to finish tying Tina's ankles. Nicola came over and tied the scarf around Cadim's mouth.

'And the girl,' said George, and he handed her his own evening scarf.

Nicola gagged Tina and then gave her a gentle push which made her collapse on to the settee from where she stared up at the three of them, her eyes large, cow-like and uncomprehending.

George took Cadim by the arm and said, 'Walk.'

They went into the hallway and out of the chalet door and down the garden path to the beach. It was a fine night, bright with a thick stippling of stars; a light breeze rippled their reflections in the water. George walked with one hand on Cadim's arm, the other on the pistol in his pocket. It was late and there was no one about. Over to the right, towards Annecy, the sky was shot occasionally with the glare of a passing headlight and from the hotel behind them came the steady thump of the dance band.

Nicola pushed the rowboat into the water and held it for Ricardo Cadim to get in. George handed Nicola the pistol and she got into the stern and George sat in the bows and took up the oars. Without hurry he began to row out into the lake.

As they had come out of the front door of the chalet, Antonio Bardi, who had been coming down the garden path to fetch Tina, saw them for a moment held by the small light over the door. More than anything else he had seen the gold smoking-jacket of Ricardo. Instinctively, he had stepped off the path into the screen of a large oleander bush and watched them go down to the beach. If he had been armed he would have had a simple course open to him, but he was not. Armed or not he was not a man to rush into unwise action. He saw the boat move out and begin to pull southwards down the lake, making for the western shore.

He left his shelter and went back through the garden to the front of the hotel. The white Mercedes was parked under a row of poplars that fringed the edge of the garden. Gian was sitting at the wheel, smoking, the car radio playing gently. Seeing Bardi he got out.

Bardi said, 'Come with me.'

He turned and began to retrace his steps quickly. Gian followed him. They went through the garden and down to the hotel *plage* and here, standing by the row of beached canoes, Bardi said, 'The man and girl who were at St Tropez have just taken Ricardo. Take a canoe and follow them. They've gone over to the western side and they're not far ahead. Follow them, but don't let them see you.'

Gian nodded and began to slide a canoe to the water. He had long lost any surprise at the suddenness of any order.

'Stay with them as long as you can,' said Bardi.

Sitting in the canoe, Gian said, 'And when I know where they are?'

'Come back here and let me know. In the chalet.'

'And if there's trouble?'

'There is to be no trouble. They will not see you.'

He turned away from the beach and Gian began paddling.

Bardi went back up the path to the chalet and into the hallway. There was a telephone in a wall niche. He picked it up and asked the hotel exchange for a number. A few seconds later he was talking to Lodel, giving him instructions, too. When he had finished, he put the telephone down and went into the main room.

Tina was sitting up on the settee, just at the point of freeing her hands behind her. Bardi made a sign to her to stop and he went over and sat beside her. He undid her ankles and then took the scarf from her mouth. As he did so, she gave a little cry. He put his arms around her and held her comfortingly for a moment.

Then he said, 'There were two of them – a man and a girl?'

'Yes, monsieur.' Her hands went up to her hair which had become disarrayed. 'They just walked in – with a gun.'

'Don't worry. Nothing is going to happen to the *maestro*. I have sent someone after him.' He stood up and went to the sideboard and fixed her a large brandy and soda. Coming back he handed it to her, his eyes going from her face over her body to the length of her legs. 'Drink this. And remember, what has happened here tonight, you must never mention to anyone. The *maestro* will tell you the same when he comes back.'

Tina drank, choking a little on the strong brandy, and

he patted her back softly, letting his hand rest on her bare shoulders.

When she had finished the drink he took her hand and pulled her to her feet, then stood back looking at her.

'You are very beautiful . . .' he murmured, looking only at her body. 'But your dress has been splashed. Go into the *maestro*'s room and sponge it and then we will have dinner.'

He held her hand and led her to the hallway and then with a gentle kiss to the tips of her fingers he let her go, watching her cross the hall to the doorway of Ricardo's bedroom. He stood there for a few moments thinking first of Ricardo and then of the two who had taken him away. Nothing would make Ricardo speak. If there was one thing which Ricardo did not seem to the world it was iron-willed. Once, during the war, the Germans had had him for a while but he had said nothing. Inside the tall, willowy frame, behind the effeminate, soft manner, there was sheer steel.

He walked across to the bedroom door, aware of the excitement in him because these were the moments that took him out of himself and gave him a great lust for living. Tina had her dress off, laid across the bed, and was sponging the hem with a damp cloth. As she bent over the dress her blonde hair fell loosely forward, her large breasts bulged invitingly, smooth and full above her brassière, and the line of her thighs and legs from a brief froth of lace was taut, moulded and strong. She turned and looked at him as he crossed to her. For a moment her bright red lips parted, full and warm, as though she were going to say something; then there was no need for her to say anything as his hands found her bare arms and slid around her and his mouth covered her lips which only for the briefest moment resisted his and then responded with an eager welcome. He kissed her passionately and, his mouth still on hers, bent her backwards until she finally lay on the bed. Then he stepped back from her, smiling, and she looked up at him and suddenly giggled, a warm, earthy, peasant sound. Slowly she half rolled over and began to unhook her brassière at her back.

They were in the small dining-room of the lakeside bungalow. Ricardo Cadim sat at the round dining-table, his elbows on the shining mahogany, staring at a glass vase full of artificial flowers, his lips pursed as though the crudity of the flowers was a personal affront to him. Fortunately for his aesthetic sense he could not see the picture over the fireplace from where he sat – a view of the lake towards Annecy, done by some ungifted amateur.

George stood beyond the table by the curtained window, looking down at Cadim. Nicola was behind the man by the small service-door that led into the kitchen.

George said, 'The position is a very simple one. A Mrs Pinnock has asked me to trace her daughter, Elsie. I just want the answers to some questions from you. So far as I am concerned, when you have answered them, you can go back to the hotel.'

Cadim's eyes went from the flowers to George's face. 'Why couldn't you have asked me these questions back at the hotel in a civilized manner? Look' – he raised his right arm and the gold of his jacket material flashed under the light – 'I'm covered in filth from that little boat.'

George said, 'Because I don't think you would have answered the questions freely back there.'

'But you think I will here – after all this underhand, melodramatic nonsense?'

'Yes.'

'Then I'm sorry to disappoint you. I don't know anyone called Elsie Pinnock.'

'Are you sure?'

'Absolutely.'

George shook his head. 'It is not going to do you any good to lie.' He nodded to Nicola over Cadim's head and, as Cadim turned to look at Nicola, George went on, 'Just keep your eyes this way and your mind on our business. Now, you and Elsie – I think her stage name was O'Neil at the time – often worked together. In England and abroad. Is that correct?'

'No. I know no one of that name.'

Behind Cadim, Nicola who had slipped into the kitchen came back and quietly placed on the floor some way from the table a large black cat.

'And you never met her mother – Grace Pinnock?'

'No.'

George smiled. 'Curious. She says she met you two or three times. She didn't remember much about you – except one particular thing. Take a look behind you.'

Ricardo Cadim turned round slowly, saw Nicola and then the cat. The cat moved towards the fireplace and began to rub its head against one of the knobs of the brass fender. As it passed close to Cadim the man stiffened and drew himself back.

'I don't understand you,' he said primly, his nostrils pinched.

'Oh yes, you do, Cadim. She remembered that you couldn't stand cats. That they gave you the most terrible asthma. It's a nice cat, black for luck. But we couldn't get all black ones. We've got seven more in the kitchen, all shapes, colours and sizes. And they're coming in here, one by one, until your memory improves. Now, let's go back to Elsie. You worked together at times – and I've no doubt that she was a good assistant: more character and poise than the one you've got now. But eventually she got married to a man called Tony Longo. You remember him, of course?'

Cadim sat up, taut, withdrawn in his chair, and he was breathing in a mechanical, deliberate manner.

'I don't know what you're talking about.'

'You will.' George nodded to Nicola.

Another cat was brought into the room, a large tabby. It gave a small mew of protest and then ran across the room and jumped up on to the back of an armchair by the window. Sitting there it began a careful cleaning operation. Cadim's eyes turned slightly sideways to avoid seeing the cat and suddenly his hands began to grip the edge of the table, the knuckles showing white.

'Tony Longo,' persisted George. 'That was his name. But he had others. Scorpio. Antonio Bardi. They were married, but eventually Elsie left him. You know this, of course – that she left him? And you know why?'

Ricardo Cadim shook his head and then, holding himself as though he were determined not to breathe any more, clipping off his words to prevent any intake of the contaminated air, said, 'Please stop this nonsense . . .'

'It's not nonsense. Elsie left her husband and she took her small son with her. Where is she now? And what name was her husband using when she left him?'

'I know nothing,' said Cadim.

George nodded to Nicola.

Another cat was brought into the room, a white monster with fight-scarred ears and untidy grey patches marking the white. It went to the fireplace, slashed a right hook at the black cat, and then rolled over on its back and began pushing its head against the rug, purring loudly.

A long, wheezing sigh came from Ricardo Cadim as he was forced to breathe and the last drain of colour went from his face.

'You know all about Elsie,' said George relentlessly. He did not like doing this, but it had to be done, and it was a help to recall Laborde in the café cellar, filling his brandy glass. 'I want to know where she is. I want to know where I can find Bardi. You know them both. You knew her when she used to visit the Aboler house in Switzerland. And you knew him when he used to go there with his mistress, a Maria Vendez. Now come on – don't be stupid.'

Cadim put a hand to his throat and jerked his evening tie loose and his fingers fumbled with the stud of his shirt collar. Then his head dropped suddenly and he gave a long, ghastly moan as he fought to get air into his lungs. With a desperate effort he started to pull himself to his feet.

George went round to him and forced him back into his chair. 'Sit there – and talk.'

Cadim's head went back, his mouth gaped a little and he said thickly, 'Damn you —'

George said, 'Just begin to talk and we'll take you into another room.' He nodded at Nicola. She hesitated for a moment, but George insisted.

Another cat was brought into the room, a thin, half-starved, wild-looking creature. It moved nervously and quickly under the table and sat there.

'Elsie,' said George. 'Elsie and her child. Where are they? Where can I find Bardi or Longo? If you can't talk now just bang your fist on the table to say you will and I'll get you out of here.'

Cadim's shoulders were working now as though they were part of some great pump thumping away to suck in air which no longer existed. His head dropped on to his chest and short, snoring noises came from his throat as he tried to breathe.

'He'll die,' said Nicola anxiously. 'George, you mustn't do it.'

'He won't die. I've seen people with asthma before.' He put out a hand and shook Cadim by the shoulder. 'Just say you'll talk.'

Slowly Cadim's head came up and he made an effort to open wide his heavy-lidded eyes. With a sudden, feeble jerk of his neck he spat at George.

'If that's the way you want it,' said George, his face suddenly tight with anger. He bent down and picked up the black cat and put it on the polished mahogany in front of Cadim. The cat struggled for a moment, the vase was knocked down and then it sat there, very still, crouching under George's big hand, its face towards Cadim.

For a moment Cadim faced the cat, then his head turned laboriously away, his mouth gaping, the breath singing in his throat as he fought for air.

'Elsie Pinnock – where is she?' George held the man's head back, looking down into his half-closed eyes. 'You hear me? Where is she? All you have to do is nod to say you'll talk.'

Cadim's head lay back, his eyes shut, gravelly, rasping noises coming from his throat. His body swayed in the chair and George held him. For a moment or two, he thought he would have to give up, that the man would pass out before he could get anything from him. Then Cadim's eyes opened slightly and there was the faintest nod of his head.

'Give me a hand.' George turned to Nicola.

She came over to him and between them they got Ricardo Cadim to his feet and dragged him out into the small hallway. They lowered him into a deck chair and George turned back and shut the dining-room door.

'Open the front door,' he said. 'He'll come to quickly with the night air.'

Nicola went to the front door and opened it wide. George went into the kitchen and came back with a glass of water. He stood over Cadim and waited.

Slowly the man began to come round as though he had been given a large inhalation of ephedrine. The noises died in his throat and the pumping of his shoulders eased off. He lay back for a while, as though he had dropped into a quiet sleep, his head thrown back, the muscles of his neck stretched, his eyes closed. George leaned forward, held his chin and made him drink some of the cold water. Cadim choked, water dribbled over his chin, then he slowly put up a hand and pushed the glass away.

Within fifteen minutes he was leaning forward, his elbows on his knees, and his breathing had steadied back to normal. Through the open doorway of the hall came the sound of a nightingale singing in the lakeside trees and the air funnelled in cool and fresh.

George and Nicola waited. Slowly Cadim's head came up. Without a word he took a handkerchief from his breast pocket and wiped his wet chin and mouth.

George said, 'The cats are still there. If you try to avoid

anything – you go back in. Is that understood? I shan't get soft-hearted.'

'I don't imagine you will,' Cadim said. His voice was low, strained, but there was no fight in him now.

'Now then,' said George, 'let's come back to Elsie. You knew her?'

'Yes,' he said sullenly. 'I knew her. We worked together on and off until she was married.'

'To Longo?'

'Yes.'

'Who is now Bardi?'

There was the slightest hesitation and then Ricardo Cadim said, 'Yes.'

'And then she left him – why?'

'Because of his infidelities.'

'Is that all – the only reason?'

'Yes.'

'I don't think so. Remember, it'll take only a few seconds to put you back in that room. And just to help your memory – I know all about the Bianeri.'

Cadim's head flicked sharply sideways at George. The tip of his tongue wetted the edges of his lips.

'You're a most extraordinary young man, aren't you? I think you're heading for trouble.'

'Stick to Elsie. Why did she leave Bardi?'

'Because of his other women – but chiefly because she found out how he made his money and' – suddenly there was a hard sincerity in him – 'she was far too honourable and decent a person to tolerate him. She gave him the choice of reforming, trying to make some restitution to the people who had been his victims, or losing her.'

'I see. And there wasn't any choice as far as Bardi was concerned?'

'No. It was impossible for him to change.'

'So what happened to Elsie and the child?'

Cadim was silent for a moment then, rubbing his long hands gently together, he said, not looking at them, 'He was not prepared to lose his child. Don't think he is a

man entirely without emotion. The child meant everything to him. And he loved Elsie. He still does. But he
wanted the child. So he took it from her. This was many
years ago. The boy is now about fourteen.'

'And Elsie let him take the boy?'

'She had no choice. He could no longer trust her not to
expose him. So he dealt with her.'

'How?'

Cadim's hands went up to his collar and neatly he began
to re-fasten the stud and knot his tie. He did it with a
quick, deft movement of his fingers that suddenly reminded
George that this man was Monsieur Magique. The tie
fixed, he made little brushing movements of his hands
down the lapels of his smoking-jacket. Although he was
clearly deeply involved with the Bianeri, Bardi and blackmail, George found it difficult to place him. Somewhere –
if only in the tone of voice which he used when talking
of Elsie – there was some quality in the man that called
for respect.

'How?' repeated George.

Cadim said, 'You're not really just looking for Elsie on
behalf of Mrs Pinnock, are you? It is the other side that
concerns you – the Bianeri and blackmail?'

'I ask the questions,' said George. 'What happened to
Elsie? Don't tell me he killed her.'

'Don't be a fool,' said Cadim sharply. 'Bardi loved her.
But he had to make sure that he was safe from her. So he
sent her away to a nursing home . . . Poor Elsie.'

'You mean he's got her shut up somewhere . . . in some
home where he's got everything nicely fixed?'

'That's exactly what I do mean.'

'And you let this happen? You had some feeling for her,
didn't you?'

'Of course.' It was said almost proudly. 'I was against it.
But as Elsie would make no promises, it was the only thing
to do. I know what you're thinking, monsieur. How could
I? It's a question I've asked myself many times. How could
I? But I did, and the answer is simple and very ugly. I had

178

myself to protect, just as Bardi did. My love for her, which was quite different from his, was just not strong enough to make me risk my own skin. At this moment I am hating you bitterly for making me remember all this.'

'Then you've got to go on hating for a bit. I want to know where I can find her, and where I can find Bardi.'

'I can't tell you that.'

George shook his head. 'Don't be a fool. Do you want to go back in there?'

'I can't tell you. Haven't you got enough, for God's sake?' His voice rose, touched with the edge of panic.

'I want to know – and you're going to tell me.'

'Please, monsieur . . . You're asking me to destroy myself.'

'I don't care a damn what happens to you,' said George brutally. 'Elsie's locked up somewhere – has been for over ten years. And people are being blackmailed, ground down, their lives bitched about by you and Bardi. What do you want me to do? Cry over you and Bardi? I don't care a damn what happens to you. Nothing that can happen could be bad enough. Now – either you begin talking fast or you go back with the cats, and this time I won't be in a hurry to pull you out!'

'George, please.' Nicola put a hand on his arm.

George shook it off. 'Don't get soft with him. He's as bad as the rest. He's going to talk.'

He stepped forward, grabbed Cadim by the arms and jerked him upright. 'I give you five seconds to make your choice!'

Then, as they stood close together, a voice from the open doorway behind him said, 'Just take your hands off Ricardo and turn round very slowly.'

Cadim's eyes closed with relief. Slowly George released him and turned round.

'That's right,' said the voice. 'Keep your hands well out. Ricardo – just make sure of him.'

Behind him, George heard Cadim move and then felt his hands running down his sides. One slipped into his jacket pocket and took out the Walther.

'Good.' It was said by a man standing just inside the hallway whom George had never seen before. He was a tall, well-built man in his fifties, dressed in a white dinner-jacket, a scarlet cummerbund above his black trousers. He had a good strong face, browned, smiling blue eyes, and he wore his whitish hair full over the ears. His hands were thrust comfortably into the pockets of his white jacket. Behind him, just flanking him on either side, were two men whom George recognized at once. One was Gian in chauffeur's uniform and the other was Lodel.

George dropped his hands to his side. For a moment he weighed the odds: Cadim behind him with a gun, Nicola backed up against the wall of the hallway, Gian and the other man with guns. There was no percentage in it, he decided.

'I suppose you're Bardi?' he said.

The man smiled and nodded. 'There's no harm in your knowing. Yes. Just go and stand by the wall with mademoiselle, and both of you turn and face it with your hands behind you.'

Slowly George went over to Nicola and, as they turned, he put a comforting hand briefly on her arm.

11

THE ROOM was circular, about ten feet high, with a light let into the ceiling behind a heavy iron grille. The walls and the inside of the door were lined with thick green canvas which had padding behind it. At about shoulder height in the door was a sliding panel, worked from the outside. Directly opposite the door, about twelve feet from it, the wall had been built out to form a small raised plat-form, with a built-in mattress which was the bed. To one side of the bed was a padded shelf projection from the wall with a few magazines on it. There was nothing else in the room except a thin strip of carpet, studded to the floor, which ran from just inside the door across the room to the bed.

At six o'clock the door panel went back, the door was unlocked and Lodel came in with another man. They stood just inside the door, Lodel with a heavy blackjack in his right hand. The other man was dressed in a long white coat with the red initials *E.S.* worked on the breast pocket. Later, George was to learn that these stood for *Etablissement Samonix*.

The attendant said in English, 'The toilet facilities, monsieur, are just down the corridor.'

Lodel stood outside the door and the attendant came out after George. He was marched six steps down a white-painted corridor without windows – he caught a glimpse of stairs at the end of the corridor – and then into a washroom. They went in, the door was locked and Lodel stood with his back to it, saying nothing. The attendant set out towels, soap and an electric razor.

George went through his morning toilet without a word being said by either of the two men. The lavatories reminded him of school: there were no doors on them.

He was led back to the room and locked in. Breakfast came at eight o'clock, the attendant carrying it on a tray which he put on the padded shelf. Lodel stood just inside the door, expressionless, looking as though he had been doing this all his life and was more than bored by the ritual. Not a word was said. He and Nicola had been brought here from the lakeside bungalow in a private ambulance which had been parked a few yards up the rough track that led from the road to the bungalow. Their hands tied, they had been locked inside with Lodel. The white Mercedes with Bardi and Ricardo Cadim had driven off ahead of them. Neither Bardi nor Cadim had said anything to them. So far as George knew, the Lancia and all their belongings were still at the bungalow for which they had paid a fortnight's rent. The only thing that he knew had been done was that Gian had got rid of the cats. Nicola had asked about them when they were unshipped from the ambulance. Gian had told her he had let them free and for a moment there had been a glint of amusement in his eyes.

George had been able to see nothing of this establishment because the ambulance had driven into a car port which was under the building. Nicola had been taken off by an attendant and Gian, and he had been brought to this padded cell.

The breakfast was good: two fried eggs, rolls and coffee. Before the attendant and Lodel came back to collect the tray, George took the small, blunt butter-knife from it and hid it in the pages of a magazine which he left lying on the floor by the bed.

When the attendant arrived with Lodel, the man ran his eye over the tray and at once said, 'You have kept the butter-knife, monsieur. Please.' He stood waiting with the tray in his hands.

George said, 'There was no butter-knife. I used the other.'

The attendant said something in French to Lodel.

Lodel came down the strip of carpet with a surprising quickness and the blackjack whipped up and down in his hand, cracking George across the collar-bone.

'The knife,' said Lodel.

George held himself back with difficulty. Then, with a shrug of his shoulders, he kicked the magazine on the floor towards them and the knife slid out into the open.

'Please don't be so foolish again,' said the attendant, and his voice was chiding, more sad than angry.

At ten o'clock the door was opened and Lodel and Bardi came in. Lodel stood with his back to the closed door. This time he carried a gun which he held loosely in his hand.

Bardi wore a dark-blue suit, dark-blue tie; the white of his shirt was crisp as frost, and he looked confident, amiable and efficient. There was a faint whiff of shaving lotion about him.

He stood a few yards from George and motioned him to sit on the bed. George sat down and lit a cigarette. They had left all his belongings on him, except his penknife and Ernst's keys.

George said, 'I've waited some time for this moment. I just regret that we're not alone. But I'm not giving up hope that the time may come.'

Bardi smiled and nodded. 'I understand that. Clearly you are not a man to give up hope. That's why you're here and not in one of the ordinary rooms like Miss Marden – if that is her real name.'

'You should know about names. How's my friend Cadim this morning?'

'He's quite recovered. He's at Annecy and will finish the week there before taking a holiday. Surprisingly, he has quite forgiven you.'

'I get the feeling that Ricardo Cadim is much more of a man than you are. Is this part of the treatment, a pleasant chat every morning?'

'No. You won't see me again after this morning. I just wanted to talk to you and make some points clear. You, of course, have no idea where you are?'

'We're about an hour's run from Annecy. Say forty miles at the most and the ambulance did a lot of climbing.'

Bardi nodded and pulled a cigar case from his inside pocket. He selected, prepared, and lit a cigar and then said, 'This is the Etablissement Samonix, a sanatorium and thermal station, a private concern with which, officially, I am not connected. Actually, however – since I like to look after the people who work for me – it is a convalescent home for the Bianeri. Even if you got away from here – which, of course, you are not going to – any investigation would be met by a façade of the most convincing lies. However, that is not the point. My chief concern at the moment is to know for whom you are working. And please don't tell me it is Mrs Pinnock.'

'I don't intend to tell you anything.'

'So I imagine. But, if you refuse to change your mind, I must tell you that within a few days Miss Marden will have told me.'

George looked at him, longing to get his hands on him. There was no point in saying anything to the man about Nicola, no point in making any plea.

Bardi said, 'You are unconcerned?'

'She is well able to look after herself.'

'Maybe, but not after a few days' treatment . . . nothing unpleasant, of course. But after a few days of treatment with the right drugs she won't know what she is saying. In fact she will happily tell the truth. You could save her that tedium – and me, of course.'

'You can go to hell!'

'Very well. Once she speaks and I know who your client is, then of course I can kill this inquiry at source. But, until she does, I keep you here as my alternative route to the truth. Some people – it's quite rare, I assure you – have been known to collapse under the intensive drug treatment which will be necessary —'

George was on his feet. But Bardi stepped back quickly and Lodel came up level with him, the gun raised.

George dropped back on to the bed. The man could be lying, of course, about the drugs. The whole thing could be a try-on to make him talk.

He said, 'You bring her here. If in front of me she asks me to talk, then I will.'

Bardi shook his head. 'Unfortunately, at the moment she is as stubborn as you are. It would be a waste of time. But later we might think about it.'

'And what happens to us, when she does speak?'

Bardi splayed out his large hands and the blue eyes, which had been full of warmth until then, went cold, almost blank. He said tonelessly, 'Nothing to which you could look forward with any pleasure.'

George shook his head. 'I get a feeling about you, Bardi. You've had a wonderful run. You've had it all sewn up for years. But somewhere you made a mistake. Somewhere you handled someone wrong. Maybe Elsie. That's the first crack. Since then you've been busy patching up cracks. But they're gaining on you, Bardi, aren't they? The whole fabric is beginning to be unsteady and you know it. And now you've got us on your hands, and you have my client who already knows a great deal. People don't give up, you know, when they see some hope of freeing themselves . . . Right down inside you're far from certain how much you can go on covering up successfully. You must wake some nights and wish you could go back to Morelli's restaurant and start all over again. But nobody can go back. And, by God, I'm glad you can't! Now, get out of here.'

For a moment George saw the man's teeth biting at his lower lip; he saw the stiff contraction of face muscle and the hard set of the big body. Then, abruptly, Bardi turned away to the door. Lodel opened it and backed out behind him.

When they had gone George sat staring savagely at the floor. The bastards! He should never have involved Nicola in this. After the business at the Café César he should have insisted on her going back to England. Now what the hell was going to happen? A few days' treatment Bardi had said it would take. He probably had some white-coated doctor to do his dirty work for him – sedation by drug and the gradual sapping of Nicola's will, and then the other drugs that produced a high, responsive state of euphoria – and Nicola would be happily babbling away in answer to their questions.

He got up and paced about the room. He had to get out of this room, this padded cell. And he had to get out within the next couple of days if he were going to have a chance of putting a stop to Bardi for good. But how? There was nothing in the room to help him, nothing but firm canvas-lined walls, a few magazines, a strip of carpet on the floor, and whatever he had in his pocket.

He turned his pockets out. He had his wristwatch, the Longines, a packet of cigarettes, a lighter, his wallet with paper money – he'd left all his loose change with the waiter at dinner at the Hôtel de l'Empire – a handkerchief, and his false passport.

He got up and walked round the room, now and again

kicking at the padded wall to relieve his feelings, trying not to think of Nicola, but knowing he would go on thinking about her.

He sat down on the bed and stared at the door. He could try something when Lodel and the assistant came back, but he knew that he would have the slimmest of chances. If he wanted to do any good and get Nicola out of here he had to escape from this room and have a good start before his loss was discovered. Annecy . . . forty miles away. Probably – since it was a thermal station – they were up in the mountains somewhere pretty remote, because Bardi would have picked an unobtrusive spot for a Bianeri convalescent home.

Lodel and the assistant would come in through the door. He had no chance of standing beside it to get them unaware. The trap always went back and they made sure he was by the bed before they entered. The assistant would come in with a tray and Lodel would stand a few paces inside the door, gun or blackjack ready. George stared at the door, at the place where Lodel would be standing . . . and then, very slowly, he got up and walked towards the door.

He walked down the long strip of green carpet which was laid across the polished boards, and a faint surge of excitement began to mount in him. Why not? The man he had to deal with first was Lodel. Lodel was the rough-house type. Get Lodel out of the way and he could deal with the assistant.

He bent down and examined the carpet. It was fixed to the floor, along its long edges, with five or six brass-headed tacks that were sunk deep into the medium pile. At each end the carpet was clipped into a brass two-foot length of metal about an inch wide through which four screws – not more than half an inch long, he thought – had been fastened. Yes, Lodel would come in and stand, eyes missing nothing while the assistant served him . . .

George examined the brass tacks along the edge. He could pull the carpet free, tearing the tack heads through it. But that would be noticed at once. What he wanted was a screw-driver to unscrew the screws holding the brass end-pieces and to prize up the brass tacks. They would all have to be in place, looking firm, but in reality loose in their small sockets. Once he had them out he could enlarge the tack- and screw-holes, put the screws and tacks back and no one would notice.

But how?

It took him half an hour to get the answer, and it meant sacrificing his watch. He couldn't get the back off the watch without a proper tool so – keeping an eye on the grille in the door – he hammered it against the small portion of one of the door hinges which was visible through the canvas. Within ten minutes the watch was a mess. But he had the back off and the sharp edge to it made a screwdriver and an instrument for prizing up the tacks. Smashing at the watch again he finally got part of the winding spindle free so that he could use it to enlarge tack- and screw-holes.

After that it was a question of patience and vigilance. During that first day, he got the tacks down one side free and their holes enlarged and the tacks back in place, and he learned something of the routine of the place. There was the toilet-round first thing in the morning, the break-fast visit, and then an inspection for a few minutes through the grille at mid-morning. Then the lunch visit, a mid-afternoon grille inspection, dinner – and an hour after-wards a last toilet-parade at which he was given a pair of coarse white pyjamas by the assistant.

As he sat, dressed, still on the bed, George reckoned that he could have the job done by the end of the next day. That meant he could make a try for escape on the morning of the third day. It would have to be at the breakfast parade. How far gone would Nicola be by then? It would be the morning. She would have recovered a bit during the night from any treatment. All he wanted was that she could stand up and move and understand him. Two days . . . if he worked during the night he could make it by the next morning, with luck. But the assistant had obligingly warned him that the light went out at nine, and it was impossible to work in the dark by feel alone. When the moment came the carpet had to be on the floor, looking to all the world as though it were firmly fixed.

Nicola's room overlooked three gravelled and balustraded terraces, joined by a wide sweep of steps. Beyond the lowest terrace was a thin strip of grass, then a belt of tall pines. Beyond the pines, a deep valley fell sheerly away and on its far side a row of mountains rose sharply to the horizon. Trees spread around the lower slopes and above them were grey cliff shoulders and towering crag pinnacles. On one of the highest peaks she noticed that there were still patches of snow in the shadowed saddles and small hanging valleys.

Through the bars on the windows she could see distantly to the left, far down, the red roofs and a church tower in some small village.

Her room was plain, a nursing-home room, with a bed, a couple of chairs, a wardrobe – all the furniture painted white – and an adjoining bathroom. All the windows were closely barred, and the door had no handle on the inside, only a lock with an empty keyhole. On the inside of the door was pinned a cardboard printed notice headed, *Etablissement Samonix*, giving the times of meals, forbidding radios, and announcing the times of the celebration of mass in the sanatorium's chapel on Sundays.

The first morning her breakfast was brought to her by a woman attendant who might have been dumb, for she just shook her head silently in answer to Nicola's questions. Nicola had the impression that someone waited outside the door while the woman was in the room.

For an hour after breakfast Nicola spent most of her time at the window. A few men and women in ordinary clothes appeared on the terraces, some of them sitting in the sun, reading and talking, others strolling about. The whole scene looked placid and peaceful, but she noticed that there were always two or three attendants in white coats somewhere on the terraces.

About an hour after her breakfast, she began to feel tired and a desperate longing for sleep overcame her, while at the same time her mind became confused, and the white walls of the room seemed to recede endlessly from her. She lay on the bed, curiously content, yet unable to prevent the drift of her body and mind into sleep. She had the impression that while she slept other people had come into the room. Once, waking, a moment of clear perception with her, she saw a woman attendant sitting by her bed. The woman smiled at her and Nicola smiled happily back and heard herself say, 'It was the coffee, was it? Something in it?'

The woman put a warm hand on her forehead and Nicola drifted back into sleep.

She woke again, late in the afternoon. There was no one in the room. She lay in bed, dressed in pyjamas which she knew were not hers, and watched the cloud shadows racing across the distant peaks. She was quite content, unworried even when she remembered George and knew that he was somewhere in this building. He was being looked after, she was sure of that . . .

The attendant, dumb as ever, came in after a while and gave her some broth and dry toast. Nicola was hungry and the meal seemed very meagre. But when she told the attendant that she wanted more, the woman just shook her head.

When the woman was gone Nicola lay in bed, hungry still, and then sleep came back to her. During her sleep she had again the half-dream, half-real sensation that people were in the room – a man's voice spoke quietly and there was the quiet chink of something being dropped into a metal tray. She felt hands on her arm and, drowsily, spoke irritably as she felt the sleeve of her pyjama being rolled up.

A few moments later the room came up into sharp focus. The woman attendant was standing at the foot of the bed, holding a white enamel tray in her hands. The lights were on and it was dark outside. A man in striped trousers and a black coat, pince-nez tipped on to the end of his nose, a man she had never seen before, was smiling down at her. Little specks of dandruff powdered the collar of his jacket from his grey hair.

In a mild voice, he said, 'You have nothing to worry about, mademoiselle. You are being looked after well. Just rest and relax. You like it here?'

Nicola nodded and it seemed to her that before she had even made the movement of her head her eyes had closed and she was away into sleep again.

When she awoke again the light was still on, but through the window she could see the faint pearly flush of dawn just brushing the tops of the mountains. Her head was aching and her mind was like some crazy cinema screen that kept going out of focus. She lay in bed, her eyes shut, fighting the dizziness. Slowly it began to wear off and as it did she had a curious conviction that it was important for her to fight this happy confusion, to fight the ache in her head. . . . Somewhere, somehow, she had forgotten something which was very important.

A voice quite close to her said gently, 'Drink this.'

Nicola opened her eyes. It made her head ache more, but her eyes and her mind were coming into control.

Standing by her bed was a woman with a glass in her hand. It was not the attendant.

She put the glass in Nicola's hand and slipped her arm around her shoulder, to raise her a little so that she could drink in comfort.

Nicola drank. It could have been whisky or brandy, she thought. She could not be sure, but it went through her body like a pain. Then the pain went and sharp focus came back.

The woman stepped back from the bed, taking the glass. She wore a purple dressing-gown, with a gold cord about the middle, and there was a frilly swirl of white lace from her nightdress at the open neck of the gown. She was tall and had thick blonde hair which, untidily but yet attractively, she had piled on the top of her head. She was, thought Nicola, near her fifties, but her face, though it was almost haggard about the mouth, was the face of a beautiful woman. In some way the face seemed familiar to Nicola but for the moment she could not place it. The woman's eyes were dark and large and she had a trick of blinking, shutting them with a tiny grimace, as though even the poor light in here hurt her. She smiled at Nicola and Nicola decided that she liked her. Ten, twenty years ago and this woman would have been a queen, a splendid blonde creature . . . even now she had an almost regal air, except for the unfortunate grimace with the eyes.

The woman said, 'I shouldn't do this, of course. So you won't mention it, will you?'

'Why are you here? Who are you?'

The woman smiled and came and sat on the bedside. Ignoring the questions, she said, 'I get the brandy from one of the attendants. They're very kind, you know, and they do little things for me.' She laughed gently and shook her head. 'But they don't know about the keys. That is my secret. More than ten years I've been here and right from the beginning I started to steal them. There was a fuss at first, but I had a good hiding-place. They thought they had lost them. What does it matter, anyway? I don't want to get out. I don't have that key. But I have the others. And I like to go visiting. . . .'

Nicola, her mind clear now, saw that the woman just wanted to talk and that the talk covered a remoteness, almost a dream, in which she lived.

Quite suddenly, watching the once beautiful face with the blonde hair piled above, the truth struck her.

She said, 'Your name is Elsie, isn't it? Elsie Pinnock?'

The woman nodded. 'Yes. Elsie. Not Pinnock, though. But you won't tell anyone about the keys, will you? You see, I'm always careful who I visit. Just the people I like, the new ones that come. I saw you at the window today, looking out. And I liked you. Oh, yes I liked you; you're tall like me. . . . Well, not quite so tall, and your hair is the same.' She laughed. 'If I were younger we could be sisters. Except that you've got nice blue eyes. Mine are so dark. Once I was very beautiful. . . .'

'You still are,' said Nicola gently. She put out a hand and held Elsie's. This was the woman who had shared a flat with her mother. Elsie O'Neil. She went on, 'Why are you here?'

Elsie shrugged her shoulders. 'Because I'm ill. Oh, I'm ill, you know. My mind wanders at times, so that I can't look after myself. Only sometimes at night, I feel better and I like to talk to people.'

'And you're happy here?'

'Oh, yes. I'm very happy.'

For a moment Nicola hesitated. Her head still throbbed and she had the impression that this clarity in her was only transient. This woman touched her, and she instinctively shrunk from hurting her in any way.

She squeezed her hand and said, 'I'm glad you're happy. But don't you miss your husband?'

Elsie laughed quietly. 'Oh no! Though he's very kind. He comes and sees me sometimes. He owns this place. But I don't miss him. You see, I left him . . . just before I had this trouble, this stupid vagueness in my mind. When I'm better, maybe I shall go back to him, because he's different now.'

'What was the matter between you?'

'Oh, so many things . . . I forget most of them. My son comes sometimes. Just for a while, during school holidays. He's a nice boy, but he's shy and I can see he is always embarrassed here, so I keep the visits very short. Children don't like the old people who are so vague. . . .'

'Where did you live before you came here?'

'Oh, everywhere. We travelled so much. But right at the end we had a home in Switzerland on one of the lakes. Do you like gardening? I love it. I have a little garden here, though it's so high up and cold in the winter that some things I love won't grow. . . .' She put a hand to her forehead and the eyes tightened, stayed fixed, as though she were suddenly in pain.

'Are you all right?' asked Nicola.

Elsie's eyes opened. 'Oh, yes . . . but I get tired on these visits. And always, you know, I'm a little bit frightened. I have to be so careful.'

Elsie stood up and walked slowly round the end of the bed. Then she turned and looked back, frowning at Nicola, 'Why did you call me Pinnock?'

'I thought that was your name, as a girl.'

'Oh . . . I wonder. No, no . . . my name's Bardi. We changed it to that during the war. Before that . . . oh, it was something.' She laughed loudly and then put a hand to her mouth. 'Oh, dear . . . I mustn't make a noise! Bardi, that's it. We changed it in Switzerland. That's where we lived. Oh, you could grow canna lilies there, right at the edge of the lake. Not up here, though. But it's the soil. I didn't want to leave Villa Margritli, you know. We'd only been there a month and I wanted to do so many things for the garden.'

'Where was this villa – Margritli, is it?'

'Yes. Margritli. It's a pretty name.'

'And it was on a lake?'

'Yes. I must go now. Dear, dear . . . I hope I've done that door properly.'

'But which lake?'

'Oh, my dear, I don't remember. There are so many lakes in Switzerland and it was a long time ago.' She paused at the door and began to slip a key into the keyhole. 'Now you go back to sleep. I'll come again some time. Not tomorrow because that's the day for my weekly big injection and I sleep solidly. . . .'

She had the door open and was around it and gone before Nicola could say any more to her.

After she was gone Nicola lay back against the pillows, the ache in her head slowly subsiding and sleep beginning to creep up on her. Before sleep came, she was worried . . . she hadn't been entirely herself while Elsie was here and there was something she should have done or asked her. Surely there was? Surely she should have asked to be let out too . . . ? And the lake and the Villa Margritli . . . why was all that so important?

George worked on the carpet fastenings all the next day and by the evening he had them all free and back in their places in the enlarged holes. To the casual eye the carpet looked as though it were still firmly fixed to the floor. That day he watched Lodel when his meals were brought. Each time he came inside the door some way and stood on the end of the carpet. This day, too, he had abandoned the blackjack in favour of a gun and, George noticed grimly, that he had taken over the Walther which Ricardo Cadim had taken from him. Why, he wondered? Perhaps Lodel was a collector, always ready to make a change.

He slept uneasily through the night that followed. At six o'clock the toilet parade was made and then the two hours' wait until breakfast seemed to stretch itself out to all eternity. Mentally, George rehearsed the scene to himself. If Lodel did not stand on the end of the carpet then the attempt must be put off until lunch time; put off and put off until Lodel did stand on the end of the carpet.

Long before the two men were due George got himself into position. He took one of the magazines that were in the room and stood just clear of his end of the carpet. The wall shelf was away to his left with the end of the bed curving round to it. First Lodel, he thought, and then the attendant.

Finally the door inspection trap was drawn back and, when it did, George stood up, magazine in hand, his feet just clear of the end of the carpet with its brass rail.

The attendant came in with the tray and Lodel followed him, gun hanging loosely from his right hand. He came forward a few steps, his eyes going round the room and then halted. Come on, you bastard, thought George, another step. The attendant moved diagonally across the floor towards the shelf. He put the tray down and still

Lodel was clear of the carpet end. For one sick moment George thought that he was going to stay clear of it. Then, as the assistant turned and began to walk towards the door, Lodel stepped forward on to the carpet to give him room to pass out.

At this moment George dropped his magazine to the floor. At the sound the attendant paused and looked back at him.

Lodel said something impatiently, jerking his head towards the door. Momentarily his eyes were off George as he started to bend down to pick up the magazine.

He got his hands on the magazine. Then, with a sudden movement, he shot them forward and grabbed the brass runner at the end of the carpet strip. It came up easily in his hands from the enlarged holes and he gave a vicious jerk, pulling the whole length of the rug towards him.

The effect was more successful than he had imagined it would be. The rug slid free towards him across the smooth boards. Lodel's feet were whipped away from under him by the moving carpet. He fell, crashing his back against the padded wall, and the gun spun from his hand to the attendant's feet.

George jumped forward, ignoring Lodel, knowing that he must make sure of the gun, and crashed his right fist into the man's face. The man went backwards and as he was falling George jabbed his left across and took him on the jaw. He fell and George got his hand to the gun and whirled round to tackle Lodel who was coming up, dazed, on his knees, the top of his head two feet below George.

George crashed the gun, butt first, on to Lodel's head. The man grunted, swaying on his knees and then started to come up again. George swung the gun and hit him again on the side of the head and, this time, Lodel went down and stayed down. George turned to the attendant. He was lying stretched out by the far wall.

Quickly George unbuttoned the front of the long white coat, rolled the man over, and worked the coat free from him. He put the coat on. It was a bit short for him and tight under the armpits. Then he went to the door which had been left slightly ajar and slipped out. The key was in the lock. He turned it, dropped it into his pocket and shut the observation trap. So far as he was concerned now, the two of them could come round whenever they liked. They would have to do a lot of shouting to make themselves heard from the padded room.

Standing outside the door, he checked the gun for ammunition and then dropped it into his right pocket, keeping his hand on it.

He went down the corridor, past the toilet entrance, towards the steps that rose from the end of the corridor. He walked without hurry, keeping his head down slightly. Just before he reached the steps he saw a half-open door on his right. He stopped and looked cautiously round it. A short flight of concrete steps led down into an underground garage. Parked in the garage were two ambulances, a Citroën saloon, and beyond it the familiar white Mercedes. From the far end of the garage a sunlit concrete slope ran upwards to the ground level.

George turned away and went up the steps at the end of the corridor. He had to find Nicola. Later, the garage would give them an escape route. But he had to find her first.

At the top of the steps was another corridor. Ten feet away was a half-glass door and, when he got to it, he found himself looking into a wide, sunlit hallway, white-painted, with large vases of flowers on a long, magazine-stacked table. Beyond the table was a reception desk and it was empty.

George went quietly through into the hall. To his right was a pair of tall doors filled with coloured panes of glass, that looked like the main entrance doors. A woman was on her knees near the doorway, polishing the wooden floor.

George went across to the reception desk, scratching the right side of his face casually to screen himself from the woman. She half turned, looked at him, and then went back to her polishing.

He slipped behind the desk and found what he wanted: a long board hung with keys and above each key a number. But which key would take him to Nicola? There were about thirty of them. How did he get over that one? Bardi ran this place as a genuine convalescent home. Every new admission would be registered. He turned back to the front of the desk. The wooden top was empty except for a leather-cornered blotter, a pen-set and a white telephone. Below the counter was a long drawer. George pulled it open and there was a black-covered, thin, ledger-type book. He took it out and opened it. Away by the main door the woman began to sing quietly to herself as she worked. Down the opposite end of the hallway a swing door suddenly opened and a white-coated woman came out carrying a tray. She came up towards George who bent low over the ledger. Then she turned and began to climb a wide flight of steps that ran upwards a few yards to the right of the desk. As she did so she called to George, '*Quel beau temps ça fait. Eh, Marc?*'

George grunted and half raised a hand, and the woman went on up the stairs. He flipped the pages of the ledger now and found the last entries. Under the Monday date he found two entries. And he noticed that Bardi – looking ahead to the possible necessity for future cover – had stuck to the right sexes but had changed the names. There was an entry for a man and against it the comment, *Observation room*, and another for a woman and, against that, the note, *Chambre 6*. There were no other entries on that day or since.

George decided to take a chance on Room Number Six. He took the key from the board.

The observation room was in the basement, but he thought that it was a safe bet that the ground floor would be taken up with kitchen, dining-room and various other public rooms. The bedrooms would be on the upper floors.

He slipped round the desk and went up the stairs. At the top of the stairs was a wide landing with two corridors running away from it and then another flight of stairs going up to another floor. Fortunately on the wall of the landing was a painted board with arrows pointing down either corridor giving the room numbers one to four, to the left; five to eight to the right.

A few seconds later George was outside Room Six. He unlocked it and slipped inside, taking the key with him and pushing the door back on the snap lock behind him. Nicola was in bed, staring drowsily in front of her.

The next half hour was an agony of impatience for George. He had no idea how much time he would have before Lodel and the assistant were missed, but no matter how short it might be, it was clear that he could do nothing with Nicola in her present state. He kissed her and her eyes shone with happiness at seeing him, but it was obvious that all sense of their danger had gone from her. She treated him as though he had just come to pay a nursing-home visit, his presence a welcome relief to the boredom of being in bed.

He talked to her, tried to make her understand, shook her by the shoulders, sat her up in bed and made her drink glasses of water, but all she did was to look puzzled, giggle a little and, whenever he let go of her, sink back in the bed. In the end he lost his temper because of his anxiety for her. He pulled her out of bed and walked her up and down the room, his arm around her, talking, talking, keeping his voice down, and wondering all the time just how much grace he was to be given.

In the end she began to come round a little and then she became angry and demanded to be allowed to go back to bed. He grabbed her by the arm as she tottered away from him and forced her into the bathroom. Without ceremony, he turned on the bath spray and, holding her head over the bath, kept her like that while he ran cold water over her head. Then he straightened her up. As she stood stupidly in front of him, he massaged her cheeks and kept talking, and slowly he saw the effort she was making to understand him. He walked her back into the bedroom and sat her on the edge of the bed. As he stepped back from her he saw with relief that, although she swayed a little, she remained upright. He left her and went to the wardrobe. All her clothes were there.

He went back to the bed and she greeted his arrival by flopping backwards on to the bed, laughing quietly to herself, and repeating, 'Oh, George . . . Oh, George . . .'

With the greatest difficulty, he started to get her clothes on. He didn't care a damn about modesty. He stripped her and got some help from her as he worked clumsily at her arms and legs. If he ever got her out of this, he told himself savagely, he would have to marry her. Not that he didn't want to marry her. He did. But no man could do this to a girl and not make the offer. And Christ . . . he'd undressed a few drunks in his time and put them to bed, but this was the first – and, he hoped, the last – time, he had ever had to dress a drunk.

In the end she began to do more things for herself, clumsily and slowly. When she was dressed, he stood her up and put his arms around her. He held her very tight, his lips against her wet, fair hair. There was something in the embrace, the feeling of his strength close about her, that finally brought her back over the border.

When he released her, she said very slowly, 'What do you want, George?'

He held her shoulders, speaking close to her. 'You're to come with me. Can you stand? Can you walk?'

'Of course.'

'Let's see.'

He released her. Nicola began to walk slowly across the room. It was only a reasonable performance, and George decided that he had to risk it. Time must be running out.

He said, 'All right. We'll try – and I'll kick the guts out of anyone who gets in the way.'

Nicola came back and sat on the bed. 'Now?' she said.

'Now,' said George.

Nicola raised her legs. 'Shoes,' she said.

George looked at her feet. He had forgotten her shoes.

'Silly George,' she said. And then, as he came back with

her shoes and began to slip them on for her, she put her hand on his head, ruffling his hair, and said caressingly, 'Silly George. Nicola loves silly George. Nicola loves silly George very much.'

George groaned. What a time and place for a love scene!

George went to the door, opened it and looked out. There was no one in the corridor. Nicola came up behind him, pulled his ear and kissed him on the side of the neck.

George rolled his eyes hopelessly at her, took her arm and led her outside. He raised his hand warningly for her to stop any talk, then he led her down the corridor. At the top of the stairs George saw that the woman from the hallway was now polishing the balustrade, sitting on the steps, her back to them.

He led Nicola down and past the woman.

Her voice came from behind. '*Vous voulez que je vous assiste, Monsieur Marc?*'

Deep in his throat George said, '*Merci,*' and shook his head. And all the way down he was aware that the woman had stopped working and was watching them.

They went across the hallway and through the glass swing doors. Once through the door, George's impatience was like a fire in him. He turned, got his arm under Nicola's legs and lifted her. He started quickly for the door of the car port, and Nicola, her arms about his neck, her face buried into his shoulder, suddenly said, 'It's all right, George dear . . . I'm beginning to be with you.'

12

GIAN WAS polishing the off-side back mudguard of the white Mercedes when George came up behind him and jerked the Walther hard into his side.

Gian turned slowly, polishing-rag in hand, his chauffeur's cap pushed to the back of his head, and stared at

George. Then, the surprise dying from his face, he slowly raised a hand and rubbed the point of his chin and smiled.

George said, 'If you give a moment's trouble, I'll let you have it. Open the rear door of the car.'

Gian moved carefully away from him and opened the door.

Over his shoulder George said, 'Nicola.'

Nicola came slowly from behind one of the ambulances and got into the back of the Mercedes and Gian shut the door on her.

Gian said, 'You are making trouble for yourself.'

George said, 'Go round to the driving side. Keep well in sight.'

Gian went round the car and George covered him with the gun. When Gian was at the far door George slid into the seat next to the driving seat and motioned Gian to get in.

Gian got into the car, and George said, 'Now drive out of this place. One wrong move and my finger's going to slip.' He pushed the gun hard against Gian's side.

Gian said, 'Don't worry. I don't fool around with guns and people like you. Why don't you just take the car and leave me?'

'To raise all hell in five minutes? Drive.'

Gian started the engine and the white Mercedes slid up the ramp and out into the open air. Before them a gravelled driveway curved down between pines.

George said, 'Is there any sort of check at the gate?'

Gian said, 'No. Just a lodge-keeper. But the gate is open all day. How did you fix Lodel?'

'Never mind. Where are we?'

'Samonix.'

'How far from Annecy?'

'About an hour. This is up near the Swiss border.'

A turn in the drive brought up the gate, two stone pillars, and a small cottage to one side, and beyond the main road dipping downhill.

George said, 'Was my car and the rest of our stuff left at Annecy?'

'Yes.'

'Then you take us there.'

Gian nodded, glanced up in the driving-mirror and smiled. 'Mademoiselle is asleep,' he said.

Without turning George said, 'Good. Now keep going, but take it steady.'

Gian nodded, settled his eyes on the road, and fell silent for a long time.

They dropped downhill, through a small village square of Samonix, and began to climb the opposite side of the valley. As they hit the top of a small pass, Gian said, 'I admire you, monsieur.'

'Just keep it that way.'

'No, I mean it. Clearly you are a stubborn man who never gives up. Les Roches-Pins, Pampelone, Paris, and now here. Why?'

'Because there's something I want.'

'Ah . . . yes, that I can understand. Something you want.'

Gian was silent again, thinking, the little smile never far from his lips.

A little later they reached Albertville and turned north towards Annecy. A sign said, 'Annecy – 45 kilometres'.

Beyond the town George said, 'I saw your mother the other day.'

Gian nodded casually. 'Ah . . . yes, how is she?'

'Well. She doesn't really believe you have a fine job as a rich man's chauffeur. She thinks you drive a truck.'

Gian chuckled. 'She is a good woman. But limited. Like my brother Pierre. Limited people just remain good and poor.'

'You don't go for that?'

'No.'

'What do you go for?'

Gian was silent for a while and then he said, 'You know, I could choose a spot and just drive us all off the road. I might be killed – but if it were the right spot so might you and mademoiselle.'

George jerked the gun a fraction harder into his side.

'Just try. I'm taking all risks.'

Gian laughed. 'Maybe. Yes . . . I think you are. So, monsieur, my instinct – right from the moment in the garage – has been for co-operation not opposition.'

'Make that clearer.'

'Willingly, monsieur.' Gian's hard brown hands tightened on the wheel. 'I am tired of belonging to someone else. It is not a good thing for a man of my temperament always to be told, "Do this, do that" – and some of the things, even for me, are not pleasant things. Your mademoiselle, for instance, damned near killed me.'

'You're paid for such risks.'

'Not enough.'

'So that's it. Money?'

'Yes.'

'For that you must have something to sell?'

'Agreed. What would you like me to sell?'

Watching the man, George decided not to rush things. 'Bardi's wife is in that nursing-home, isn't she?'

Gian nodded.

'But she won't be left there long now. Correct?'

'Correct,' said Gian.

'Bardi will take her off. To some place – perhaps his permanent home – where he keeps all his papers. Where I could get my hands on him?'

'Correct,' said Gian.

'I'd pay money to know where that place is.'

Gian pursed his lips. Then he shot a little look sideways at George. 'The price would be high.'

'How much?'

'You would have to arrange this with whoever you work for? It would not be your money?'

'I would have to arrange it, yes.'

'How long?'

'Two days, no more. It depends what arrangements you want to make.'

They were dropping down to Annecy now on the N508. In a little while the lake would be in sight. Gian overtook a lorry skilfully, putting his foot down hard and then, when they were clear, he said, 'I want it in American dollars. And I want it in Switzerland.'

George said, 'Why do I bother? I could drive you straight to the police now. Once they heard the story, they'd make you talk.'

Gian shook his head. 'It wouldn't work fast enough. I could hold out for a few days. By that time Bardi would be away – every trace covered. He'd pay me well afterwards for my loyalty.'

In the back, Nicola suddenly woke and said petulantly, 'I'm thirsty.'

'In a little while,' said George soothingly. 'Go back to sleep.'

'American dollars,' said Gian. 'How much is it worth to finish Monsieur Bardi for good?'

'Five thousand?' suggested George.

'No. What I sell is worth more than that. And there is my security afterwards. Ten thousand is the price.'

'I think it can be arranged. How do I let you know?'

'You send a telegram to my father, Andrea Palloti. He works at the Schweizerhof in the Bahnhofplatz at Bern. You just say, "Everything OK", and give a telephone number for me to ring you. After that I ring you and give you a place to come. But if you come without the money it is no good.'

George nodded. 'All right. But you watch your step. Can you trust your father? He's a Bianeri.'

Gian smiled. 'So am I. My father will just think it is something to do with a woman. I have used the arrangement before. Sign your telegram, say, "Clara". It is agreed?'

George, the gun still close to Gian's side, said, 'Yes, it is agreed.'

Behind them there was the sound of Nicola stirring and her voice, more petulant said, 'I'm dying of bloody thirst, George. George, dear.'

Ahead of them the lake came into view.

Gian, relaxed comfortably at the wheel now, began to whistle gently to himself . . . his eyes shining with the prospects of new horizons widening before him.

At the bungalow Nicola got her drink and then, while George kept an eye on Gian, she packed their cases and brought them out to the Lancia.

George got into the driving seat, covered Gian still, and said, 'It's a deal?'

Gian nodded. 'I have given my word. Bring the money and you shall get what you want.' He leaned into the Mercedes and pulled out the ignition key. He held it up. 'I shall tell them that when you left me here, you took the car key. So, I have to walk a long way to the nearest telephone. By the time they get here and have another key you will be well away. OK?'

He leaned against the mudguard and began to light a cigarette.

Five minutes later George, still in a dirty crumpled dinner-jacket, and Nicola, still in her evening dress, were driving through Annecy. Five miles beyond Annecy on the road to Geneva, they turned down a by-lane, found a wood with a stream, and spent half an hour changing and talking.

Nicola, sleepy but normal, told George about Elsie and George outlined the deal he had made with Gian.

Nicola said, 'It's clear that Bardi has kept her there all these years. I felt terribly sorry for her, though she seemed oddly happy.'

'She won't be there now,' said George. 'He couldn't take that risk. I'm looking forward to a few moments alone with him. I'll bet he's been on the phone already to Ricardo Cadim telling him to pull out and go to ground for a while.'

Back on the road they stopped later for coffee. George put through a call to Synat and was lucky enough to catch him at his office. Guardedly he gave him what news he felt safe to pass and then outlined Gian's proposition.

Synat said, 'You're doing damn well. Ten thousand is steep, but we've got to try it. You're going to Geneva?'

'Yes.'

'All right. You can pick up the money tomorrow by showing your passport at my bank there. But don't you hand over the money until you're certain you're going to get something.'

'I'll make sure of that.'

'And listen, Constantine – the moment you know where to pick Bardi up, hold everything and let me know. I want to be in on it. It may not be entirely straightforward. A lot's going to depend on his nationality and the extradition laws. This Bianeri thing means that he can pull strings. Get me?'

'Yes. The thing is not to give him time to wriggle.'

In Geneva, they found themselves a couple of rooms in a small hotel on the Quai-du-Mont-Blanc, and then George telephoned a friend of his in the British Embassy at Bern who was a Second Secretary.

A voice over the phone said, 'Sorry, you're a bit out of date. He was transferred to Stockholm last year. Who is this?'

'George Constantine.'

'Oh, yes – I've heard about you. Exploring and that kind of lark. Anything I can do? Hotel trouble? Lost passport? Woman trouble? Temporary loan? That's a sample of the things his pals usually phoned about. No offence, of course.'

Why, thought George, do I always get the chatty ones?

He said, 'Yes, you could help. I want to trace the owner of a Swiss car. Can do?'

'Well . . . not strictly our affair, but try me. What was it? Brief romance. Wonderful girl sweeping by in an Alfa-

Romeo, can't sleep at nights for thinking of her. OK none of my business. Let's have the number and so on.'

George gave him the car number of the Mercedes, the telephone number of the hotel and said that if ever he were in Bern he would buy him a drink.

He then sent a telegram to Andrea Palloti at the Schweizerhof, Bern. The next morning they went to the bank and picked up the ten thousand dollars from a cashier with a light ginger moustache who did not even give George a glance as he counted out the bills for George to slip into his briefcase. As George snapped the catch the clerk looked up and winked at Nicola.

Once outside, George said, 'Blast him, for even looking at you.'

'I rather liked him. Or was it just the moustache?'

At their hotel that evening, in the middle of a badly-mixed Martini, George was called to the telephone.

It was his new-found friend from the Embassy.

'Sorry, old chap,' said the voice. 'Great disappointment – or maybe she was driving her father's car. Taking a dim view – it could be her *fiancé* or husband, of course. Name is Hans Lodel. Only address is that of a bank in Zürich. No help, eh? Sorry.'

George went back to Nicola and told her the news.

'Our friend is very careful, isn't he,' said Nicola. 'A villa at St Tropez that belonged to Dorothée Guntheim and now to a Brazilian – if that's true. And a nice white Mercedes for touring, registered in Switzerland under Lodel's name. He likes people to go round in circles when they make inquiries. What about this Villa Margritli on a lake?'

George shrugged his shoulders. 'Switzerland is stiff with lakes and villas called Margritli. It would take weeks to sort them out. No, Gian is our best bet.'

'So long as Bardi doesn't suspect him.'

'Why should he? Gian's no fool.'

The Villa Margritli stood on a small out-thrust of land,

the lake water coming round it, closing in to leave only a narrow neck of driveway from the main road. It was an old-fashioned conglomeration of gables, slate-roofed little towers, and windows with chocolate- and cream-painted shutters laid back against the walls. Pines and monkey-puzzle trees flanked the drive. A wide, stone-flagged terrace in front of the house had a set of steps which went down to the lake water. The terrace urns and flower beds were blue and red with agapanthus and canna lilies.

Across Lake Thun the Neisen peak was crowned with a little roll of summer cloud in the evening light. Behind the villa the waterside mouth of the Justisthal was stepped with vine gardens and ran, steepening quickly, pine-studded, up to the flanks of the Neiderhorn and the Rothorn.

Bardi turned back from the window of the bedroom from which he had been looking at the lake.

A woman was sleeping in the four-poster bed behind him. Her face was sideways on the pillow, her blonde hair loose across it. He stood looking down at her and for a moment his face softened. Ricardo had been right, he thought. She was the only woman he had ever loved, and the one woman now from whom he could never hope for love. Now that the Etablissement Samonix had been made impossible for her, he would have to find another place. She could not stay here for long. Long ago she had first loved and then violently hated the place, hated it because of him.

He put out a hand and touched the loose hair, listened to the heavy, drugged breathing. Then, abruptly, his hand came back and his face went stone-hard, as he thought of the Englishman who had made all this change necessary.

He turned and went out of the room and down the wide stairway to the hall which had great windows at the far end looking out over the lake. He went through a small door to the right.

It was a long, high-ceilinged room. The walls were panelled in pale pinewood, the vertical stiles of the mouldings carved with tumbling swags of fruit and birds and animals. The ceiling was ribbed with a framework of pine beams – a shallow run of curves like the skeleton of a light-draught barge – and between the ribs the plaster was painted with a profusion of allegorical figures. At the far end of the room was a small gallery approached by four steps, the steps and the edge of the gallery lined with a low, ornamented railing with the centre bosses of the panels picked out in gold leaf. In a wall niche at the back of the gallery three candles burned before a small figure of the Madonna holding a child.

The tiles were ivory-coloured, quite plain, and rafted with carpets and rugs. A long Shiraz rug with a red-and-green seed pattern lay in front of the fireplace, and at the foot of the gallery stairs was an enormous Senneh carpet with a great centre medallion of flowers and a vivid blue border. Over the marble fireplace, in which a small fire of pine cones burned, was a Chippendale oval giltwood mirror carved with rustic branches and foliage. Silver and porcelain glowed from wall cabinets. From the centre beam hung a great chandelier, coming down in eight circular tiers of icicle drops and spreading into four cut-glass branches. On the wall at the back of the gallery was a modern Lorcat tapestry of fighting-cocks. Just inside the entrance door was a suit of fluted Maximilian armour. The only window was opposite the fireplace and looked out over the lake. A long refectory table stood immediately under the chandelier. On it a wide bowl spilled over with ivory-coloured roses.

Standing by the table was Lodel.

Bardi went to the window and stood watching a pair of swans move across the water, wings ballooned, necks arched like serpents. He lit himself a cigar and turned to Lodel. 'Is there no news of the two English people?'

'No.'

'There will be. A green Lancia car . . . and they must stay somewhere. Sooner or later we shall know. And when we do we shall be very direct. Is that all?'

Lodel shook his head. 'No. There's Gian.'

'You mean Gian and Maria?'

'That – and also this. Look.'

Lodel's hand came out and tossed something on to the table. It slid across the polished wood, ringing briefly.

Bardi went over and picked it up. It was an ignition key on a small tab-ring.

'Where did you get this?'

'In his room this morning while he was swimming in the lake. It was in his breeches.'

Bardi said, 'This is the old key – the one Gian said the Englishman had taken.'

'Yes. He lied.'

'The fool – and he keeps the key.'

'He could have arranged something with the Englishman. He wants money – and Maria. Do I deal with him?'

Bardi shook his head. 'Not yet.' Bardi's eyes went cold, remote with thought. A too lusty and uncontrollable desire for happiness was Gian's weakness. He hadn't the intelligence to control it and make it work for him efficiently. It was not often that he made mistakes in the people he took into his personal service. Some instinct in him had suspected Gian from the start, but he had taken him to please his father – old Andrea Palloti. One shouldn't do things to please people. It led to trouble. Still . . . in the old days Andrea had been useful to him when he had worked as a valet for Aboler. Aboler – a clever man, but only with money. Even Andrea had been able to fool him, to break into that beautiful security about money and affairs on which he had prided himself.

Bardi said, 'Gian still keeps in touch with his father?'

'Yes.'

'He's still in Bern?'

'The Schweizerhof.'

'I'll telephone him. And you, Lodel – it is agreed about Gian. But it will be my way. In the meantime, you watch him. Keep him here in this place so that if he has to telephone it must be from here. You know what to do about the telephone?'

Lodel nodded.

'I want a record of every call he makes. Does he know about the tapes?'

'No. But Maria does.'

'He will say nothing to her until he has arranged whatever it is he is going to arrange. Yes, I see . . .' Bardi blew a thin jet of cigar smoke. 'Our Gian wants money, a lot of money . . . it is fortunate for us that he is such a fool.'

13

GIAN'S TELEPHONE call came through just after breakfast. He was brief but explicit, a businessman in no mood for generalities. On the north side of the Thunersee, not far from Interlaken, was a place called Beatenbucht. Above this was a ski-lift that started from Beatenberg station and ran up towards the Neiderhorn. The lift went up through three or four staging-points. George was to take the lift at five o'clock that afternoon and get off at the second staging-point. He was to wait there until Gian arrived and then follow him to a small patch of pine trees that lay to the east of it. He was to be alone and to have the money with him.

Before Gian rung off, George said, 'I shall be alone and I shall have the money. But I shall be armed.'

Gian said, 'It makes no difference.'

They drove from Geneva around the lake to Vevey, then north-west up over the Juan Pass and down to Spiez on the south side of the lake. From there it was only a short run to Interlaken where they found rooms at a faded Edwardian hotel full of whispering old ladies and glossy-leaved aspidistras. From Interlaken it took some fast driving along a second-class road to make the Beatenberg station by ten minutes to five. George left Nicola tucked well out of sight with the Lancia, and bought himself a ski-lift ticket.

There were quite a few summer tourists coming down the lift but not so many going up. At this time of the year the lift was used by walkers who dropped off at the various stages and went for long hikes across the hills.

A little way up the first stage he could turn and see the Thunersee spread out below him and the crowding peaks reaching up to the south.

The trouble with this business now, George told himself, was that, with the prospect of closing in on Bardi, one's instinct would be to go charging in. But that would have to be resisted. Bardi was slippery. The net would have to be drawn closely and carefully before any final action could be taken. This man held villas in other people's names, and registered his car in the same way. But somewhere he had to have a permanent base, somewhere he kept all his papers. Somewhere he had to be known in such a way that he could not avoid identification. It was this information he had to have from Gian before he handed over any of the money which he now carried in a small parcel in his pocket. The Walther he carried in his trouser pocket, bulging the material out as though he were packing a wad of tea-time sandwiches.

The first stage of the lift followed a small valley, grey stones thrusting out from the green turf and a few pines scattered here and there. Over the clack of the rollers at the supporting pylons he could hear the endless tinkle of cow bells, a sound that always gave him the impression that he was living inside a musical box that for ever played a rather limited tune.

There was a small hut at the first-stage station. Three or four people got on the descending side of the lift as he approached. There were three clear sets of chairs in front of him, and as the one immediately ahead of him moved into the station he saw a sturdily-built girl – thick boots, a brown skirt, dark sweater and sunglasses – get into the chair. He grinned as he watched her wriggle about to get the big rucksack on her shoulders comfortable. Some of the summer tourists took their walking very seriously. . . .

A small path dribbled up the slope below the second stage and was flanked to the right by thick woods. Now and again, because of the ground contours, the chair came down low, almost to the level of the tree tops, and then soared. Two girls coming down the path waved at him and he waved back. The girl in the seat ahead had a camera out now and was taking shots.

The second-stage point came up and he slipped the protective bar clear in front of him. Ahead of him the girl hiker got off, too, and plunged, shoulders bent, over the turf and upwards as though someone had called stirringly, 'Excelsior!'

George got off and, staying close to the moving lift, leaned against the wooden rail and lit a cigarette. There was no one at this point waiting to get on, but a dribble of people coming down.

He turned and watched the ascending line of seats. It was ten minutes past five. Far below him were the wooded shores of the lake and he could see the thin wake of steamers. Away to the right a rocky ridge marked the fall-away of the Neiderhorn shoulder into the Justisthal and the lake village of Meringen. Once, long ago, he remembered, he had spent a boyhood holiday around these parts with the Professor and his wife. It was odd, he thought, how lately he had found the Professor slipping from his mind. Only Scorpio occupied it coldly, determinedly. Get Scorpio. Beyond that there was nothing.

He saw Gian coming when he was about seven chairs away. Between him and Gian only one of the chairs was occupied. It was a chair about three ahead of Gian. A young man was sitting in it. He wore a small billycock hat, leather trousers and bright-blue braces over a red shirt. He was reading a book, and he passed through the station without looking up.

George stepped back a few paces and waited for Gian. The chair came up with its slow, processional movement, dignity without haste. Gian was bare-headed, his copper-coloured hair taking the sun, the brownness of his face and throat sharp above a white shirt, his legs crossed comfortably as he sat slumped back in his seat.

George watched him. As the chair came within a few yards of the alighting platform he waited for Gian to move, to drop aside the holding bar. But Gian made no movement. He came sailing in, looking straight ahead of him, making no move to get off.

George stepped forward, raising a hand, but the chair sailed by him. It went by him with a steady rattle of the overhead rollers, and Gian stared unmoving at the slope ahead. And in the few moments of Gian's passing, George saw why Gian had not alighted. His head was tipped a little to one side and from below a neat hole in his left temple there was a little trickle of blood that had spotted the breast of his white shirt. The chair went out of the station, soaring over a sharp contour lift, cleared a pylon about fifty yards away, and then George saw Gian's body slip, the shoulders sliding downwards. For a moment he hung like that, and then the body slipped again, sliding under the chair bar and falling. Ahead, the young man in the billycock hat went on reading, unaware of what had happened behind him.

George jumped off the platform and began to run up the steep turf slope. Fifty yards ahead was a clump of pines that had masked the end of Gian's fall. He went through them and found Gian on the far edge, sprawled on the turf at the side of a rough path.

He knelt down and turned Gian over. The brown, sun-tanned face stared upwards and then flopped slowly sideways. George saw then that as well as the bullet hole below the temple, there was another just behind the left ear, though no blood had come from it: two little holes, drilled neatly and precisely into the young man's skull. He did not have to be told what weapon had been used. He'd hunted himself for some kinds of game with a ·22 rifle, and he did not have to be told that to drill a man's head while he moved in a ski-car was more than just good shooting or good luck – it was championship class.

Somewhere, as Gian had come up the slopes, there had been two shots, sharp, decisive; and Gian had paid for reaching too clumsily for happiness, and the young man ahead of him had gone on reading his magazine.

He stood up and stepped back into the cover of the pines behind him. The movement was instinctive. It was the kind of movement he'd made before in other places. Suddenly he had the cold feeling that he was naked. There was a feeling of helpless vulnerability between the shoulder blades and he had the sensation that his skull was as brittle as an egg-shell. There was nothing he could do for Gian, but there had to be a great deal he must do for himself. Somebody had known Gian was coming up here. If they knew that, then they knew it was to meet him. Why had he been allowed to come as far as the second stage unharmed, while Gian had been picked off? It wasn't hard to work that one out. If they'd picked him off some of the passengers on the lift or maybe the attendant at the top – which he could have reached before Gian got on at the bottom – might have discovered him and the lift might have been stopped. To Gian below that would have been a panic sign, maybe. No, someone wanted him up here and had been quite happy to pick Gian off as he came up. They didn't care if the lift stopped now. They had him up here. Nearly five thousand feet up and only a rough track to take him down – unless he cared to risk the lift back. Which he didn't . . . not when there would be someone tucked away behind a pine who could shoot rings round a William Tell.

He went through the pines to his left and when he reached the edge of the trees he paused. Ahead of him was a broken slope, studded with rocks. High up on his right hand was a long rock ridge, steep-faced. To the left, down-hill, was a long sweep of grass and shrub-covered plateau with the crests of pines just showing beyond it. Between him and the far edge of the plateau, and the prospect of a further tree cover, were about three hundred yards with a certain amount of rock cover. If he could get to the far pines he could go on working his way downhill, bearing always to the right, and finally make the bottom of the Justisthal and the lake. He pulled the gun from his pocket. He had at this moment no faith in anyone except himself. Nobody was going to help him.

He picked a clump of rocks about a hundred yards away and, bending low, began to run for them. He was within twenty yards of them when the proof came that he was being hunted. There was a sharp crack away to his left and something tore through the loosely-swinging flap of his jacket pocket. He made the last five yards in a long dive that almost beat the breath out of him. Another shot clipped the edge of the rock behind him and sent up a cloud of stone chips.

There was no doubt in his mind where the shots had come from. Somebody had been waiting just below the edge of the plateau, between him and the pines. He sat up and examined the ground ahead of him. A small cattle-track ran from the rocks along a shallow scoop of ground that rose after about fifteen yards to a stretch of turf about fifty yards long which would expose him to the plateau, before he could gain the cover of the next outcrop of rocks. He started to crawl along the track, keeping out of sight. The Walther was useless unless he could get to close quarters, and he didn't see anyone with a ·22 rifle letting him get within a hundred and fifty yards – which made the gun about as useful as a boomerang. As he crawled forward he tried to recall the ·22-calibre rifle he had last used. It had been a lever-action repeater and the magazine had held twenty-five short or twenty long rifle cartridges. Give his present stalker the benefit and say twenty-five shots. Two already gone on Gian and two on him. That made twenty-one to go. He spat dust from his mouth and felt the sweat running off his forehead. He came to the end of the cover and halted, eyeing the open track ahead.

He let his breathing even down. He looked back over

his shoulder. Above the far line of the pines he could see the ski-lift moving and the black silhouette against the sky of the occasional passenger. The General Public were a great help, as always. They could hear shots, they only had to look down and see the dead Gian on the track below them, or over this way and wonder why he was crawling along a cattle-track like a slow-worm . . . but they saw nothing and probably had only the briefest curiosity about the shots.

He got to his knees and began to dash across the open turf for the next outcrop of rocks. He was hardly in the open before the first shot came. A red-hot poker was whipped lightly across the back of his neck and the shock sent him stumbling sideways. He fell heavily, but even as he hit the ground he kept rolling, knowing that two seconds of immobility would be enough to make him a perfect target. Another shot whipped the turf into a long ragged ribbon in front of his face. Then he was on his feet, running and zig-zagging and praying, keeping his head down, and the gun in his left hand up across the side of his face. Another shot whined by him as he flung himself into the shelter of the rocks.

He lay in their shelter, sobbing for breath, and somewhere dully in his mind he heard a score-keeper count. Three more shots gone. That made eighteen left. He didn't fancy his chances. The man had been ready for him the moment that he broke cover. He would have given himself halfway across the open patch before the shot came, but it had been slammed at him within the first two steps.

He sat up and found a niche in his rock cover and looked down over the plateau. There was no movement at all, except far to the left where an old woman, in a black dress and white lace bonnet, sat placidly knitting while a handful of cows tinkled and cropped the turf. For relief he cursed her. She was either deaf or carrying Swiss neutrality too damned far.

From this clump of rocks he had the choice of two

routes. A little gully ran away steeply upwards towards the distant ridge of rock above. It would give him cover all the way up to the ridge. But he didn't want to go upwards. He was longing for the lower slopes. Downwards was a low bank of turf behind which the cattle-track had worn a depression. It slanted away towards the edge of the Neiderhorn ridge that overlooked the Justisthal. The trouble was that it only went for about fifty yards and then the bank petered out, leaving a hundred yards across open ground before he could make the cover of a mass of broken, rock-studded ground. He sat for a while, trying to make up his mind. Upwards was safer but it led nowhere. Downwards meant a hundred-yard carry in the open — but if he made it, he was on his way. As he glanced up the gully towards the ridge above him, he saw a movement on the topmost rocks. For a moment the sweat in his eyes and the westering sun made it hard for him to see what it was. Then a figure moved. He recognized it at once. It was the girl in sunglassses with the heavy pack. As he watched he saw her hands raised before her face and caught the glint of sunlight on metal. For God's sake, he thought, she was sitting up there calmly taking photographs for her album while he was being hunted like a rat down here. Couldn't she see what was happening? All she had to do was to dash away to the ski-lift and get some help. He cursed her, now, aloud and in stronger terms than he had used on the old woman.

The cursing made him feel better. He took out his handkerchief and dabbed the back of his neck. The blood was running but not in any way that suggested he was going to bled to death in the next few hours.

In the cover of the mound he began to work his way down the cattle-track. A lark sang somewhere above. The distant cow-bells tinkled. Out over the lake a kite went round and round in lazy, loose spirals. There was a beautiful growing evening peace over the whole world, and George cursed himself for being so lenient with Gian. He should never have agreed to buy information. He should have held Gian in the Annecy villa and beaten the facts out of him.

When he got to the end of the cover, he squatted, looking at the open stretch ahead of him. It was a beautiful stretch of turf, carpeted with thyme and small heaths and busy with the noise of bees. He hated every yard of it, but knew that he had to make it somehow. He glanced backwards and upwards. His hiking girl had moved farther along the ridge towards the Neiderhorn shoulder. She was standing, legs widespread, and still using her camera. Just for a moment she lowered it from her face. It was then that he caught the glitter of the sun on something behind her, something that stuck up over her right shoulder. It hit him then, almost as though someone had smacked him in the face. So that was it! What a sucker he'd been! Dark glasses to hide her face, and the loose sweater and ugly skirt to hide a figure that he had once had displayed for him in Paris. Standing up there, watching every move he made, was Dorothée Guntheim, and it was no camera she was using but a walkie-talkie mouthpiece, the set in the pack on her back and the antennae shining in the sun over her shoulder. Every move he made down here was being relayed. The moment he moved out of this cover she was going to call, 'Now!'

He squatted there and thought hard, forcing memory back to his boyhood years. How did the fall away from the Neiderhorn shoulder go to the Justisthal valley? He had walked the ridge with the Professor long, long ago. His memory presented him with a recollection of a sharp, steep crag face dropping to loose moraine slopes. There might be a chance that way. There certainly was no chance for him on this route, not with Dorothée Guntheim calling the moves above him.

He turned back along the cattle-track and then took the gully that led upwards to the ridge. Here, he could walk upright in cover and he went fast, moving up towards the girl. She saw him coming and began to move along the ridge, away from him towards the Neiderhorn shoulder.

When he had gone a hundred yards, which he reckoned would make him about three hundred yards from the edge of the plateau below, he climbed the side of the gully and looked back, keeping in the cover of a rock. Three hundred yards range made him fairly safe from even a first-class shot.

It was no surprise to him to see, already out in the open and coming up towards him, a man wearing a wind-breaker and a beret, a rucksack on his back, and carrying a rifle across the front of his body. It was Bardi, complete with his walkie-talkie.

George put his gun in his pocket, slid down into the gully and began to run hard. Above him Dorothée moved farther along the ridge and he was almost at the foot of the steep face when there came a shot from directly behind him. He dropped flat and looked back. Two hundred yards away along the foot of the ridge another man had appeared and George recognized him at once. It was Lodel and he realized now that Lodel had been there, always in his rear, as a back-stop in case he tried to turn on his tracks and make for the ski-lift. Up above, he thought bitterly, Dorothée was doing a good job of work. Both men wore packs on their backs and he could see the sun glinting now on Lodel's antennae.

He realized then that, with Lodel closing in behind and Bardi below rapidly narrowing the range, there was only one hope for him. Dorothée above calling the moves made any hope of playing cat-and-mouse hopeless. He hadn't a chance in hell of losing them in the rocks or getting to the top of the ridge into new country where he could outflank them. He had one line to take, and that was to go hard and fast along the bottom of this ridge towards the Neiderhorn shoulder and keep the range open between him and the two men as long as possible.

He was on his feet and running hard as the decision formed in his mind. In the first hundred yards there were two shots somewhere wide of him and then no more. He looked back once and saw Bardi below running across the plateau, covering his left and Lodel behind, coming more slowly along the loose rocks and gravel at the bottom of the ridge.

He spurted hard, watching the ground, choosing his places and knowing that every yard he made now was going to count later. When he came to the shoulder he would have no chance to pick and choose. He would have to go down fast and trust that he would find cover before they reached the edge and let loose at him.

Five yards from the edge of the shoulder, he glanced back again. He had made up some ground on the men. Two hundred feet above him Dorothée was standing close to the shoulder edge, able to see every move he made.

He was on the edge, and had a flashing vision of the great valley running far below him, widening towards the lake: then he was over, going down a steep grass slope towards the first rock fall, his shoes digging into the turf to brake his progress. At the edge of the first drop he took four seconds to run his eyes over the crags and falls below, picking a route. He let himself over the side and went downwards faster than he had ever thought he could take any descent, hands and feet swinging for holds.

He was within twelve feet of the bottom of the climb when he heard a shout above him. He glanced up. The two men were at the edge of the rock. He knew then that there was only one chance in the world for him. The rifles were coming up, holding him in their sights at eighty yards range. He had to let them think they had made their kill.

At the foot of the fall, there was a long loose slide of gravel and stones that sloped steeply down to the next rock face.

Moving down still he waited for the shots. They came – two of them. One seared right down the length of his jacket at the back, and the other punched into his jacket sleeve, tearing through the loose flesh of his armpit. He fell off the rock face, let himself go, let himself fall, letting every muscle relax. He hit the loose stones ten feet below and rolled. He rolled, making no effort to control himself, his body sliding and bouncing as the body of a dead man might cascade. Gravel, stones and dust roared around him. He saw the lip of the next fall coming up, the edge pocked with large boulders that had come to rest at the foot of the slide. Only then did he begin to use his feet and hands, movements that no one from above could possibly detect. He had to hit a boulder to save himself from going right over and falling free. When he hit the boulder he had to slide sideways round it, with the slow motion of an inert body, and drop away over the side, then pray that neither of the men would face the steep climb down to check on his death.

He hit a boulder with the side of his body and, without having to force it, felt himself swing sideways from the shock and his feet drop out over space. It was then that he dug his hands into the ground, braking his progress, fighting for a hold as he went over. For a moment, he thought that he was lost. He began to fall free and then his left hand found rock. He swung away, his chest coming clear of the cliff face, the screwing round of his body-weight almost breaking his wrist. He hung on and then swung back, and his feet found a hold. He hung, panting, blinded by dust, to the cliff face. He had no idea how long he clung there, but the world slowly came back to him. His eyes cleared, and he saw that he was two feet below the edge of the cliff, spread-eagled against its face, with a long drop below him and, at its foot, the green spear-pointed crest of a clump of pines waiting. As he looked a cascade of stones poured down over him; then, missing him by inches, the large boulder he had hit, came blackly past him, disturbed from its precarious poise. He clung to the rock as stones and dirt poured over him . . . far below, he heard the thundering crash of the boulder into the pines. He shut his eyes then: clinging to the rock face, his body trembling. A kind of rage possessed him, making his body cold with shock and filling his mind with white-hot, searing, swearing fury, robbing him of all thought.

After that it was like some crazy film, cut and pieced together purely to confuse. Now and again the film broke down and there was nothing but blackness through which he seemed to be crawling, with no sound except the laboured pump and wheeze of his own breath. He was an ant on the face of a smooth concrete wall. He was everything in turn: a climbing, walking, burrowing, sliding creature trying to get somewhere, not knowing where, and in the end he gave up . . . or it seemed to him that he gave up, though the crazy film went on. Finally he shut his eyes against it, tired of the nonsense.

When he opened his eyes again, it was to see a thin slip of moon over the crest of the pines above him, and to hear the sound of running water. The sky was studded with a few random stars. His head was clear but his body was full of protest, dozens of small voices of bruise and cut nagging at him.

An arm held him round his shoulders, and he could feel the warmth of a hand through his shirt. His jacket was off, one shirt sleeve ripped short, and the whole of his right shoulder was wet with water. He looked down and saw the blackness which could only be blood streaked down the white side of his shirt. The arm and hand moved, held him firmly, bringing him upright.

'Drink,' said a woman's voice.

Metal touched his lips and he swallowed obediently, feeling the bright sting of brandy against his throat. He coughed and sat forward, but the brandy was in him, warm, alive, like some hot-blooded creature.

He straightened and turned. Against a backdrop of cliff, pine and stars, he saw the face of Dorothée Guntheim.

'What are you doing here?' he said slowly.

She gave him the brandy flask. This time he held it himself and drank, watching her over it. She was dressed as she had been on the mountain, thick skirt, a beret, and a plain white collar of a blouse above her sweater neck. The starlight caught her thick glasses.

'I came back,' she said flatly, 'because the others said you were dead — but I knew they had to be wrong. I knew there had to be a day and a man when it would all finish. I've dreamt about it and wondered what I would do. This is the day and you are the man.' Her voice was strained, almost as though it were full-charged with static electricity that might at any moment break from her control.

George put the flask on the grass. 'Somebody's always wrong, somewhere. What the devil are you talking about?'

Dorothée took out a cigarette case and lighter and lit a cigarette for him. George took it obediently.

Dorothée said, 'You will be all right. I've fixed a bandage under your arm. The bullet just went through the flesh. By any reasonable calculation you should be dead. But the thing has gone beyond reason — it had to one day, for some man.'

'Am I the man?' he asked the question, matching her mood.

'Yes. When you came to my room that Sunday morning I had the feeling that you might be. I know now that you are. From that moment I began to change . . . I should have hated you because I loved him. But everything began to change.'

George could sense that there was no easing of the strain in her. He had the impression that she was completely indifferent to him, neither friendly nor hostile, that she was being compelled now to finish some task, to free herself.

Gently, he said, 'Who is this one you love? Bardi?'

She nodded. 'Bardi. He uses people, men and women. They like it. I liked it. Oh, yes, at first I liked it. That was in Germany while his wife was still with him. He needed me. He used me and I was enchained.' She spoke slowly, her English correct, accented, always the strain behind it.

George said, 'But now you want to be free?'

'Yes. Because the day and the man had to come. Bardi is no longer untouchable. No man could be for ever, and with him it has been a long time.' She gave a little laugh, and it echoed among the close-packed pines. 'Pleasure, his own pleasure, always he has to seek it, tearing it from other people because he has no way of creating it for himself. Do you know the pleasure you gave him? To plan the hunt? To let Gian bait the trap? To drive you across the hills? When he fired and you fell, his pleasure was something wild, rampant inside him.'

George said, 'And now you hate him?'

'I don't know! I don't know!' The strain broke in her voice, making it edged and shrill. 'He sent Lodel away, back to the villa, and we were left alone on the mountain. And he was like a giant, drunk with pleasure. Lodel was hardly out of sight before he began to take me. And I let him. My God, I let him. But for the last time, for I knew then that it was not, nor ever had been, from any gratitude, love, or thought of my pleasure, but because he wanted the ecstasy to go on, and on, and on . . .'

She broke off suddenly and slipped off her glasses with her left hand, held them in the corner of her mouth by one wing, and wiped her eyes with a grubby handkerchief which she took from her skirt pocket. She looked ludicrous, pathetic and broken, and George felt anger stir in him against Bardi, stir and turn, and grow strong and violent.

He stood up stiffly and looked down at her. Coldly, he said, 'Where can I find him?'

Her head came up and she blinked at him. Then slowly she put her glasses on, and, surprisingly, smiled, saying, 'Yes, you are the man. I knew it in my room. I knew it in that Paris cellar . . . it was here' – she pressed her hands hard against her chest– 'like a hardness that would never stop growing.'

'Where can I find him?' said George.

She stood up then and held out to him his jacket which she had picked from the grass. The air was cool. Somewhere a nightjar called harshly and distantly a train horn scratched one long note across the night.

'Go down the valley path to Meringen. The Villa Margritli. It is the first house on the lakeside towards Interlaken. You will find your friend there. They took her as she sat in your car, before Gian arrived. Laborde drove her back.'

'How many of them are there in the place?'

Dorothée took a step past him, upwards into the pines.

'Four. Lodel, Maria, Bardi – and his wife. Laborde has gone back. I was sent back, too. But I came up here. Why do I tell you all this . . . ? Why . . . ?'

She was past him now, going up the small path that followed the stream, away from him, away from the lake.

He stood there and let her go. There was nothing he could do for her. A long time ago the destruction had begun, at the moment of meeting Bardi. . . . He saw her standing, poised, half-naked, in her flat . . . saw Ernst slumped in his chair . . . saw Laborde holding the Remy Martin bottle . . . saw Gian, head cocked over, the blood above his ear . . . and then he turned and began to go down the valley, towards Meringen, towards the Villa Margritli . . . towards Scorpio. . . .

14

IT TOOK him an hour: down the rough track of the Justisthal, into Meringen with the lake spread flat and moon-silvered before him, then along the road to Interlaken, to the grey pillars of the drive entrance. The name – Villa Margritli – was cut into a slab of slate, gold-lettered. The driveway running up to the house was shrub-lined, flower beds in an heraldic maze of stars and crescents, all colour taken from the canna lilies, the geraniums and the edging lobelias by the night. And he walked, feeling his body wakening, feeling muscles lose stiffness, warmed and cherished by the anger and the desire in him to reach Bardi; knowing now that nothing was going to stop him, that the first man or woman who stepped into his path would be ruthlessly overcome, for something of Dorothée Guntheim's fatalism had entered him.

There was a light showing from one of the high windows, and another to the left of the house on the ground floor. He went across to the left, past the light, and found a side door where the driveway curved around the end of the house to the garage block. Pausing for a moment at the door he saw the white Mercedes parked in the moonlight on the grey concrete. Beyond it was the long low body of the Lancia.

He took the Walther from his pocket, pushed open the door and went in. A cream-painted corridor, with a squat deep-freeze cabinet at one side, led to a half-open doorway through which came the sound of voices.

He opened the door wide and went in. It was a kitchen, polished, gleaming: copper pans on the walls, a white Aga stove, a long table with red Formica top, steel-legged chairs, and a smell of coffee.

Maria was sitting at the table, her face resting in her cupped hands, and her face had the dullness of heavy grief over it.

Lodel, wearing a white jacket and black trousers, was standing with his back to him, a mug of coffee in his hands.

George took two paces towards him. The man turned. George saw the instinctive movement of the hand with the mug, the moment of self-preservation, but his own right hand went up, crashed down, the butt of the gun taking Lodel on the forehead. The man went down, his head thumping against the base of the Aga. A runnel of coffee spread over the black- and white-tiled floor.

Maria sat unmoved at the table and her eyes came slowly up to George. For a moment they looked at one another and George, feeling it in himself, knew that it was in her, too – a madness, in this night, that had to run its course because every ingredient of fantasy, darkness, evil and death had long ago been slowly worked into the fabric of these hours that were upon them.

Ignoring her, he jerked a nylon drying-line free from

its patent container on the wall, bent and rolled Lodel over and began to tie his hands behind him. The man breathed heavily, his forehead bruised, small beads of blood, too small to break and run, spotting the skin.

Maria said, 'You were on the mountain?'

George stood up. 'Yes.'

'They said you were dead.' She stood up wearily. 'Tell me, it is true, Gian is dead?'

'Yes. I saw him.'

'I knew, but I had to hear it from someone else. He was standing there, drinking his coffee, telling me, "Gian is dead".' For a moment the weariness in her was broken by a bitter smile. 'And I knew it had to be. I told Gian, but he was full of his own strength . . . so full.'

George said, 'Where is the girl?' He held the Walther covering her.

Maria shook her head. 'You won't need that for me. Stay here and I will bring her to you.'

She turned and went to another door at the end of the kitchen. George followed her but she did not look round. He stood in the doorway and watched her cross the servants' hall to a door at the foot of a narrow stairway. She took a key from the pocket of her dress and opened the door, standing outside, making a motion of her right hand.

George saw Nicola come out, puzzled, cautious. Then she saw him. She came running and he gathered her to him with one arm. As Maria came back to them, he said to her, 'Where is he?'

Maria said, 'You go up the stairs into the main hallway. There is a red-leather door, studded with nails, bright golden nails. Inside.' She paused then, looking hard at him, grief making her face ugly, the wide mouth free of lipstick, her eyes dark with despair, and said, 'You want me to stay?'

George shook his head. 'I need only him.'

She went past them back into the kitchen and the door was shut upon them.

Holding Nicola's arms, George went towards the narrow stairway. She began to talk but he shook his head, and something in his manner silenced her. The presence that was part of this night took her, bound her to him, and made her unquestioning, loyal to all his movements.

They went up into the great hall together. The curtains were drawn over the far lake window and two chandeliers blazed with light. Facing them on the far side of the hall was the red-leather door and to their right ran upwards the wide, curving main stairway.

As they stood there, taking in the scene, poised on the lip of movement, they heard the sound of feet coming down the great stairway, a sound which was soft and whispering. With it was another sound, the dry, crisp rustle of silk, dragging and clinging over the polished boards.

Both heads turned upwards, and then movement was suspended in them, for at the last turn of the stairs a woman was framed against the far blaze of a higher chandelier.

It was Elsie, but an Elsie transformed, held, too, by the spell of this night; awakened, drug-freed by long sleep, escaping from slavery into a world of memories that no longer confused her. Her pale hair was piled loosely on top of her head; from the throat of her heavy flame-coloured silk robe a great froth of white lace fell from her nightdress and, with each step she took, there was the quick gleam of silver slippers. She came down the stairs, tall, splendidly regal and, behind the phantom of the being she was now, there walked the memory of all she had been, of a tall, full-breasted, vibrant woman, her body rich with promise – and for a moment or two she was that. But as she reached the bottom of the stairs, George saw that her face was dead and cold and drawn; the only life was the glitter in her eyes that now and then flickered as though she were in pain.

She went by them, without seeing them, and crossed to the red-leather door. She pushed it open and went in, the door swinging behind her with a deep, sighing sound.

George went across the hallway and put his hand on the door. He waited a few moments, then pushed it open gently and slipped in, Nicola following him.

The only light in the room came from the wall sconces and from the candles that burned in the wall alcove that held the Madonna and Child at the back of the far, raised gallery.

George and Nicola stood in the shadows by the great suit of armour and watched, held and commanded by the power that was still gathering strength this night.

Bardi, in evening clothes, was standing by the fireplace. There was a whisky glass under the Chippendale mirror, and a cigar burned in an ashtray beside it. He was turning over a sheaf of papers in his hands mechanically. The movement slowly ceased as he turned and watched Elsie come across the room to him: beyond her he saw nothing.

The silver slippers gleamed across the Senneh carpet. A few petals had dropped from the ivory roses and lay, frail coracles, on the polished wood. At the back of the gallery, the Lorcat tapestry had been raised high up the wall and the door of a small vault stood open, electric light shining within it, showing shelves stacked with tin boxes and piles of files.

Bardi said, 'Elsie, my love. *Cara* . . . you shouldn't be here.'

He dropped the papers to an armchair.

Elsie moved past him to the foot of the gallery stairs and turned, looking down the full length of the room and then at him.

'Why did you bring me back here?' The voice was cold, accusing, yet oddly remote as though she spoke in some unbreakable trance.

'*Cara —*' he began.

'Don't call me that.' Her voice was level, no emotion in it, only the coldness which was part of her coldness.

He frowned then and said sharply, 'Stop this nonsense. You must go back to your room.' He began to make a move towards her, but she put up her hand, the loose sleeve of the red gown falling, showing the bare arm. Her bare palm, facing him, halted him.

'Why did you bring me back? I thought it was a dream – that it had never been. But it is all here still. You, alone here with your papers. This —' she half turned and pointed to the vault door. 'All this filth and horror. Nothing has changed. I thought it was a dream, but nothing has changed.' For a moment her voice broke, sobbed and then her eyes came back to him.

'Elsie . . . you are ill. This is wild talk. Let me take you back to your room.'

She shook her head. 'You have lived in filth. And you have made me filthy. How can that be forgotten or forgiven? How can the filthy be made clean? There is only one way.'

'*Cara*, stop this at once,' he cried angrily, moving rapidly towards her.

From the back of the room George stepped forward, gun levelled at Bardi.

'Stand back from her, Bardi.'

Bardi spun round. Momentarily his mouth dropped loosely. Then, maybe because he too at that moment was suddenly caught by the slow, inevitable movement in the night, yet would fight it, break it, and use it as he had used so many other things and people, he raised a hand to his forehead, his face suddenly taut with passion, and turned, ignoring George.

George, his voice harsh and commanding, cried, 'One step – and I'll shoot you in the back!'

Bardi halted.

Ahead of them, Elsie – untouched by this intrusion, ignoring it as though it had no real existence, not seeing, perhaps, that there were others in the room – said with a long shuddering tone of anguish in her voice, 'It must be made clean . . . Oh God, it must be made clean. It must be ended.'

She went up the gallery steps and she seemed to float

more than walk, tall and terrible, like a priestess going to the altar. She took one of the candles that burned in the alcove before the Madonna and went into the vault, bending low at the doorway. She set the candle on a shelf, picked up a bundle of papers and threw them out on to the gallery floor. She took tin boxes and shook their contents free over the floor of the vault and the papers skimmed and fluttered in the air like released birds. When the floor was thick with them, she turned and shuffled her feet through them, holding back the edges of her gown as though she trod in filth. Then she bent and picked up a sheet of paper and set the edge of it to the candle, watching it flare, holding it, turning it so that the flame rose high, before she dropped it to the ground amongst the others.

From behind Bardi, edging up to him now, George saw the desire to move work in the broad shoulders, and he said quietly, 'Move one inch, Bardi. Just move, and give me the chance to fire.'

And Bardi stood where he was. Behind him George and Nicola watched, and deep in both of them they acknowledged the rightness of this hour which belonged to the tall, splendid woman who had once been Elsie Pinnock – Elsie who now moved, tall, remote, golden-headed like a queen, possessed, bending with the candle, leaving flame behind her, holding it now, not to papers, but coming clear out on to the gallery, touching the flame to the hanging side curtains, waiting with a cold patience for the fire to take, to spurt, live and then run the length of the material. Behind her the light in the vault grew stronger and the room began to wake with the noise of flames, the roar and the lusting sigh of fire, and the air began to fill, rich and warm with the heady redolence of burning pine as the panelling behind the curtains smouldered, sparked, spat and then blossomed into flame.

And when she had done she turned, walked back across the gallery to the alcove, put the candle in front of the Madonna, bowed slightly and crossed herself. She came back to the gallery steps and looked down on Bardi. The coldness was gone from her face and she nodded gently as though a promise, long made, often forgotten, had now been honoured. She stood there, tall, a red pillar against the redness of the flames behind her.

'You bitch!' Bardi screamed suddenly, and the sound was no man-sound. It was a night sound, the sound of this night. He spat at her, turned, and ran for the wide windows that overlooked lake and garden, bursting through them, glass shattering as the french doors swung before his bulk.

George followed him, leaving Nicola to take Elsie from the room which was doomed, from the house that would follow it to black ashes, clean ash without memory.

He caught him in the garage yard at the side of the house.

The white Mercedes was moving and Maria was at the wheel. Bardi, a few yards from the car, shouted and ran towards it, but Maria ignored him and drove on, the night suddenly burdened with the surge of power beating free from the exhaust pipes, the headlights flashing on, powdering the pines and canna lilies with a moving frost.

Bardi paused, shouted again after her, and then turned and ran for the Lancia. His hand was on the door when George caught him.

He spun him round and the man stumbled away from him, almost fell, then found his feet. With his back against the wall of the garage building, great swags of bougainvillaea tumbling from the trellis that faced it, Bardi waited. For a moment or two they faced one another in silence, Bardi's large face a white blur in the shadow of the wall. Then from behind them, escaping from the house, flames somewhere reached up into the night, and the yard became a black-and-gold pool of moving light.

Bardi came for him and George waited, the coldness in him deep and violent, filling him with mercilessness.

Bardi flung himself forward, his hands reaching for George. Controlled, as though he were in a ring, tactics fixed, George stepped aside and quickly uppercut him to the chin.

Bardi went back and hit the ground. A cold voice in George, as he watched Bardi come up, chanted, 'For the Professor, for Nadia Temple . . .'

The man came at him again, and George's right fist swung across, smashing him to the ground, and the voice cried inside him, 'For all of them . . . all the unknown ones.'

Bardi came back again, and George smashed him down, like a machine pounding at some great edifice, demolishing the long-rotten fabric.

In the end Bardi lay on the ground and rose no more. But he half turned and looked up, breath sobbing, face bruised and bloody, the eyes remote, unmoving, at George, and he found one action, one word to write his own epitaph.

'Bastard!' he cried.

Then, as George stood rocking on his feet, feeling his own tired body mauled, protesting, the roar of the burning house behind filling this mad night with a hundred mad voices, he saw Bardi's hand go to his jacket pocket and then come back to his mouth. He saw the lift of the head in the moment of swallowing, saw the cold eyes fixed on him. Then, from its support on one elbow, the man's body slowly collapsed and legs and arms writhed in one sharp spasm; the big head tipped back on the cobbles, the eyes, wide open, were suddenly fixed sightlessly on the sky which was reddening in the glare of the burning house.

George turned away and walked towards the main door of the house. Coming down the steps were Nicola and Elsie, Nicola's arm around the woman.

Nicola said, 'Where is he?'

George said, 'He's dead. He took poison. He must have known that a time like this would come. Take her to the car. I'll get Lodel . . .'

He went on past them towards the side entrance.

EPILOGUE

THE SOUND of rain woke him, hard, splashing September rain with the lick of a rising gale behind it to shake the window panes. He came drowsily out of sleep, half-dream, half-memory still with him, and he lay looking sideways at the runnels of water coursing down the glass of the window.

This was the time of day when he remembered it all most clearly, when it all came back in broken, vivid fragments of time . . . Elsie, now safely in England with her son, but then a tall, Hellenic priestess moving to the compulsion of a duty that had slept too long . . . And Scorpio lying on the ground, his big face washed with the glow of flames . . . and the fierce spit and roar of the house burning.

He slid out of bed and walked to the window, staring out at the sea which creamed before the wind over the rocks below, watching the top hamper of the palms sway and toss, and the long, swirling wraiths of sand whipped up the beach by the wind, the red-and-yellow hotel awnings bellying with it, full-charged, straining to take wing. A great roller thundered against the sea wall, spouting high and spreading a great fan of foam that blocked everything from his sight.

Her voice from behind him said, 'What are you doing there?'

'Watching the storm. If this keeps up the hotel will have to put out a sea-anchor.'

'What's the time?' Her voice was still half-drowned with sleep.

'Five o'clock.'

'Oh, no . . .'

He smiled without turning. He heard her turn in the bed and then her voice came again, 'Do you always get up at five and wander about the place?'

'You'll get used to it.'

She said sleepily, 'Come back here at once. And look at your shoulders. You're sunburnt to hell. You'll have to rub them with something.'

He turned then. 'I will? Isn't that your job? You'd be failing in your duties.'

She smiled up at him, fair hair loose over the pillow, one arm and part of her shoulder bare above the sheet, and she patted the rumpled pillow at her side invitingly and said, 'Have I done so yet?'

He crossed to her and, as he slid in beside her and held her so that their lips almost touched, the gale smashed at the window and he said teasingly, 'It'll be a great morning for a walk in the wind and the rain.'

She rolled her eyes in despair. 'Why didn't someone warn me. . . ?'

The words died as his lips closed on hers.

VICTOR CANNING

Acclaimed as 'one of the six finest thriller writers in the world'.

QUEEN'S PAWN 30p

'Beautifully engineered plot, hair-trigger suspense, set-piece climatic excitements aboard QE2: typically compulsive Canning.' THE SCOTSMAN

'Canning at his best . . . a master of invention and suspense'. THE TIMES LITERARY SUPPLEMENT

THE WHIP HAND 30p

'An excellent book for any spy fans . . . Canning plays out another tense, fast-moving tale. Rex Carver, private detective, follows a beautiful girl from Brighton to the Continent and into a spider's web of danger and intrigue.' EVENING STANDARD

THE MELTING MAN 30p

'Few more macabre settings for a climax could be imagined than the private waxworks of a mountain chateau . . . Crisp, polished and as tense as they come.' BRISTOL EVENING NEWS

A SELECTION OF POPULAR READING IN PAN

CRIME

Agatha Christie
THEY DO IT WITH MIRRORS   25P
John D. MacDonald
PALE GREY FOR GUILT   25P
ONE FEARFUL YELLOW EYE   25P
Dick Francis
FLYING FINISH   25P
BLOOD SPORT   25P
James Eastwood
COME DIE WITH ME   25P
Ed McBain
SHOTGUN   25P

GENERAL FICTION

Mario Puzo
THE GODFATHER   45P
Rumer Godden
IN THIS HOUSE OF BREDE   35P
Kathryn Hulme
THE NUN'S STORY   30p
George MacDonald Fraser
ROYAL FLASH   30p
Rona Jaffe
THE FAME GAME   40p
Leslie Thomas
COME TO THE WAR   30p
C. S. Forester
THE MAN ON THE YELLOW RAFT   30p
Andrea Newman
A BOUQUET OF BARBED WIRE   35P
Arthur Hailey
HOTEL   35P
IN HIGH PLACES   35P
Nevil Shute
REQUIEM FOR A WREN   30p

Kyle Onstott
DRUM 40p
MANDINGO 30p
Kyle Onstott & Lance Horner
FALCONHURST FANCY 35p
THE TATTOOED ROOD 35p
Lance Horner
HEIR TO FALCONHURST 40p

ROMANTIC FICTION
Juliette Benzoni
MARIANNE Book 1:
The Bride of Selton Hall 30p
MARIANNE Book 2:
The Eagle and the Nightingale 30p
Georgette Heyer
COUSIN KATE 30p
FREDERICA 30p
BATH TANGLE 30p
Sergeanne Golon
THE COUNTESS ANGELIQUE: Book One
In the Land of the Redskin 30p
THE COUNTESS ANGELIQUE: Book Two
Prisoner of the Mountains 30p

HISTORICAL FICTION
Frederick E. Smith
WATERLOO 25p
Colin Forbes
TRAMP IN ARMOUR 30p
Jean Plaidy
MADAME SERPENT 30p
GAY LORD ROBERT 30p
MURDER MOST ROYAL 35p

NON-FICTION

Dr Laurence J. Peter & Raymond Hull
THE PETER PRINCIPLE   30p
Peter F. Drucker
THE AGE OF DISCONTINUITY   60p
Jim Dante & Leo Diegel
THE NINE BAD SHOTS OF GOLF (illus.)   35p
Adrian Hill
HOW TO DRAW (illus.)   30p
Maurice Woodruff
THE SECRET OF FORETELLING YOUR
OWN FUTURE   25p
William Sargant
THE UNQUIET MIND   45p
Graham Hill
LIFE AT THE LIMIT (illus.)   35p
Ken Welsh
HITCH-HIKER'S GUIDE TO EUROPE (illus.)   35p
Miss Read
MISS READ'S COUNTRY COOKING   30p
Gavin Maxwell
RAVEN SEEK THY BROTHER (illus.)   30p

Obtainable from all booksellers and newsagents. If you
have any difficulty, please send purchase price plus 5p
postage to P.O. Box 11, Falmouth, Cornwall. While every
effort is made to keep prices low, it is sometimes necessary
to increase prices at short notice. PAN Books reserve the
right to show new retail prices on covers which may differ
from the text or elsewhere.

I enclose a cheque/postal order for selected titles ticked
above plus 5p a book to cover postage and packing.

NAME..

ADDRESS..